Mastered

IN HIS CUFFS

THE 10TH ANNIVERSARY EDITION

SIERRA CARTWRIGHT

In His Cuffs

ISBN # 978-1-80250-762-1

©Copyright Sierra Cartwright 2024

Cover Art by Kelly Martin ©Copyright January 2024

Interior text design by Claire Siemaszkiewicz

Totally Bound Publishing

IN HIS CUFFS

Dedication

For one of the most brilliant women I have ever
known: Claire Siemaszkiewicz.
You are my heroine!

Chapter One

Finally.

She'd made it.

Maggie smoothed the front of her short leather skirt and followed her friend Vanessa through the front door of the Den, Colorado's spectacular BDSM club nestled in the Rocky Mountains.

Music blasted from the back patio, and the bass shook the walls. Half-naked people — men, mostly — were everywhere, and cool air whispered in through open windows.

Gregorio, the Den's caretaker, met them in the foyer.

"Welcome to Ladies' Night." His dark eyes were sharp, taking in everything. At times she wondered if he saw into people's souls as well as their hearts.

As he moved, the wink of his silver earring made him resemble a pirate, sending a shiver through her.

"I'm here for the debauchery," Maggie said. After the week — *week? More like weeks* — she'd survived at work — she needed it.

"You've come to the right place," he assured her with a grin.

Maggie had been looking forward to this outing for over a month. Not only had she spent her lunch hours shopping online for a new outfit and killer shoes but she'd also purchased a sparkly collar.

Every day at five o'clock, she'd happily slashed through the date on her calendar.

The fat, red mark served as a reward for surviving another workday with the insufferable David Tomlinson, and it was a visual reminder that she was closer to a night at the Den, where she would hopefully receive a spectacular spanking that would take her away from her everyday life and satisfy her deepest cravings.

"Are you planning to scene tonight, Maggie?" Gregorio asked.

She nodded. *Definitely.*

"Sex?"

With the right man – Dominant – possibly. "I'm not planning to, but I won't rule it out."

"Condoms are provided in all the private rooms. House Monitors also have them. I take it you want to participate as a sub, not a Domme?"

"That's correct." She wondered how he managed to keep up with the particulars of each guest. But then, that was why he ran the place.

"Are you looking to play with a man or a woman? Both? Multiples?"

Oh. It definitely is Ladies' Night. "Strictly het," she replied.

Several different colored wristbands lay on a nearby table. Gregorio selected a white one and affixed it to her wrist.

"Switches are in yellow," he continued.

"That's the one I want," Vanessa chimed in.

"Seriously?" With an eyebrow raised, Maggie looked at her friend.

Vanessa shrugged. "You never know what opportunities might present themselves."

"As always, Tops have red bands," Gregorio informed them. "So that's what you'll be looking for, Maggie."

"Got it," she replied, anxious to start the festivities.

Over the years, she'd visited the Den often enough that she could take Gregorio's place at the door. But she also knew he wouldn't hurry through the ritual, despite her impatience.

"House Monitors have black HM bands around their upper arm. House subs have purple ones. The Den's safe word is 'halt'. Use it at any time. Enjoy yourselves."

"I will, for sure," Vanessa said.

Brandy, a woman Maggie knew as a house sub, took their jackets and purses. Her motions were easy and elegant, something Maggie would never be able to replicate.

Any night at this glorious property owned by Master Damien was fabulous, but four times a year, the owner went all out for the house's single ladies, providing entertainment, demonstrations, Doms and Dommes, exotic non-alcoholic beverages, and the most mouthwatering desserts imaginable.

For over a week, she'd saved up her calories with the intention of indulging in all her favorite things. Not that it mattered, really. If she had her way, she'd burn plenty of energy during a BDSM scene or two.

Playing would also help with her stress level. Orgasms had a magical way of soothing most of her emotional upsets. Tonight, though, she'd need at least a dozen of them to forget the crappy hell her life had become.

With luck, it would take less than half an hour to find someone to take her to the downstairs dungeon.

She and Vanessa made their way toward the kitchen and looked out the patio doors.

A fire danced and popped in a pit. People in all sorts of outfits, from street clothes to club wear, milled about. A stage had been set up near the back of the paved area where a band rocked out, led by singer and guitarist Zephyr 'Zeph' Rockwell who all but made love to a microphone.

"I'll have a double shot of that deliciousness," Vanessa said against Maggie's ear.

"Zeph?"

Oozing sex appeal, he wore an unbuttoned black shirt, and unbelievably tight leather pants that left nothing to the imagination. A recent video of him had gone viral, thanks to a publicity stunt by Chelsea Barton, one of the Den's members. The sensational musician was now giving women all over the world heart palpitations.

"I'd let him put his guitar under my bed," Vanessa replied enthusiastically. "And he can strum any part of me that he wants to."

At her friend's outrageousness, Maggie laughed.

"But no. I'm talking about the Top standing to the right of the stage. I think he has on a black band. I love a man who has authority and knows how to wield it."

Since the party attracted so many newbies, Master Damien brought in extra House Monitors—male and female—to ensure everyone's safety and answer questions.

"I don't know who you're talking about." Her platform shoes added much-needed inches, but even they couldn't help Maggie see through the crowd.

"Over there." Vanessa pointed. "Near the speaker. Short dark hair. Jeans. No shirt. Can you see him yet?"

"No."

"Wait. I think that's a pair of handcuffs on his belt loop." She made a show of exaggeratedly fanning herself. "Damn."

Maggie craned her head.

"Do you need me to lift you up?"

She glared at Vanessa. Vanessa was five inches taller than Maggie and never missed an opportunity to point that out.

"Would you care for a chocolate-covered strawberry?" a server inquired, distracting them.

"Oh, God, yes," Maggie said.

Vanessa and Maggie both turned away from the huge glass windows and toward the sexy man standing near them. He was over six feet tall, with long hair she itched to run her fingers through.

She took her time selecting a treat from the silver serving platter. After all, she enjoyed keeping him next to her for an extra few seconds. Not only did he smell of expensive, spicy cologne, but he had on a bow tie and remarkable, tight shimmery gold pants. His chest was devoid of hair, and his skin glistened as if oiled. Master Damien *definitely* knew how to please his guests.

Finally, Maggie chose the strawberry with the most chocolate coating, and since she'd done that, Vanessa selected two. "You got more chocolate than I did," she explained.

Where Maggie was deliberate, Vanessa seized every opportunity that came along. The fact they were so different had made the friendship all sorts of interesting over the last eight years. Maggie nibbled at her dessert while Vanessa bit hers in half.

"Another, ladies?" the man tempted.

"Could you leave the tray?" Vanessa asked.

"*No*! Don't you dare," Maggie countered.

Vanessa picked up another treat while Maggie shook her head. The man winked at Maggie before moving off.

"The gorgeous man I was looking at earlier is gone. You never saw him, did you?"

"Not like it's a loss. There's plenty of them here."

"True enough. But I like handcuffs. So do you, right?"

Enthusiastically, Maggie nodded. She loved any kind of restraint.

"So, have you seen anyone you're interested in?" Vanessa asked.

After she finished her strawberry, Maggie surveyed the crowd in the kitchen and great room. "I wouldn't mind sceneing with the Top I played with last time, if he's here. He knew his way around my body without a map." The man had flogged her hard and had gotten her off. "How about you?"

"I'm greedy. I want two men."

"Two?" Even though Gregorio had mentioned it, Maggie hadn't considered trying a ménage, but now that Vanessa said she was interested...

"It *is* Ladies' Night," Vanessa pointed out.

Maggie laughed. "So it is."

The music trailed off and raucous applause followed. After wiping her hands on a cocktail napkin, Maggie joined in. Zeph was so much better than the wanna-be rocker who used to perform up here.

A few seconds later, Zeph introduced his next song—a single that was accelerating up the charts—then nodded to his band who cranked up the sound.

"Ready to get your kink on?" Vanessa asked.

"Almost." As always, nerves assailed her, a heady combination of adrenaline and expectation.

"If we don't leave at the same time tonight, we'll meet up at the Chalet?"

Maggie nodded. Because it was a special evening, they'd splurged on a hotel room in Winter Park. Master Damien had thoughtfully provided a shuttle between the Den and several stops in the nearby tourist town. "If you go home with anyone, send me a text. Let me know where you are and who you're with." Even though the Den's members were vetted, it didn't hurt to be safe.

"Same for you."

"Yeah." Maggie rolled her eyes. "As if."

"Hey, you could shock the world and do something totally out of character."

"That's definitely not happening."

After she'd managed to escape from her most recent relationship—with Samuel—Maggie had vowed to never to lower her guard again.

Unlike a lot of men she'd met, he'd seemed at least a little interest in learning about her and BDSM... Well, he'd watched some videos, even though he wouldn't read any blog posts or books. Nor would he attend munches or play parties.

When he lost his job, she'd made a huge mistake by letting him move in with her.

One evening, after living together for over two months, she'd arrived home from work exhausted and stressed. There was nothing more that she wanted than hot sex and to go to bed. A butt paddling would have been the icing on the cake.

He'd been planted in front of the television, playing video games. An open pizza box and an empty beer can were strewn across the coffee table, and he barely looked up when she entered.

After cleaning up his mess, she asked about sex.

Throwing his controller, he stood, face furrowed in anger, calling her a selfish fucking bitch and screaming that no man could satisfy her and her fucked-up demands.

His cold, calculated words had devastated her. But after she'd recovered and talked to friends, she'd been resolved.

Less than a week later, she packed up his belongings, put them outside, and changed the locks.

As he filled her messages with more vile accusations, she hardened her heart and promised herself that she'd never let anyone that emotionally close again.

Keeping her distance was the only way to protect her heart.

Since then, she'd gotten her needs met at the Den where she wasn't shamed for her desires and could play with a different Top every time she visited. The exhilaration of not knowing what to expect added to her delirium.

As a bonus, she could dash away as soon as the scene was over, avoiding any messy entanglements.

Though it had taken time, she'd learned to embrace her single status.

Now, she enjoyed it.

She no longer had to answer to anyone if she worked late. If she didn't feel like getting out of her pajamas on a Sunday morning, she didn't have to. In fact, she could eat ice cream for dinner or skip vacuuming for so long that dust bunnies threatened to strangle her.

All in all, that suited her, especially with her awful boss's ridiculous work-hour demands.

"Targets acquired." With a little wave, Vanessa confidently headed toward a group of men in the great room.

Maggie snagged a virgin piña colada from the granite island in the kitchen then walked into the backyard.

She stood to one side and watched a few couples dance in front of the stage. Off to the left, a tall, broad male knelt in front of a woman who wore a red wristband. Though the image was erotic, it didn't do much for her.

At the office, she engaged in constant battles with her self-appointed boss and had to be on guard all the time. Letting go and surrendering to her submissive tendencies was critical to her mental health.

"Would you like to dance?"

She turned and smiled at a man who'd approached her. He was tall and lanky, wearing a plaid shirt. At least he'd skipped the pocket protector.

Part of her knew she was being unfair. He had an earnest smile, and she was sure he was a nice man. He had on a red band, but somehow, she didn't see him as a Top. His tone was chatty rather than confident. And his eyes were drawn together in a way that seemed more hopeful than assertive.

She waited a few seconds. Though he continued to look at her, she had no compulsion to cast her gaze at the ground, and not a single spark of attraction raced through her.

If she was going to bare her body — or at least parts of it — to a stranger, she longed for a Dom with a razor-edge of danger, but one who wouldn't get too attached. "Thank you." She tightened her grip on her glass as a lie rolled easily off her tongue. "Perhaps another time."

"It was worth a try," he said with a shrug before moving onto the next possibility, a woman who was swaying as she listened to Zeph.

Maggie sipped her cool drink, loving the blend of pineapple, coconut, and whipped cream on her tongue. Since the mocktail had juice in it, she told herself the beverage was somewhat healthy.

She was ready to take a second drink when she caught sight of a gorgeous, shirtless man. Her knees weakened and the glass almost slipped from her fingers.

David Tomlinson!

Her bosshole.

The one man on the planet she couldn't stand.

Her nemesis.

The man who tormented her days and haunted her nights.

What the hell are you doing here?

Her heart stopped.

How could this be possible? After all, she'd come here tonight to escape him.

Trembling, she lowered her hand as a thousand thoughts collided. Her boss was kinky? And she had no doubt he was six-foot-three of raw dominance.

Tomlinson stood near a speaker, arms folded. His dark hair was spiked, and he could have been poured into the jeans that showcased his muscular legs in a way that dress slacks never could.

Then he turned slightly, enough for her to glimpse the black band on his rippled biceps.

You're a House Monitor?

Crap.

It was bad enough that he was here, but she hated that he also held a position of authority.

Then silver flashed in the dim lighting, cold, hard, unmistakable, making her heart slam into her throat.

Handcuffs.

Was this the jackass Vanessa had noticed?

If Maggie didn't know him so well, she might have agreed that he was sexy. But his good looks were a shell that hid the fact no heart beat in his chest. If he had a soul, she'd be surprised.

With her own eyes, she'd watched him manipulate people to his own ends. Sure, he was one of the smartest people she'd ever met, but so what? He never did anything good with it. Instead, he used his intelligence for shitty purposes.

Still staring at him in shock, she took a few steps back into the shadows, as if that ridiculous act could somehow make her invisible.

How the heck was she supposed to proceed now? Should she offer a nonchalant hello? Ignore him and hope he didn't see her?

With a sigh, she considered catching the shuttle back to Winter Park.

Immediately she dismissed that idea.

She was here to have a good time, and under no circumstance would she allow her relentless boss's presence to stop that.

Then she exhaled. Pretending she hadn't seen him wasn't her style, and she didn't intend to spend the entire night skulking around and looking over her shoulder.

That meant she had to face him.

With a resigned sigh, she straightened her spine.

As if sensing her gaze, he looked at her.

He scowled—a ferocious, all-too-familiar expression.

Obviously, he was as surprised and as unhappy to see her as she was to see him. *Good.* She shouldn't suffer alone.

A tall, willowy sub walked up to him, claiming his attention.

Relieved at the interruption, Maggie pushed out a hot breath, then took a sip of her drink, desperately trying to regroup.

We're both adults. And they'd each sought out the Den for a reason. There was absolutely no reason their work relationship should have any bearing on what happened here.

With determination, she pivoted and strode back inside to wander into the living room. A trio near the fireplace were placing bets on the outcome of tomorrow's football game.

Near the window, a Dom rested his shoulders on the wall.

Though he wasn't overly tall, he was broad, and his T-shirt revealed beefy biceps. He could probably wield a flogger for a good long time.

After pointedly glancing at her wrist, he returned his gaze to her face.

Her heart rate increased, and she tightened her grip on her drink as she cast her gaze at the ground, silently signaling both her submissiveness and willingness.

A ridiculous amount of time later, she raised her head, stunned to see him striding away from her, out of the room.

In his place stood David, considering her.

Now that he had her attention, he strode over to her.

"What was that about?" she demanded. "Did you say something to him?"

"Yeah." His voice was rich and deep, and rigidly controlled. "I told him if he touches you, I'll fucking kill him."

"You... *What*?" When she caught her breath, she tipped her head back to look a long way up into the dark blue, unfathomable eyes of her adversary.

His jaw was set, and his arms were once more folded across his chest.

"Who the hell do you think you are?" She set her chin in a stubborn line. "You ruin every one of my days. I will not allow you to spoil this evening for me."

"When we're here, it's *Master* David, or I'm open to Mr. Tomlinson. I've always wanted to have you over my lap for the good spanking you deserve." He captured her hand, raised it slightly, then traced the wristband that informed him she was a sub. "You're here to suffer, Maggie? I'll ensure you do."

"Thanks, but I've had my fill of that from you." Despite her bravado, a frantic pulse lodged in her throat, strangling her.

"I see. But you're still standing here."

Why am I?

"And since you are..." He leaned in closer, branding her with his crisp, masculine scent. "When you speak, you'll damn well call me Sir. Understand?"

Chapter Two

Shocked into silence by his words, Maggie blinked. Since they'd met, David Tomlinson—nicknamed the Tyrant—had been standoffish. Business was the only thing they'd ever discussed. And he'd harbored thoughts of having his hand on her ass?

"Maybe we should satisfy our mutual desires."

"Not in this lifetime, David," she fired back primly.

"Tonight even," he countered.

She laughed, hoping it didn't sound as brittle as it felt. "Even for you, that's an arrogant statement."

"I spent the last few minutes watching your reflection in the glass, Margaret—"

"Maggie," she corrected. "I hate being called that." Especially since he used it at work.

"My apologies."

The soft note of sincerity in his tone caught her off guard.

"It won't happen again."

This side of him disarmed her, and she wasn't sure she liked it.

"You're wearing a white wristband."

Automatically she clamped her free hand around it.

"And you lowered your gaze for that Dom."

Damn you for noticing.

She waged an internal battle to keep her guard up. "Do you know how to mind your own business? Ever?"

"I pay attention to detail."

"There's an understatement." During the first weeks that he'd taken control of her family's firm, he'd scrutinized every file, analyzed spreadsheets, sat down with each employee in private, insisted on personally meeting each of their vendors, and reviewed all current and past customer files. At this point, it seemed he knew as much about Elevated Edge as she did.

"For example, I know you're flustered," he continued.

"So you're a psychic in addition to having superior business acumen?" If sarcasm were arsenic, he'd be dead.

"You're thinking about lifting your skirt for me and lowering yourself over my lap. You're wondering if I'll give a hard spanking, one like you need."

Frantically she shook her head. "That's insane." But now she pictured that very thing, and heat traced through her.

"You're hoping I'll let you keep your underwear on. And yes, you are wearing panties."

She scowled. *How the hell do you know that?*

"If you were as calm as you'd like me to believe, you wouldn't be stabbing the bottom of your glass with your straw."

She froze, not realizing she had been betraying her inner turmoil.

This David confounded her.

In typical fashion, his dark hair was spiked and swept back from his broad forehead. His eyebrows were drawn together in an arrogant, masculine slash.

As she'd noticed earlier, he wore a pair of dark denim jeans, but she hadn't seen the scuffed, black motorcycle boots.

Except for his trademark arrogance, he didn't resemble the man she knew from work.

Normally he wore expensive power suits with crisp button-down shirts. The only concession to an occasional casual look was a loosened knot in his requisite red or blue tie.

She'd spent so much time being irritated by him that she'd never really noticed him as a man.

But now…

His shoulders were broad, and his waist was trim. The black HM band emphasized the size of his arms. Clearly, he had a gym membership, and he used it.

But heaven help her, she couldn't help but stare at the thick black belt encircling his waist. Add in the cuffs that refracted the overhead light… He made breathing difficult.

"How about it, Maggie?"

She looked up at him. His use of Maggie rather than Margaret had been intentional, as if he knew exactly the effect it would have on her. She would never scene with a man who didn't respect her wishes, and he was proving he would. "What happened to your no fraternizing policy?"

Several more people entered the room, and the noise level increased. He took hold of her shoulders and moved her back a little. She didn't protest. Why, she couldn't say. Maybe oxygen deprivation was suddenly making it impossible to think?

He released his grip, but he'd effectively trapped her in a corner, her back to the wall. The act seemed symbolic of their entire relationship. He was adept at maneuvering her to suit his wishes.

Six months ago, when he'd acquired Elevated Edge for far less money than Maggie believed it was worth, she'd put up a fiery verbal protest. Rather than deal with her directly, David had taken her mother aside.

He'd told Gloria that Maggie's help was critical to the success of the firm. Without it, he wouldn't move forward with the purchase.

In a brilliant strategic move, he'd then called Maggie into a private meeting and presented a deal that gave him everything he wanted.

If they met his lofty goals — meaning Maggie worked her ass off and brought in sales — her mother would be rewarded with almost a million dollars at the end of two years. He hadn't promised Maggie a penny beyond her regular wages, but he'd known that ensuring her mother was taken care of was the biggest incentive of all for Maggie.

Her mother had told Maggie she didn't have to accept his terms. Another deal, perhaps a better one, would come along. Together, they'd figure it out.

But once David had shown her the reality of Elevated Edge's fiscal picture due to her mother's mismanagement, Maggie had realized she had no other options. She loved her mother and desperately wanted her to have freedom from the financial struggles she'd always endured.

If he had simply waltzed in as lord and master, Maggie would have flipped him the bird on the way out of the door. But he was far too smart for that. Still, that didn't mean she liked or appreciated his manipulation.

Once she'd agreed to his terms, he'd pulled out an employment contract. With short, angry strokes, she'd signed away her life. In corporate speak, she was shackled to him with golden handcuffs.

And that wasn't much different from the metal pair dangling from his belt loop. Despite her resolve, she kept glancing at them.

He took the glass from her nerveless fingers and gave it to a passing waiter.

Leaning toward her, David crowded her space. They breathed the same air, and his scent intoxicated her — power, spiced with raw masculine confidence.

"I think we can both agree this is an exception. You wouldn't be doing this to get ahead at work. I wouldn't be forcing you to do it to keep your job. At the office, we'll have the same arrangement we have now."

He sounded both reasonable and convincing. But she needed to keep her distance to save herself.

"Meaning you'll set my schedule, tell me what to do, organize my life, prioritize my tasks, and I'll agree with you."

"Much the same way as it'll be tonight, yes." His smile was predatory.

She shuddered then regretted she'd allowed him the glimpse of her vulnerability. "I have no intention of sceneing with you."

"The choice is always yours." He shrugged easily, as if convinced of her ultimate decision. "Do you know the club's safe word?"

She blinked. "We're not having this conversation."

"Do you know the safe word?" he repeated.

The man was nothing if not persistent. "Of course."

"Then tell me what it is."

She felt as if she were involved in a game whose rules she didn't understand. "Halt."

"If you want me to walk away, say it."

Awareness of him simmered in her, slowly heating her blood. One word would end their discussion. So why was she still here, feeling tempted? "You don't play fair."

"I like to win," he agreed. His plainly stated words took away any further argument. "You and I both know that in any D/s relationship, the sub has the real power. You get to set the rules and the pace. If I don't agree to your terms, we have no deal." He paused. "In a way, the tables are turned. It seems to me you should relish that after six months."

"It won't be your butt that's being blistered."

"Or legs," he added. "Or shoulders. Or breasts." He moved a fraction of an inch closer, and she was on fire. "Or pussy."

Needing support, she pressed herself harder against the wall. "I'm not saying I would ever agree to your insane suggestion…"

"Go on."

"If I did, we wouldn't talk about it at the office."

"What happens here, stays here, if that's what you're afraid of."

"I'm not afraid of anything, David," she said, her words infused with bravado she was sure he could see through.

"No?" He leaned closer, and she shrank back even farther.

Maggie reminded herself she didn't like him.

But she couldn't deny her full-on attraction to his dominating manner.

Every day, she watched him in action. When he wanted something, he pursued it with single-minded determination. A very feminine part of her wondered what it would feel like to be the focus of that attention.

"Do you have your own safe word that you prefer?"

"Halt is fine."

"How about a word to slow things down?"

"Eclipse."

He tilted his head to the side.

"I'm more likely to say accelerate," she told him.

"I wouldn't have figured you for an extreme player."

"You think you're all knowing and all seeing, Mr. Tomlinson," she said. "But you've misread a few things about me."

"I'll give you that. Based on your behavior at work, I would have taken you for a Domme."

"It might be fun to strap you to a Saint Andrew's cross," she said, raising one of her eyebrows.

He laughed.

She blinked. The sound was so foreign it startled her. "I'll take that as a no, then."

"Not a chance in hell," he affirmed. "The only one feeling a lash will be you. And feel it you will."

Before she could respond to his flat, arrogant statement, he continued, "I assure you I will be very observant about your reactions." He captured her chin and tipped her head back. "I want to know what quickens your pulse. I'll find out what dampens your panties. I want to know all of your erotic sounds and what each means."

She wished she had met him here first, that she'd seen him as an exciting Dom, felt the connection, and agreed to scene. But she couldn't pretend their relationship wasn't already laden with hostility and distrust.

"For tonight," he reminded her. "Just tonight. Say yes, Maggie Mine."

If she was smart, she'd tell him no. She shouldn't want this, him. But every nerve ending zinged. Need won the battle over common sense. "*Yes,*" she whispered.

Desire flared in his eyes, widening them and making her knees weak. When he spoke, approval made his voice deep and rich. "Good."

After releasing her, he stepped back, and she was grateful for the physical space. This close, she noticed how male he was, sexy, sensual, and threatening.

"Any hard limits?" he asked.

This part of a negotiation was familiar, and she relaxed into it. She was good at asking for what she wanted. "No blood, edgeplay, permanent marks."

"How about formal protocols?"

She'd had enough experience to know that Doms differed on what that meant. But in this setting, since they weren't a couple, she doubted he would ask for anything she'd find objectionable. "If it suits you, I'm okay with it."

"I don't require strict adherence, other than being called Sir or Mr. Tomlinson."

She scowled. Maggie called him Mr. Tomlinson to drive distance between them, not as a term of respect. Calling him that would alter their dynamic. "Well played," she said begrudgingly.

"Any objections to that?"

"No."

"No...?" he prompted.

"No, Sir." With him, the word was unfamiliar on her tongue, but the mere utterance of it made her knees weak.

He gave a tight nod. "I expect straightforward communication and honest answers to any questions I ask."

Goose bumps chased up her arms. "Sounds fair."

"What are your limits around humiliation?"

"As long as I'm not left alone for long periods, I'm fine."

"I won't leave you alone, ever." He cracked a smile, and it scared the hell out of her. "If you're suffering for me, I want to watch and enjoy every moment of it."

The set of his jaw, combined with the husky purr in his voice—part promise, part threat—made her tremble.

Maggie would have never suspected she'd willingly experience anguish for David Tomlinson, let alone offer herself to him, but in this moment, there was nothing she wanted more.

"And suffer you will, Maggie," he vowed.

Maggie froze as her boss reached forward to tuck a few stray strands of hair behind her ear.

His gesture was tender, a contradiction to what she knew lay ahead.

"Your wristband indicates you're open to having sex, but given the nature of our relationship, I think we should discuss it." He lowered his hand to trace a finger around the top of her collar.

His gentle touch was a distraction, and his question loomed large. She considered his comment.

She'd have to face him on Monday morning and every workday for the next eighteen months. Maggie hated awkward emotional entanglements, so she'd never slept with anyone she worked with. She also knew she could compartmentalize with the best of them. "We're both adults," she said. "If the scene leads to sex, and it feels like a natural progression, I'm sure there won't be any repercussions."

"I want to be very clear about this." He slid his finger beneath the collar. "You're open to it?"

Am I? "Yes."

"I can fuck you as hard and as long as I want?"

The words, so raw, natural, caught her off guard. "I thought you were a House Monitor. Don't you have things you need to do?"

"I'm off duty for the next two hours."

"Master Damien agreed to that?"

"I asked for three. We compromised at two." With his fingertip, he drew her a little closer.

"Pretty sure of yourself," she said. "No one can sustain a scene for that long."

His grin told her he welcomed her challenge. "We're wasting time. Anything else you want to discuss before I take you downstairs?"

"Ah…" The moment was here. It was real. "No. I'm fine."

"Then if you're ready, I think it's about time to get on with it."

She nodded.

"Please respond verbally."

"Yes."

He waited, and she drew a steadying breath before saying, "Yes, Mr. Tomlinson."

He looked over his shoulder and signaled to Brandy. The house sub moved toward them, and he let go of Maggie's collar. Instead of letting her go entirely, he rested his fingertips on her shoulder. Even through her shirt, the warmth and firmness of his touch reassured her.

"Please fetch me a leash," he said when Brandy joined them. "And the bag I checked when I arrived. Brown leather."

"Of course, Master David."

Maggie had never been leashed. She'd bought the sparkly, hot-pink leather strip around her neck as a fashion piece. She hadn't anticipated it would actually be used as part of a scene.

Within a minute, the blonde sub returned. With her head bowed, she extended the items he'd requested.

After thanking her, he placed the toy bag on the floor then accepted the black nylon lead.

With a quick curtsy, Brandy left them.

Maggie's gaze was fixated on the leash. His motions were quick and efficient as he attached it in place.

"I'll expect you to keep the tension taut so that you keep the appropriate distance between us," he told her. "Please keep your hands behind your back, except for when we are on the stairs. Your safety matters, so I want you to hold on to the banister. Do you have any problems with my instructions?"

"No...Mr. Tomlinson." Damn, the formality of the address, especially minus her implied sarcasm, sounded odd. But she was sure it had his desired effect. They were Dom and sub, not coworkers, not friends.

"Say that again, please," he instructed.

He'd spoken softly, with a velvety steel undertone. With her, it was far, far more effective than if he'd been harsh. She met his gaze, and her heart rate decreased as she began to slip into a submissive mindset. "I understand your instructions, Mr. Tomlinson, and I have no problem with them."

"Very good."

His approval made her relax her shoulders.

"You look very pretty on my leash, Maggie."

"I... Thank you, Mr. Tomlinson." Resisting the urge to tug on the hem of her skirt and cover herself, she laced her hands at the small of her back.

He wrapped the length of nylon around his hand twice, obviously planning to keep her close. "Ready?"

"Yes, Mr. Tomlinson."

With a brief nod, he turned and began to walk.

It took her a couple of steps to match his pace and get accustomed to being led. No one paid attention to them as they moved through the main level of the luxurious mountain retreat.

At the top of the stairs, he gave the leash some slack. He descended slowly, and she appreciated his thoughtfulness.

The main room of the house's dungeon buzzed with activity. A kneeling sub was attached to a ring on the wall. A couple waited for beverages in front of the bar, and servers moved through the space, carrying bottles of water and more trays filled with delicacies.

Master Damien walked over to talk to them. "I see Maggie has agreed to play with you."

The house owner looked at her, rather than David. She knew Master Damien was checking on her, giving her an out. "I did, Sir," she told him.

"He'll make you cry," Master Damien warned.

She hazarded a quick glance at her temporary Dom.

David shrugged. "It has happened once or twice."

"As you know, Sir," she said to Master Damien, "I don't cry."

"I'm afraid you might have just issued a challenge," Master Damien said with a quick grin.

The club's owner was an enigma to her. Although she saw him every time she came to the Den, she knew very little about him. Sometimes he wore a suit, other times he was much more casual in jeans and a T-shirt. Tonight, he wore slacks and a black lightweight sweater.

On occasion, she'd seen him with his hair pulled back and secured with a thin strip of leather. Now, it was loose, with the ends curled against his collar.

Rumors about him were rampant. The only thing people were pretty sure about was the fact he lived in seclusion. She'd heard he had another job and spent some time at the Den but didn't call it home. Everything beyond that was wild speculation. He'd either had a sub who'd shattered his soul, or he was heartless to begin with and had never allowed anyone close.

All she knew was that she appreciated the way he ran the Den. Nothing happened here without Gregorio or Master Damien knowing about it. Some of the playrooms had an exposed wall in case the players wanted to be seen. Other places had doors for privacy, but even then, there were windows so that someone could periodically check on the sub's safety.

To her knowledge, no one had ever witnessed Master Damien participating in a scene. Maggie knew she wasn't the only one who'd wanted to play with him.

"Is there a private room available?" David asked.

"First door on the right."

David wound up the leash again, bringing her in close. "I'd like you to keep your hands behind your back," he reminded her.

She immediately did as requested, but he continued to regard her. "Yes, Mr. Tomlinson." While she was accustomed to having Master Damien look in on her scenes, being corrected in front of him embarrassed her. She looked at the floor, wishing it would open up so she could disappear.

"Let me know if you need anything," Master Damien said.

"Thank you," David replied, answering for them both.

A tug on her leash yanked her out of her musings and refocused her on her submission. She forgot about herself and her feelings as she followed him down the hallway.

Once he had led her to the room, and the reality of what they were about to do set in, the first tendrils of nerves rippled through her.

From her numerous visits, the room was familiar. Each of the play spaces had similarities — they were all stocked with cuffs and various spanking implements. But each room also catered to a different form of play.

This one had a table that resembled something out of a doctor's office, but not exactly. There appeared to be a cradle for her head, so that she could safely be situated facedown. In that way, it looked more like something a massage therapist would use.

Like a table in a doctor's office, it had a small shelf that could slide back, leaving her bottom hanging suspended. How much pressure she'd be under would depend entirely on how he secured her. There were attachments that could be extended for her heels. She had no idea how he intended to use the piece of furniture, but the numerous possibilities intrigued her as much as they made her anxious.

He closed the door behind them.

Suddenly they were alone, and her nerves slammed into overdrive.

The dungeon walls had been soundproofed, or so she'd learned on her first visit to the Den. It could be disconcerting to others to overhear screaming, and when she was the one screaming, she liked having some privacy.

Since the area also served as a studio for exclusive video shoots, keeping down outside noise was important. Despite all those efforts, the walls still seemed to softly vibrate from Zeph's band.

David detached her leash. "Please kneel while I set up the room." He pointed to a spot on the floor.

The instruction at least was expected, something familiar in the oddness of sceneing with him.

He stood still while she lowered herself into position.

Maggie rarely played with the same man twice. There was something about the thrill of the unknown with a new Dom. The fact she knew David, but in a different context, enhanced her excitement and apprehension.

Since he hadn't instructed otherwise, she watched him hang the leash from a hook in the wall before placing his bag on the countertop. He unzipped it and pulled out several condoms — he hadn't been joking when he'd said he wanted to fuck her.

He laid out various-sized cuffs, likely some for her wrists and others for her ankles. He pulled out a tawse, a paddle, and three different floggers, each crafted from different colored leather. The strands varied in thickness. Her mouth watered as she wondered which he'd select and if she'd ever get to try them all.

The man was compulsive in his need to have every part of his life organized, and he never went home for the evening without straightening his desk and angling every chair in a precise way.

As she watched, he placed each item on the counter in a precise order, with nothing touching.

There were other items she couldn't see without craning her neck, and that would be bad form.

She did manage to catch a glimpse of him taking out a bottle of water before he placed his bag on the floor and turned back to her.

Those dratted nerves returned, their intensity skyrocketing.

Without speaking, he picked up a chair and moved it close to where she knelt.

After sitting, he finally shattered the quiet by telling her, "Please stand and remove all your clothes." He offered his hand to help her up.

For a moment, she hesitated.

This was the perfect chance to flee.

She drew in a sharp, steadying breath.

Run. While you still can.

Those thoughts were immediately followed by others. *Am I smart enough to listen to my intuition?*

Chapter Three

Wondering where her common sense had gone, Maggie took a steadying breath, then accepted his help.

David's—*Master David's*—grip was strong, firm, reassuring.

Their bodies were close, and the setting pulsed with intimacy.

He released her, and she drew her tight-fitting shirt over her head.

"Purple?" he asked. "Another surprise. I'm betting your panties match the bra."

"Why would you guess that, Mr. Tomlinson?"

"The bra isn't as risqué as I expected. Therefore I figured you bought a matched set."

He was right.

She dropped the shirt to the floor before unzipping the skirt and wriggling out of it. Maggie felt as if she were doing a striptease for him.

"Very nice," he said as he swept his gaze down her body, taking in her thong, stockings, and garter belt.

Now she was doubly glad she'd made the purchases.

She stepped out of the skirt.

"Do you dress this way at work?"

"You'll never know, Mr. Tomlinson."

The air seemed to hum with a sudden electrical current, like she'd felt in lightning storms on high mountain peaks. She hadn't meant it to sound like a challenge, but it had come out that way.

"Please continue," he said into the seething tension.

The first few minutes with a new Dom always made her uneasy, until she slid into the place where nothing interfered with her thought process, where doubts buckled beneath the heartbeat of instinct.

Aware of his scrutiny, she reached behind her and unhooked the bra clasp before drawing the straps down her arms. Still looking at him, she dropped the lacy lingerie and pulled her shoulders back.

He tapped his forefingers together. "You have gorgeous breasts," he said. "How sensitive are your nipples?"

"Somewhat. But not overly so," she replied. Beneath his appraisal and the room's overhead fan, they began to bead. "When I masturbate, I enjoy stimulation, so I put clamps on them."

"And would you like me to put a pair on you this evening?"

"If it pleases you, Sir. I mean, yes, please, Mr. Tomlinson."

"I understand why you're the company's lead salesperson," he said with a slight nod of respect. "You're highly adaptable. This side of you that wants to please must be helpful in business development. It seems sincere."

"Thank you for saying so."

"You could try it when you enter my office."

"And you could release me from that employment contract," she countered.

"Without your talents, Elevated Edge stands to lose a significant amount of sales revenue. If you opened a competing business or moved to one of our rivals, it could devastate us. So the answer is no."

The argument was a familiar one. If she were honest, she'd admit he was right. Their customers liked her. Her mother was the firm's creative talent, though. She had an eye for web branding, from actual design to implementation. Together they made a hell of a team, and customers were loyal to her mother, often returning for additional campaigns.

David stood and crossed to the counter. "Tweezers or clovers?"

"Clovers. That way you can tug on them, and they'll stay in place." She licked her lip. "Please."

He selected a pair and tested the pressure on his little finger before discarding them in favor of a second set.

"Are those harder or lighter than the previous ones?" she asked.

"Harder."

Her pussy dampened in anticipation.

"Give your breasts to me."

For a moment, she looked at the clamps. A chain ran between them, and they hung from his index finger. Then she met his gaze, as if he'd urged her to look at him.

At work, he insisted on having his way. In this private room with just the two of them, her naked and vulnerable, him bare-chested and in charge, she saw him in a new way. There was a quiet, observant intensity in his blue eyes. He was listening to and respecting her every wish, changing his style to suit her while still asserting his will. That would make him an even better Dom. And she was looking forward to it.

Obediently she cupped her breasts, drawing them up and together. "Please, Mr. Tomlinson, will you put the clamps on me?"

"It will be my pleasure."

The first touch of her boss's fingers on her skin sent shockwaves through her.

Before tonight, she would have said she'd never allow him to touch her. Now she was all but begging him to.

He played with her nipples, his touch extra light. She moaned, wanting more.

"I'll set the pace," he told her.

"Of course, Mr. Tomlinson." Unable to help herself, she swayed toward him.

"So needy."

"Yes," she whispered.

He pinched her nipples then released the tips, only to grasp them again and roll the swollen peaks between his thumbs and forefingers.

"Oh, thank you. Thank you."

"Lovely manners you have, my little pet."

Even though she was petite, she was curvy, and she wasn't accustomed to being called little. Near him, though, she was small. He could tuck her under his chin and hold her close…not that she wanted him to, she told herself.

Most men gave her nipples a few perfunctory tugs, but he turned this torment into an art form.

He responded to her unspoken demand by increasing the pressure, making her nipples fully erect.

"Now they're ready for me. Keep holding your breasts," he instructed.

He let her go only long enough to take hold of her right nipple, extend it, and affix the rubber tip.

"Ah!" She sucked in a breath.

"More than you thought?"

"Yes," she admitted.

"Can you bear it?"

The shock of it had already begun to fade as he took hold of her left nipple and stroked it, distracting her. Finally, her breathing returned to normal. "I'm better now, Mr. Tomlinson. Thank you."

"You have expressive features. I'll have to watch you more carefully when we're together outside of here."

"I'm better at hiding my thoughts when I'm not involved in a scene," she told him. Before she was mentally prepared, he attached the second clamp, compressing her nipple.

She squeezed her eyes shut to deal with the sharp bite of pain.

"At some point, I may add weights to them," he told her when she had centered herself and looked at him again.

"If..." She breathed out. "If it pleases you."

"I'll give you a few more moments to adjust before I amuse myself with your breasts." He took his seat again. "When you're ready, remove the rest of your clothes."

She worked down the ankle straps of her platform shoes then kicked them aside. The movement caused the clamps to sway, so she moved a bit slower.

"Beautiful," he approved. "Nothing pleases me more than this."

"Mr. Tomlinson?"

"Your femininity. Your graceful motions."

Under his scrutiny, she removed her underwear. She stood before him in nothing but the garter belt and black stockings.

"Nicely groomed," he said.

From his tone, she couldn't tell whether he approved of her shaving or not. She settled for saying, "Yes."

"I like my subs completely naked so I can see every red mark. Remove the rest of your lingerie if you please, Ms. Carpenter, so we can get on with it."

After peeling off her thong, she released each clasp on her garter belt and rolled down her stockings, one at a time, again taking care to minimize her movements.

Then she unfastened the hook behind her waist and allowed the delicate, lacy garter belt to float to the floor.

As he gazed at her, she fought the onslaught of nerves that urged her to cover herself.

"Very pretty," he said.

His tone sounded so sincere she believed him. Either that, or he was a skilled Dominant who knew how to put a sub at ease. It didn't matter. She gained confidence from his compliment.

"Turn all the way around for me. Slowly."

When she faced him again, mouth dry, he nodded in apparent satisfaction.

"You truly are beautiful, Maggie."

Not quite believing him, unsure what to say, she remained silent.

"As I've been fantasizing about it, we're going to start with an old-fashioned over-the-knee spanking. But first..." He stood again, collecting her discarded clothing and placed everything in a neat pile before selecting a pair of substantial-looking weights.

She reminded herself she'd given tacit agreement, but that didn't stop her from swallowing deeply as he approached her.

"I don't mind tears," he reminded her.

"Do you have onions in your pockets, Mr. Tomlinson? That's the only way you'll see me cry."

A hint of a smile curved his lips. "Defiant until the end, are you?"

Instead of immediately attaching the weights, he squeezed her breasts. Heat shot through her.

"I'm going to stroke your pussy."

Since he hadn't instructed her to part her legs or move, she stayed where she was. He plumped one of her breasts while he slid a finger between her labia.

Masterfully he teased her, coaxing her response.

"Could you come from just this?"

"I... I imagine I could, Mr. Tomlinson." She wondered if he'd experiment, but he stopped and lowered his hand.

"I want you more aroused when I let you come."

"Of course, Sir." She'd been with enough Doms to know that some preferred she wait. Others enjoyed making her come multiple times. In case the evening didn't go as well as she hoped, she'd packed her trusty vibrator in her overnight bag.

"Ready for the weights?"

"Yes, Mr. Tomlinson."

He grinned at her. "I do like the way that sounds."

"Don't get accustomed to it past this evening. At work I'm going to start calling you David."

"Cheekiness earns you extra spankings."

Yes, please. "I'm not afraid."

His smile faded, and once again he was all stern and fierce. Part of her knew she shouldn't torment him, that it was akin to pulling a tiger's tail, but this side of her boss intrigued her. At work, she didn't dare answer back. Her mother's future hung in the balance. But here... There was a certain freedom in being on footing that they both understood, that had rules. If things spun out of control, she could use her safe word. The truth was, for her, the dynamic they had elsewhere enhanced the scene, adding an air of danger.

Dispassionately, he added the silver disks. She did a little dance as her nipples were dragged downward.

"Damn, that's beautiful." His words were a soft purr of approval.

"It hurts."

"When you're a bit more aroused, you'll forget about it," he promised.

Though she knew he was right and she often moved from one set to another at home, having him in charge seemed to magnify the experience. She closed her eyes and gritted her teeth.

"Would you like to use your slow word in order to have me remove them?"

Maggie considered his question. She liked being pushed past what she thought she could endure. The pressure was tolerable, and she suspected it would enhance her spanking. And she knew it was one more experience she could relive while she masturbated during the coming weeks. Some things that she had disliked at the time added memorable detail to her fantasies. "Thank you for asking, Mr. Tomlinson. I'm fine."

He fisted the chain and drew her onto her toes. She gasped for air, but damn, it turned her on as well.

"You're an absolutely perfect pet," he told her.

She closed her eyes, willing herself to surrender rather than struggle against the pain.

Suddenly he released his grip, but he captured her shoulders to steady her as she balanced again on her bare feet.

When she looked at him, she saw his gaze was intent, focused on her face. He had apparently been honest earlier when he'd said he would watch and enjoy her suffering.

Of all the Doms on the planet, she would never have expected to want to please him. But the look of approval in his deep, thoughtful eyes sent a shiver of submissive recognition through her.

"Now for that spanking."

He took her wrist and drew her with him to the chair. He sat. Her mouth dried. She could ask for a drink of water, but she knew it wouldn't help. She was parched from the sudden onslaught of trepidation, nothing more. For a moment, just a moment, she wondered if she'd been smart to goad him earlier. Now she was having second thoughts about exposing her buttocks to a man who obviously relished the idea of reddening her skin.

Suddenly this seemed all too real. It was more complex than her usual scene where she would say, 'I've been bad, Sir, please punish me'. Rather, this had the knife-edge of reality added to it.

Releasing her, he said, "Over my knee, Maggie."

She moved toward him. He offered a hand for support, but he didn't grip her. Symbolically he was letting her know it was her choice.

But as she neared, he helped her into position.

The weights on her clamps pulled her breasts and nipples toward the floor — the pain was relentless.

Beneath her belly, his thighs were strong. His jeans were rough against her bare skin, and the coolness from his handcuffs teased her hip for a fraction of a second.

He jostled her so she was more secure. He placed his large palm in the middle of her back.

She expected him to trap her legs between his, but he didn't.

"I want to see you flail. If you try to get away, I want to drag you back. A little resistance feeds my inner beast."

He traced a finger up the inside of her right thigh, making her tremble. He flitted across her pussy, sliding just a fingertip inside her.

"So responsive." He rubbed her thighs and buttocks with light motions, then, as he continued, he used a bit more force, bringing blood to the surface to diminish the chance of bruising.

She tried to relax, but anxiety held her motionless.

He didn't ask if she was ready, instead he swatted her hard. She cried out from the impact and she squirmed, making the clamps jump. "*Damn.*"

"We haven't even started."

It certainly felt like it to her.

He smacked her again, burning her buttocks.

"Your skin turns pink quickly."

Without waiting for a response, he seared her skin again, this time on her right thigh.

Though she had intended to remain still and calmly take anything he gave, she flailed about. Each motion jerked her breasts, increasing the agony in her nipples.

He shocked her by moving her onto her side so that she was facing him. The position changed the angle of his impact.

For self-preservation, she curled against him. The dichotomy awed her—she was seeking stability from his body while he mercilessly spanked her.

"Your beautiful ass was made for this," he told her.

As he blazed her rear, she drank in great gulps of air, trying to reach a peaceful space deep inside her head. Normally when she received this kind of physical stimulation, she was able to bathe in it. David—the Dom—didn't afford her that luxury.

His smacks were random, some horrible, others almost gentle. He didn't pause between them. Instead, he landed them everywhere, keeping her on edge. Her brain couldn't process the information fast enough to figure out where he was going to strike next. She was wading in darkened waters, yet she didn't want to end it.

He heated the tender flesh below her buttocks, the force jolting her. The weights jangled together, and gripping pain assailed her. As a way to orient herself, she tried to count his spanks, but they were so frequent that she couldn't keep up, and she lost herself.

Struggle went out of her, replaced by surrender.

Almost without her noticing, he slowed down the number of spanks.

Warmth bathed her body.

David sat her up and drew her against his chest. Her limbs felt numb, so when he placed her head against his shoulder, she didn't protest.

He stroked her hair and uttered words of approval. Between that and the steady thud of his heart beneath her ear, he soothed her on a soul-deep level.

In just a few minutes together, they'd connected in a way she never had with another Dom.

"I'm going to take off the clamps," he informed her some time later. "Hopefully your nipples are sore enough that my touching them later will hurt."

He cupped her right breast tightly and parted the rubber-tipped clamp. Before she could even suck in a breath, he pinched her nipple and squeezed it several times, allowing circulation to return by measures.

"Ah… Thank you, Mr. Tomlinson." Often her Doms released the clamps and allowed blood to rush back in painfully.

He repeated the process with the other side.

By the time he'd finished, she was holding herself away from him a bit.

"How was your spanking?"

She gazed into his eyes. The act of allowing him to see her at her most emotionally vulnerable left her exposed in a way that was terribly intimate.

He waited.

"It was…" She debated how honest to be. Polite? Or real?

As he had earlier, he pushed hair back from her face. His eyebrows were furrowed, and she fought an insane urge to smooth his forehead. "Amazing," she admitted. "Thank you, Sir."

He smiled, and she was glad she'd told the truth.

For a moment, she settled back against him once more.

His chest was more than broad, it was inviting. The HM band emphasized the ripple of his biceps. If she were the type of woman to lean on a man, she'd be tempted to rest against him again.

"I like your manners."

His constant approval turned her inside out, making her crave more of it.

"I wouldn't have punished you for not expressing your gratitude, but I appreciate it."

"Punish?" she asked, looking up. "I've only ever scened. I've never actually been punished… Well, outside of role play, I mean."

"For something like that to happen between us, we'd have established rules, completely understood ahead of time."

And since she never planned to repeat this experience, that would never happen.

"The reality of spanking your beautiful bottom was even better than I imagined."

"Oh?" Curious, she pressed her hand to his chest and pushed away a little so that she could look at his face.

"I wanted to gauge your reactions, see what you disliked, what you liked, notice how your skin responded, where you're most sensitive, what made you wince or cry out or sigh." He threaded his fingers into her hair and pulled back her head.

"And?"

"You're responsive in every way."

Again, his words took her off guard, and she drank in his approval as she considered everything he'd said.

And while he'd been learning about her, she'd discovered a number of things about him. He paid attention to her. He'd given her enough without pushing her too hard or too far.

"When you're ready, I want to tie you to the table and torment you further."

"Is there an orgasm involved in that?"

He tightened his grip in her hair. "I wouldn't dream of sending you home unsatisfied."

"How about two?" she asked.

"Greedy sub."

"I prefer the word needy," she corrected.

"Do you?" He inclined his head toward the apparatus that came complete with extensions for her limbs. "Shall we find out just how needy?"

Restlessness filled her. The spanking had left her wanting more, emotionally as well as physically. "Yes, please."

"In that case, get on with it. I want you to lie on your back with your head in the cradle." Without another word, he slid her from his lap.

Chapter Four

Damn. This woman, this perfect sub, delighted him.

As Maggie walked the few steps to the table, David studied each of her movements, much as he had for the last few months. Ever since he'd first been introduced to her, he'd been partial to her curves and the elegant way she carried herself.

The pencil skirts she favored during business hours were professional, but the way they hugged her full buttocks inspired some thoughts that were not appropriate in a work environment.

At the office, she kept her black hair pulled back, and she wore blouses that gave no hint as to how sexy she really was.

When he'd seen her here tonight, sipping her drink, her hair spilling invitingly over her shoulders, wearing a short skirt, tight top, platform shoes instead of pumps, and topped off with a sparkly collar, she'd riveted his attention.

For a moment he hadn't been able to believe she was the same woman who challenged him on a daily basis.

She'd appeared soft and approachable, so different from the woman who'd once entered his office without knocking, then slammed the door so hard that the solid wood had jumped in its casing.

She'd stalked over on her sensible, I-mean-business-and-won't-be-intimidated-by-you pumps, had planted her hands on top of his polished desk then leaned toward him and threatened to quit if he fired a certain employee.

For five minutes, she'd presented a logical — if heated — case for keeping the overheads so high.

Her passion had captivated him. Her employment contract was ironclad. Her mother would lose out on a significant amount of money if Maggie walked away. That meant she had a lot to lose. So if she were willing to put that on the line for a coworker, he'd listen.

She'd convinced him. To her credit, she had not gloated.

From that confrontation, amongst others, he'd taken her for a straitlaced, if not uptight, woman who might be sexually repressed. That hadn't stopped him from imagining her luscious ass upturned over his lap as he spanked her. On many occasions, he'd jacked off in the shower with that picture in his mind, particularly after she had annoyed the hell out of him at work.

The reality of her glorious, naked body surpassed even his wildest fantasies.

Maggie Carpenter was as intriguing as she was responsive. She had told him earlier that she would encourage him to move faster, but he doubted she would need to. When he'd spanked her hard, she'd made mewling sounds and had kicked her legs. It seemed he hadn't got her close to tears, but his ministrations had definitely been hard enough to secure her attention.

After keeping her waiting in silence for two full minutes, he stood. The chair legs scraped the floor. She didn't try to see what he was doing, but he saw her belly move as she took a breath. "No doubt you've had some training," he said as he walked around her.

She followed him with her gaze. "I've had a little bit, Mr. Tomlinson. I took some classes at a club in Denver. And I've had relationships that had a few BDSM elements."

He was discovering more and more layers to Maggie. Their remaining time together wouldn't be nearly enough to uncover them all. "Extend your arms."

Unhesitatingly, she did so. He adjusted the table so that she was stretched gently, then fastened her helplessly into place.

"Now your legs. Spread them wide." When she was in his preferred position, he tied her ankles then strapped down her thighs, leaving her pussy exposed to him. "Too bad I can't keep you like this at the office."

"In your dreams, Mr. Tomlinson."

"Yours as well, Ms. Carpenter."

She shivered a little. Oh, yes. Doubtless his defiant employee would remember this. Perhaps she'd walk into his office on Monday morning and picture herself over his desk. Or maybe battle a compulsion to strip and kneel for him? It was impossible, he knew, but he couldn't banish the thought. "Are you comfortable enough?"

"Nothing that is causing muscle cramps."

"You can squirm without injuring anything?"

"It shouldn't be a problem."

"Shall we find out?" He touched her clit.

She tightened her buttocks and pulled back a little.

"How was that? And I'm not talking about your cunt. I'm asking if you experienced any discomfort in your thighs or arms."

"I'm fine, Sir."

He was going to enjoy this experience immensely. Bringing off the woman who constantly confronted him would be a great pleasure, better, he imagined, than spanking her had been. Listening to her cries as she called his name and begged for his touch would be intoxicating. "I'm planning to flog you, Maggie," he said.

"Thank you, Mr. Tomlinson."

His cock hardened. He was trying to give her a way out in case she didn't want a dozen strands of leather biting at her flesh, especially since she was face up, leaving her most tender flesh exposed. Instead, she encouraged him.

He walked to the counter and selected a flogger with fairly thick strands before returning to her. Her nipples were pebbled, and he could still see small indentations from the bite of the clamps. "So inviting," he said.

"Please."

After laying the toy across her body, just above her pubic bone, he pinched her pretty nipples as he watched her reactions.

She sighed.

He did it again and she closed her eyes.

The third time, he held on tight and pulled hard, distending her nipples, and forcing her to arch her back and shift in her restraints.

Her abandon was intoxicating.

David released her only to take hold again, squeezing brutally, rolling the flesh for added pain.

This time, she breathed hard and opened her eyes, fixing her gaze on his. Trust was reflected in the wide, liquid, green depths.

He continued to watch her reactions as he pulled up even farther. Her breaths were forced out in little bursts, but she never protested.

She didn't gasp until he released her. "Sexy, Maggie." He stroked her pussy, not surprised to find her wet. Damn, he wanted to take her hard, now. But he'd promised her an orgasm or two and he intended to deliver.

Telling himself the wait would make it better for him, he moved between her legs, leaving the flogger where it was. "I'm going to push back the part of the table where your butt is resting."

Though she wiggled, her restraints prevented her from moving more than a fraction of an inch.

Within moments, her bottom had nothing beneath it. Even if she wanted to, she couldn't escape his lash. "Your damp cunt is a beautiful sight, Maggie."

David moved away to take off his armband, then he returned to pick up the flogger. The ability to mark all her skin was one of the reasons he favored this particular toy. He just needed to be careful about the distance and power he used. As he danced the suede tips between her breasts, then down her chest and across the soft swell of her belly, he murmured, "I want you to cry."

Apparently unconcerned by his words, she met his gaze. "I won't."

Despite the millions of reasons she might have been intimidated by him, she didn't appear to be. Her trust was a powerful aphrodisiac. "There's not a part of you from the chest down that will escape me." She offered him a small smile that hardened his cock. "Shall we begin?"

"Yes, Sir."

He started with the soles of her feet, using the leather lightly, enough to elicit a soft moan from her.

"Ticklish?"

"Not particularly, Mr. Tomlinson. That's just..."

He waited.

"A new sensation."

"And...?" He resumed what he'd been doing.

"Ah!"

He studied her reactions. That wasn't pain on her face, more like confusion.

Before she could become too accustomed to his touch, he moved to the front of her feet, including her toes before working on her ankles. He loved to mix things up for his subs, so they didn't know what to expect. He didn't mind staying in one place if he was giving an orgasm, but otherwise, he wanted her entire body sensitized.

He continued with her calves, knees, and the fronts of her thighs, flicking his wrist to alternate on each of her legs.

As he moved higher, she lifted her body as much as she was able, silently offering her pussy.

Because that was her expectation, he skipped the sensitive area and landed the falls on her stomach.

"Mr. Tomlinson," she protested.

His lovely sub knew what she wanted. "In due time," he promised.

"But..."

"Turn yourself over to me. You'll get what you want when I decide you're ready."

As much as possible, since there was no support for her bottom and she was partially suspended, she tilted her pelvis, as if that would change his mind. With a grin, he reminded her, "You're submitting to my pleasure."

"I thought I was getting to an orgasm."

"You're not nearly ready enough," he said.

"I promise, I am."

"I'll decide that."

She exhaled as she narrowed her gaze at him.

"You're beautiful when you're mad."

"I am not beautiful," she shot back.

In silent reprimand, he landed a stroke across the inside of her right thigh. Then he explained himself. "You are, Maggie. I won't tolerate you saying otherwise."

She met his gaze and didn't look away.

"You've got a perfect body." He adored her curves. He knew she watched her weight and he'd seen her refuse the pastries that staff brought into the office. From what he'd observed, she allowed herself the luxury of an unpronounceable frothy coffee drink only on Fridays. "Made for spankings and sex."

"I don't—"

"That's my opinion and, at the moment, the only one that matters. Say, 'Yes, Mr. Tomlinson'."

She pursed her lips.

He withheld the lash. "Say it."

"Are you serious?"

"Deadly." He lowered the implement so that it brushed his calf.

Her exhalation was anything but agreeable. "You won't flog me unless I agree that I'm beautiful?"

"That's correct." To reinforce his determination, he reached to release one of her wrists.

"Wait!"

He paused.

"I agree. Just… Can we go on?"

David brushed his thumb across her lips. "The pleasure is mine."

She closed her eyes and drank in her breath, relaxing her body in an outward sign of her compliance in a way that was more meaningful than any words could ever be. That much, at least, she was willing to accept.

In life, people were often dishonest, small untruths mainly, as they tried to spare others from hurt or hide their own feelings. In that regard, he supposed, a scene wasn't much different from any other area of life. Employees and associates, even professionals he hired, often told him what they thought he wanted to hear. But involuntary gestures revealed what lay beneath the surface.

Deliberately, keeping her off guard, he went on, changing up the pattern she might have expected from earlier. He laid gentle strokes on her ribs, arms, and shoulders, turning her body the most tantalizing shade of pink.

"You're driving me mad," she protested in a whisper.

"Mmm." At his own pace, he wended his way back down her chest.

"Sir! I want…"

Even though he knew what she was going to say, he wanted to hear her beg.

"Will you please do that harder?"

"Where?"

She kept her eyes closed, as if finding courage were easier that way. "Everywhere."

"I'll give you everything you can take," he promised.

"On my breasts, Mr. Tomlinson. And my pussy. I'm crawling out of my skin."

At her words, pre-cum leaked from his cockhead. He wanted nothing more than to be buried balls-deep inside her delicious body.

Exerting his iron will over his baser needs, he continued, focusing on her and this time increasing the pressure.

As much as she could, she offered her breasts, silently beseeching him.

Her nipples were still hard. Now that she was warmed up, he gave her what she wanted.

He caught the tips and areolas with the very edge of the leather, flicking his wrist quickly to torment the tender flesh.

"Yes! More."

"You'll have marks when you dress for work on Monday."

She opened her eyes and looked at him, making sure he saw her consent. "I'll wear them happily."

Fuck. "Oh, Maggie."

"Flog my breasts, Sir."

Her beautiful pleas and facial expressions guiding him, he gave her what she craved.

As he continued, she lifted her hips in demand, crying out, begging for an orgasm. This, this, was the music his soul demanded.

Whimpers becoming cries, she thrashed her head.

"So perfect." Heavy with desire, his cock pressed against the confines of his jeans. "That's it. Give me everything." *Including your tears.* He adjusted the grip on the handle of the flogger so he could land the broad sides of the leather strands rather than the tips.

She screamed his name when he caught the underside of her creamy flesh, but she continued to seek more rather than trying to escape.

David took great care with her, ensuring his pain was deliberately inflicted.

She rewarded his efforts with tiny moans punctuated with screams.

Without warning her, he let the strands fall on her pussy.

"Yes. *Damn. Yesss.*"

He blazed across her inner thighs and her pussy, giving her no quarter as each piece of leather bit and caressed.

Within a minute or two, her breathing settled into a regular pattern. Everything he dished up, she hungrily accepted. "You love this," he marveled. Really, she couldn't be any more perfect.

"Please, please…" She beseeched him. "Please… *Sir.*"

Her wild abandon had earned her an orgasm.

He rubbed the flogger's handle between her slick folds as he slid two fingers into her damp heat.

Meeting his gaze, she went still. "I want to come," she said.

"Beg." He stroked in and out while pressing the flogger against her clit, giving her just enough pressure to keep her on edge but not enough to kick her over it.

"Oh, God, please. By all that is holy, let me fucking come."

He hid his delighted smile. "That's not exactly what I had in mind, Ms. Carpenter."

She struggled for purchase that she couldn't find. After gasping a couple of times, she said, "Please, Mr. Tomlinson, I'm begging you. Please let me come."

Much better. He finger-fucked her hard as he stimulated her clitoris.

"Sir? *Please.* Mr. Tomlinson."

Her entire body shook as she fought to obey him and suppress the imminent orgasm. He'd known her for months, and yet when it came to this side of her, he'd been clueless. Maggie — and her responses — were perfect.

"I can't..." She whimpered, tossing her head back and forth.

"Come for me," he instructed. "Come *now.*"

Faster and faster, she moved against him, and he responded to her silent entreaties, finding her G-spot, and pressing against it.

Tremors overtook her, and she screamed out as she climaxed around his fingers.

On and on he went, until she shivered, spent. Then he eased the handle away from her and slowly withdrew from her hot, damp pussy.

Moments later, she blinked open her eyes as she blew out a satisfied breath.

"You're a very sexy woman, Maggie." He walked around to the top of the table, keeping a hand on her at all times in reassurance, mindful of what she'd said earlier about not wanting to be left alone.

Her body was pink from his attentions, and there were several deeper, very satisfying patches of red.

He traced her cheekbone. "How are you doing?"

"I…" Momentarily she closed her eyes. "Thank you for that."

"You're more than welcome." He could spend the entire night satisfying her, and he'd do so, given the chance. "Are you up for more?"

"Really?"

"Unless you need a break?"

"This is what I've been fantasizing about."

Would she make that same confession if she weren't floating in the peaceful sensation of bliss? "Does that mean you want to continue?"

"Give me your best, Mr. Tomlinson. I can take it."

He grinned. Maggie, with her complex vulnerability, ensnared him. "I'd like to leave you restrained."

"If it pleases you, Mr. Tomlinson."

"I need to know if your body is able to tolerate the stress."

"I'm not uncomfortable."

"In that case…" Satisfied she was all right mentally as well as physically, he stripped and fetched the clamps again.

Her eyes widened, and she tracked his every move.

He removed the weights from the chain before saying, "Your nipples have had enough of a break, I think."

"I'm sure you know best, Mr. Tomlinson."

"How is it that no one has spanked you for your impudent tone?"

She gave an impish smile. "There's been no need as I'm always sincere."

"Honest, too." He shook his head.

"You have a beautiful cock, Mr. Tomlinson."

The feminine purr in her voice caught him off guard.

"Your body is gorgeous." She swept her gaze over him. "Sir."

Her scrutiny made him harder.

"Are you going to fuck me, Mr. Tomlinson? Surely you're not going to let that erection go to waste?"

"Sub—"

"I could suck it for you, Sir."

"That would be one way to shut you up."

"It's effective," she agreed.

The mechanics of that would be difficult, but not impossible.

And to be sure she was as aroused as possible, he clamped her nipples. Even though she'd said they weren't particularly sensitive, he'd given her plenty of stimulation. "Too much?"

"I can manage it."

"Good." He moved in closer and cradled the back of her head in his palm. Taking care to protect her neck, he brought her closer to him.

Surprising him, she opened her mouth and stuck out her tongue, seeking his cock. With his free hand, he stroked his shaft, then he guided it toward her mouth.

She pressed her tongue underneath his cock and opened wide to accept him. He fed her his cockhead, and she closed her eyes and made tiny sounds of pleasure.

He'd had his dick sucked dozens, maybe hundreds of times, and he enjoyed it more when his sub was into it.

She took him as deep as she could with the awkward position and she strained against her cuffs in a vain attempt to use her hands. The image combined with the sensation of her tongue and suction of her mouth was almost enough to make him spill.

When she took him even deeper, he gently squeezed her jaw and withdrew his cock. "Not so fast."

"But, Mr. Tomlinson…" She licked her upper lip. "I was enjoying that, and I want—"

"Quiet," he instructed. "This is about what I want."

She looked at him, but she closed her mouth.

"What a smart little pet."

"Asshat." Maggie snapped her teeth together.

"Don't be disrespectful," he warned with a deep growl, fisting the chain that ran between her clamps.

"Anything you say, Mr. Tomlinson."

Though she used the right words, her tone lacked sincerity. And she glared at him rather than looking away to express her contrition. And with the training she'd had, no doubt she knew the difference.

He crouched next to her, dug a hand into her hair, and her eyes widened in shock.

"If you have something you want to discuss, say so." He chose his next words deliberately to emphasize the differences in their stations as well as his displeasure. "Am I clear, sub?"

"Crystal, Mr. Tomlinson."

He loosened his grip on her hair and waited for her to explain herself.

"I object to you being condescending with the princess comment."

"Thank you for saying what's on your mind." He traced the outline of her lips. Keeping his voice soft and gentle, he said, "I was not being condescending, Maggie. It was a term of affection as I acknowledged your compliance and that you'd chosen the correct path. I liked the way you were sucking my dick and I appreciate that you would have continued. But I have a scene in mind and that was not part of it. I should hope you know me well enough to know I respect you and your brain. Here, I need you to trust me."

She blinked. "I…"

Despite everything, she hadn't safe worded and she hadn't asked to have her bindings removed. "Communicate with me, Maggie. That's all I'm asking."

She exhaled.

Their dynamic was complicated. More than anyone, he recognized that. "Any further questions?"

"No, Sir, Mr. Tomlinson."

"Then tell me you understand what I said."

"I should communicate with you."

"Perfect," he said. "Then we're clear."

"I'm sorry," she whispered.

Her sincerity undid him. "I accept your apology. And thank you for giving me the chance to explain myself." By slow measures, he released his tight grip on her hair. He also dropped his other hand so that he wasn't touching her and influencing her decision when he asked, "Shall we continue?"

She bit into her lower lip, appearing thoughtful.

What am I going to do?

And why does your decision matter so damn much?

Chapter Five

It was a scene, nothing more.

Or so David tried to tell himself.

But the truth was, her answer mattered to him, almost as much as she did.

Maggie remained silent for a few tension-filled moments.

Finally, she spoke. "Yes, Sir. I'd like to continue."

He uncurled his fist, one he had no recollection of actually making.

With a nod, he debated his next action, aware of his responsibilities to her, to them, to the scene. Tension lingered in the atmosphere. "Do you need me to loosen or remove any of your cuffs?"

"No, Mr. Tomlinson."

"Do you need a break?"

"No. In fact, I'd rather get back to our scene. You need to return to your duties."

Never had he been more tempted to remove his HM band.

Gently, he placed a kiss on her forehead before warning her he was going to remove the clamps.

"I'm ready."

The moment he removed each, he sucked on her nipple to soothe it and distract her while the blood rushed back into the tips.

When he was finished, he captured her chin between his thumb and forefinger. "Not so bad?"

"Better than I could have hoped. Thank you."

Determined to give her a night she'd never forget, he asked, "How do you feel about butt plugs?"

She was forced to exhale so she could answer. "Sir?"

He kept a careful eye on her as he crossed to the counter. She liked to be pushed, and he enjoyed doing it. Knowing he had her full attention, he held up a glass plug.

"Yikes." She gulped.

He had no intention of starting her with that one, but she didn't need to know that. She just needed to slip back into the correct state of mind before he touched her sexually again. "Do you object to me using it on you?"

"I am okay with plugs, generally. But that one seems a bit extreme."

"And if it's my pleasure?"

For a moment, she was silent. Then she drew a small, steadying breath. When she finally spoke, her voice was soft and a bit uncertain. "Then I will do whatever you ask."

He believed her and appreciated her.

Relenting, he swapped the plug for one that was crafted from surgical grade stainless steel. This particular one was a favorite since it had a circle on the end that he could place his finger through and move it as he desired. "I'll make sure you're prepared first."

"You're too kind, Sir."

"I presume you'll be appreciative?"

"Most certainly, Mr. Tomlinson."

After coating his forefinger with lubricant, he returned to press his finger against her tightest hole. "Open up," he instructed while easing in as far as his first knuckle. Then he withdrew to re-enter, stretching her as he went. "Relax, pet."

He knew that wasn't necessarily easy as there was no support beneath her hips. But it also prevented her from pulling away.

After several strokes, he sank his finger all the way inside.

She exhaled softly. "Mmm."

"That sounds like pleasure."

"It is. I'm ready for more if it suits you, Mr. Tomlinson."

"You are into this." She had warned him that she would ask for more rather than using a safe word, and that delighted him.

"I don't get to scene as often as I would like, so I want to enjoy every moment."

"Anything to ensure your satisfaction." He crossed to the counter, rinsed his hands then rolled on a condom before liberally dousing the plug with lube.

In the few seconds he was gone, he heard her slight movements as she adjusted her body against her restraints. "I'm right here," he assured her. "Do you need to be released?"

"No. I just want…"

He returned to her.

"Connection."

"Understood." He stroked the outside of her thigh, and almost instantly she settled back in. "I'm going to put the plug in you."

Despite his warning, she stiffened when he placed the tip at the entrance to her anus.

"That's cold," she protested.

"Next time I'll warm it for you." *Next time? When the hell did I start thinking in those terms?* They'd agreed to once. Nothing more.

He began to ease forward on the toy, twisting slightly as he went then pulling back only to repeat the motion, going deeper each time.

As he pressed the fattest part of the toy against her, she tightened her muscles and her body stiffened. "You're almost there."

He ached to have his cock in her pussy. With the angle of her pelvis and the fact her back channel would be stuffed, the tight fit would be orgasm inducing.

She whimpered. "Sir!"

He gave a firm push and the metal slid in, the base settling into place.

She sighed and shifted, accommodating the intrusion and its not-insignificant weight.

"I... That's... Wow, Sir."

He stepped back to admire her. The hilt refracted the overhead light. Her eyes were closed. Thick, dark hair spilled everywhere in untamed, sensual disarray. Her nipples were hard, and goose bumps dotted her lower arms.

Then, maybe aware of his scrutiny, she met his gaze. "Please do me," she whispered, straining to lift her head so she could look at him.

"Perfect princess," he responded. He squatted between her legs and parted her labia to lick her pussy.

"Oh, Sir!" She struggled against the restraints, seeking purchase with her heels.

Instead of giving her permission to orgasm, he teased her clit with his tongue, then slowly rotated the plug, making her cry out.

"I want you in me," she said around a gasp.

He continued to torment her until she jerked against his mouth in unspoken demand. Then he stopped.

She slowly relaxed her body but didn't protest his denial. Instead, she said, "Thank you for your attention."

His beautiful, temporary sub certainly knew how to behave. "I'll make sure you're rewarded for your behavior."

"The only thing I want is your pleasure, Mr. Tomlinson," she said.

"Perfect response." Why the hell was she available? Some deserving Dom should have snapped her up a long time ago.

He stood, taking care to keep a reassuring hand on her. He placed his cockhead at her pussy's entrance. In silent entreaty, she moved toward him as much as her bonds would allow. *Fuck.* This woman hit all his sexual hot buttons.

He took his cock in hand and began to enter her.

She blew air out through her pursed lips. "That's tight... Oh."

"Damn." As he'd guessed, with the plug in place, he didn't have a lot of space. "Tell me if I need to stop."

"It's... Don't stop. Just...overwhelming."

He nodded. "I don't want to hurt you."

"I want to feel everything," she replied.

Restraining his urges was more difficult than he might have imagined. The time playing with her, rough as well as gentle, had banked his desires. He wanted to slam into her, fuck her, ride her, claim her, let her know that — right now — she belonged to him.

"Take me."

"Patience, princess." He put his thumb against her clit and manipulated the sensitive flesh.

"Sir! Oh, Mr. Tomlinson, I need to come."

"While I'm fucking you, you can come as often as you like." Concentrating solely on her satisfaction required every bit of his self-control. He kept his thrusts shallow and continued to toy with her, easing back the hood of her clit so that he had greater access to that bundle of nerves.

She tightened her buttocks as she called out his name.

Focused on her, he stroked her faster.

"Please, please put your cock all the way in me."

Even if he'd wanted to, he could deny her nothing. He buried himself so deep his testicles touched the hook on the end of her plug.

"Fuck me, Mr. Tomlinson."

He did, stroking in and out, then grabbing her buttocks and lifting her slightly so as to stimulate her G-spot.

Her breathing became shallower.

"Come for me."

Whimpering, she obeyed.

Her pussy muscles contracted around him, almost driving his orgasm, but David gritted his teeth, forcing himself to hold back. He wanted her to shatter at least one more time.

When her body stilled, she whispered, "That was…"

He waited.

"Wow."

It had been a long time since he'd enjoyed fucking a woman so much.

"The plug intensifies everything," she said. "Well, along with Sir's massive cock."

He grinned at her teasing comment. "Of course." He pulled back slightly to smack her pussy.

She yelped but tightened her internal muscles. "Keep that up, Mr. Tomlinson, and I'll be coming again."

"That's the plan."

She squeezed her eyes shut. "I'm not sure I'll survive the night."

She would, but his scent would be on her when she went home, along with his lingering sensual marks.

When her breathing had evened out, he asked if she was okay. Once she'd reassured him she was ready, he began to thrust again, this time, in long, slow movements.

"*Oh,*" she murmured.

He changed his angle so that he could grasp her tormented nipples and pull up hard, adding a small amount of pain to the mix.

"Oh my God!" She strained against her bonds.

If she were free, he knew she'd wrap her legs around his waist, but he liked having her like this, at his mercy, even if the other way appealed. "Come for me," he demanded, twisting her swollen flesh.

She tossed her head as she whimpered.

So, so fucking sexy.

Her insides tightened and she milked his cock. He could no longer hold back. He jerked his hips, feeling the rigidity of the stainless steel that filled her ass, a sensation-filled contrast with the soft wetness of her pussy.

"Do it," she begged. "Do *me*."

Her reactions to the erotic beating and to the sex were open. It was obvious that, to her, this was no act. The purity of her response was what he hoped to find every time he scened with a woman. Ever since he'd been introduced to BDSM in his early twenties, he hadn't been interested in vanilla sex. Giving a woman more than she knew was possible appealed to him. This experience with Maggie, though, went beyond that. Satisfying her was of utmost importance to him. The way she embraced everything he offered only enhanced his enjoyment.

He released her nipples and grabbed her hips, tilting them and holding her in place.

Lost in her surrender, David fucked her hard. The bass from the music outside drove him. He had to have this woman. *Now.*

His balls drew up and he groaned.

A fraction of a second later, his hot seed spurted, filling the condom.

For long moments, he held on to her tightly, shuddering.

When the last drop of cum pulsed from him, he was satisfied in a way he hadn't been for years.

"That was amazing, Sir."

It sure as hell had been for him.

Aware that his fingers were biting into her, no doubt leaving behind bruises, he forced himself to release his grip.

"You made my muscles tender. I like that."

David gave a wry smile. "That wasn't my intention, princess. I generally have more control during an orgasm."

"The way you made me come… I'm glad you had the same reaction," she whispered.

Earlier this evening, when he'd seen her across the room and another man had shown interest in approaching her, fury had flared and a need to possess had galvanized him to claim her.

He'd imagined spanking her curvy ass, but he hadn't thought much beyond that.

He certainly hadn't anticipated that the woman who fought him so hard at the office would be so captivating that he'd never want to let her go.

Slowly he withdrew his spent cock from her.

Because she had to be as exhausted as he was, he slid the bottom part of the table back into place to support her body. "Are you okay for a second?"

"I don't think I could move if you paid me."

Grinning, he quickly disposed of the condom then returned to her.

Slowly, he released her wrists and rubbed circulation back into her arms. "Take your time."

As she shrugged and wiggled her fingers, he unfastened her ankles. Gently, he massaged her lower legs, then worked the area of her hip flexors. "When you're ready, I'm going to remove the butt plug."

"I, ah, I can do that myself, Mr. Tomlinson."

She delighted him. "Embarrassment at this point, Maggie?"

"That seems a little personal," she admitted.

"Get over it."

She turned her head to one side.

He teased her pussy to focus her attention while he pulled out the plug. "Not so bad, was it?"

"If you say so."

"It's not too late to give you a few more swats."

"I was agreeing with you, Sir."

"Ah." He went to the sink and washed the plug and his hands before returning to her and helping her to sit up.

Once she'd rolled each of her shoulders, he picked her up and carried her to the chair. With a soft sigh, she snuggled into his chest, and he wrapped his arms around her tightly, stroking her hair, enjoying the sounds of her gentle breaths, inhaling her soft vanilla scent.

In that stupidly ridiculous moment, he never wanted to leave her.

Fuck.

Come Monday, Maggie wasn't a woman who wouldn't thank him for this intimacy.

Even knowing that, he didn't want the moment to end.

When she started to stir, he asked, "How does your body feel?"

She wiggled her toes and fingers. "Well used." Pushing away from him slightly, she tipped her head back to look at him. "Thank you, Sir."

"Thank you." He lowered his head toward her, determined to kiss her, but she scrambled from his arms and slid from his lap.

Goddamn it.

He generally didn't make tactical mistakes with women—or subs—but with her, he'd fucked up hard.

Because she'd moved so quickly, she wobbled slightly, and he immediately clamped his hands on her waist to steady her.

"Once more…" She cleared her throat. "Thank you."

A fraction of a second later, she escaped his grip, putting distance between them. Despite that, her tone was still much softer than it was when they were at work.

She donned her garter belt, then slid back into her stockings. For the time being, he was content to remain where he was, taking in her appealing, feminine movements. It was almost as erotic as seeing her naked. But with her reaction when he'd tried to kiss her, he didn't dare say that.

With great, masculine approval he savored her graceful movements as she clipped her stockings into the garter belt. All the while, he wondered if he could revise the company dress code to require she wear sexy undergarments to work every day.

Immediately he nixed that idea.

He'd have a hard-on all day and the company would be bankrupt inside a month.

Finally, she slipped the bra straps over her shoulders and fastened the hooks. He was pretty damn sure he'd spend a lot of time in the future fantasizing about taking it right back off her.

She fought with the tight shirt, and that galvanized him into action.

"Stop." After standing, he closed the distance between them. "Sorry, Maggie. I can't watch you struggle," he said, taking the material from her.

Their gazes locked, and neither looked away.

Momentarily she seemed to stop breathing.

She was fucking gorgeous, and he was smitten.

With a small shake of her head, she blinked and severed their sudden, intimate connection. "Thank you."

Taking his time, he helped her into the shirt and smoothed it into place.

She kept her fingertips on his forearm as she slipped into her shoes.

"Make me a promise, Mr. Tomlinson?"

He inclined his head.

"Don't wear that armband to work."

"Too much of a reminder about who you really are and who you belong to?"

His words made her tremble, and his cock hardened again.

Instantly, she glanced at the floor before lifting her gaze back to his. "The HM stands for House Monitor, not His Majesty," she said in a clipped, professional tone. "Remember that."

Is that how you want to play? Having none of it, he struggled to suppress a smile. "You know, Maggie, you may need to remind yourself of that fact." His touch gentle, he traced her sparkly, alluring collar. "This tells me all I need to know."

"It's part of my attire for the evening."

"I see." He allowed his finger to linger at the hollow of her throat.

"It has no more meaning than my earrings."

He didn't respond. "Wear it for me anytime you want."

Her sweet, sexy lips parted. "That'll never happen."

"We'll see."

She tipped her chin as stubbornly as she might at the office. "Enjoy your evening, Mr. Tomlinson."

Nothing would ever compare to what had already happened. "Likewise, Ms. Carpenter."

Without another word, she turned and hurried from the room, closing the door behind her with a loud and decisive *snick.*

It bothered him that she'd vanished before he could ensure she was completely okay. He'd hoped to spend a few minutes caring for her, even talking. He wished she'd waited long enough to at least have a few sips of water.

Christ. She might not have needed a few minutes of aftercare, but he needed to give them.

In the past, he'd been accused of being relentless.

He didn't take time off for vacations, and that had caused trouble on his honeymoon when his bride had caught him on his laptop in the middle of the night. During stressful times, he'd get in two workouts. He didn't require much sleep and he had boundless energy. He saw each day as a task list, and he methodically checked things off and kept moving.

Lack of cuddling and intimacy had decimated his marriage.

So why the need to care for a woman who clearly doesn't want it?

By the time he'd dressed, washed his toys, packed his bag, collected the leash, and returned to find Damien in the sunroom, she'd already left the Den.

Goddamn it.

"It's not like you to mix business and BDSM," Damien observed, sipping from a glass of mineral water, enhanced with a twist of lime.

David didn't need long to think about that. "If the woman in question wasn't Maggie, it wouldn't have happened tonight."

Damien waited.

"Until now I've never before wanted to paddle someone who reports to me."

"I can understand the temptation."

A house sub accepted David's bag and left them alone without ever saying a word.

"How did it go?"

David frowned. "You tell me. Obviously, you saw her before she left."

"You'll have to ask her yourself," Damien said after what seemed to be a considerable silence.

"Fair enough. She was okay, though?"

"It doesn't appear you made her cry."

"Maybe I'm losing my touch."

Damien shrugged. "Or she's tougher than we gave her credit for. At any rate, you needn't worry about her, I'd say."

David knew he'd get nothing more out of Damien. That was something confounding and reassuring about the Den's owner. The man knew everything and revealed no one's confidences.

From the corner of his eye, David saw Brandy put up her hand to push away a man. "Brandy may need us to intervene."

Damien looked.

Niles, another House Monitor, had obviously already seen what was happening and had moved toward the pair. David wasn't surprised at the man's quick action, but he was surprised to see Niles at the Den. He hadn't attended many public functions since the death of his beautiful wife and sub.

"I'll handle it," Damien said, following David's gaze. "If you're back on duty, the patio needs an extra set of eyes." He turned away then paused and looked back. "Unless you require a little more time to collect yourself?"

"Not at all." David welcomed the responsibilities. Having something to do suited his personality better than worrying or fretting over Maggie. He was the type of man who shoved aside mental and emotional entanglements. Or he had until Maggie had fled without them having the serious talk they needed.

Confounded woman.

"That's what I expected." With a brisk nod, Damien left.

David took up his post outside near the speaker. Thankfully, Zeph was on hiatus, or whatever a band break was called. David wasn't sure how much more his eardrums could take of that racket. And some people considered it music.

As it was Ladies' Night, there were dozens of subs inside and outside, all shapes and sizes, all of them appealing in some way, from soft curves to lean lines. Some women he'd seen before. From their behavior, others were obvious first-timers.

None of them interested him.

It went deeper than the fact that he'd recently had sex. But that was where it had to end.

David was a man of his word. He intended to keep his end of the deal he'd made tonight with Maggie. He didn't fraternize. He kept his professional boundaries firm so that no employee would try to curry favor. Each week he signed paychecks, and he didn't want anyone worrying that if they rebuffed an advance or didn't invite him to a party that their job was on the line. Everyone knowing where he stood made life simpler.

Since he didn't socialize much, he spent considerable time by himself.

Not that he minded.

It had taken him a while to admit he was probably better off alone. His ex-wife had called him selfish.

When he'd gotten married, he'd thought it was forever. He'd never wanted a divorce. Worse, he hadn't seen it coming—even though he should have.

One day, six years ago, he'd arrived home from work, hours later than he'd planned. A plate of cold food had been sitting on the table. All of Sandra's belongings had been gone.

It had taken that for him to admit he had an obsessive personality. His single-minded focus on what he wanted excluded everything else in his life.

In the settlement, he'd instructed his lawyer to give Sandra everything she asked for. She'd unselfishly given him three years of her life—she deserved financial compensation as well as the happiness he hadn't provided for her.

He wasn't bitter, he was just wiser. Avoiding relationships was better for the woman, if not for him.

Allowing himself the freedom to think about Maggie for even five minutes would be a bad decision. They'd work together until her employment contract was up, and that would be the extent of their future involvement.

Still, he fingered the handcuffs hanging from his belt loop.

Despite his most powerful intentions, he couldn't help but think about tightening them around her wrists.

He wanted her on her knees and in his cuffs.

And he wasn't sure he was strong enough to resist the temptation to make both happen.

Chapter Six

What was I thinking?

Maggie stared out the window of the shuttle bus, breaths ragged, gaze focused on the Den's front entrance, back held rigid, praying that David wouldn't follow her.

Finally, finally, the driver closed the door, and she exhaled a shaky breath.

But it wasn't until he turned onto the main road that she let down her guard enough to collapse against the seat.

When she'd first noticed David this evening, she'd been filled with bravado.

She'd decided it would be easy to strip down, accept a spanking that she desperately needed — even if it was from her boss — and finish with him fucking her. Why not? As she'd said, they were both adults. The incident would be a pleasant distraction, an interlude in their lives and wouldn't have any bearing on her normal life or their work relationship.

Because their scene was so amazing, she was able to detach from her ordinary life and surrender to the moment — the exact thing she'd come to the Den for.

But afterward, when she realized she was snuggled up against her hated boss's bare chest, reality had returned with a horrible rush.

She hated how much she'd momentarily enjoyed him taking care of her. Even worse was the fact she hadn't wanted to put any distance between them.

Which clearly meant she wasn't thinking straight.

There was no way that she could allow her boss — the Tyrant — to mean anything to her.

Desperate to find a sense of normalcy and put some distance between them, she'd scrambled off his lap.

She shouldn't have allowed him to help her dress, but when it came to him, she was weak. Then, when their gazes had connected, she'd realized she'd been lying to herself.

The scene had been scorching hot and unlike anything she'd ever experienced.

Over the years, she'd been with many Doms. Most of them had been fantastically good and had made sure she was satisfied. But David had been solely focused on her. He'd pushed her, not allowing her to retreat or hide, and he'd demanded her full participation. And the sex...? It had been spectacular.

David had affected her on a deep, profound level, and she'd struggled to put any emotional distance between them. Desperate to protect herself, she'd run.

Before she'd reached the stairs, she'd run into Master Damien.

It would have been rude to brush past him, and when the house's owner requested a moment, a sub gave it to him, no matter what he or she was dealing with.

He'd looked at her inquiringly and let her know he'd checked on her while she was sceneing.

Though her heart was thundering, she'd promised him she was okay, reassuring him that her one-night Dom had been considerate, but she suspected Master Damien had seen through her tremulous smile.

After a few more questions, he'd allowed her to leave, and she'd dashed outside, grateful a shuttle was waiting.

When the distant lights of Winter Park came into view, her remaining energy vanished, and it took a ridiculously long time for her to walk to her room once she exited the bus.

Since Vanessa wasn't back, Maggie stripped off, dressed in a robe, then filled the bathtub with hot, steamy water.

For maybe an hour, she soaked, eyes closed, trying to think about anything but David. Master David.

But the harder she tried to shove away memories, the more frustratingly persistent they became.

Giving up, she flipped the lever to drain the water.

As she was drying off, she caught sight of her reflection, and a couple of faint marks on her breasts and belly.

They would likely disappear before she went to work on Monday, and even though she told herself just to wrap herself in the towel, she ran her fingertip across the tiny red streaks, savoring them.

Then, frustrated, she sighed.

She shouldn't be entranced by the reminders of her boss's domination. And yet she was, helplessly and completely.

Maggie forced herself to go through the motions of washing her face and smoothing moisturizer into her skin. Then she pulled on a pair of pajamas.

She was sitting on top of her bed, cross-legged, flipping through channels on the TV when Vanessa finally returned, sometime after midnight.

"I was hoping you were still up."

"And if I wasn't?"

"I would have made enough noise to wake the dead." Vanessa grinned. "I mean, you know how nosy I am."

With a small laugh, Maggie shook her head and hit the Mute button on the remote. How many times had she been grateful for the distractions Vanessa provided in her life?

Vanessa headed for the mini fridge to pull out a bottle of white zinfandel. "I'm going to want all the deets." As she spoke, she poured more than a generous amount into two glasses. "Did you play with the Handcuff Dom? I saw him leading you toward the stairs."

After plopping down on the mattress, right next to Maggie, Vanessa handed over one of the glasses.

In all the excitement, she'd forgotten that Vanessa had seen David at the party. "I... Yeah."

"He's gorgeous." Vanessa tipped her glass in Maggie's direction. "Well done."

They clinked their glasses together, only for Maggie it wasn't in celebration. "That was... He's..."

"I'm waiting." Vanessa took a sip.

"My boss."

"What?" Vanessa gasped. "The Handcuff Dom is David Tomlinson?" she demanded. "The *Tyrant*? You have to be kidding me?"

"I wish I was."

"Girl, what were you thinking? Oh wait. Don't answer that. I know exactly what you were thinking. The same damn thing I was. He is one fine man."

Until tonight, even she hadn't realized just how captivating he was.

"How come you never told me he was such a hot dish?"

"Honestly, I never noticed."

"How could you not?"

She rolled her eyes. "Seriously? When I found out about the takeover, I had a few other things on my mind."

Ever since David Tomlinson had bulldozed into her life, Maggie had spent hours talking to Vanessa about the entire fiasco, and she'd been wonderfully supportive when she'd dealt with the sense of betrayal by her mother's lack of honesty about the firm's dire financial situation.

Gloria's lax attitude about bills and collections had put them in a precarious position to begin with. And she had singlehandedly opened the door to the takeover all the while pretending everything was *fine*.

Vanessa had been there every step of the way.

More than anyone, her friend knew how complex Maggie's relationship was with David.

Vanessa studied her over the rim of her glass. "How did you two end up talking in the first place?"

Maggie took a deep fortifying sip of her wine. "I saw a Dom I might be interested in scening with. And David scared him off."

"No!"

She nodded.

"Which meant he owed you a scene."

"I hadn't thought of it that way."

Vanessa took a couple of drinks and waited for Maggie to go on before finally sighing in exasperation. "How was it?"

"Complicated." In order not to down the rest of her beverage in a single gulp, she placed it on the nightstand.

"Terrible?"

"No."

"Was it amazing? He's a great Dom?"

"Yeah." She propped up her knees and hugged them to her chest. "And the sex was great."

Vanessa winced. "You were right. That complicates things."

"And I have to see him every workday for another year and half." Even if she had a do-over, she'd probably make the same choices that she had tonight.

Still that will make Monday morning awkward.

"Has it changed the way you feel about him?"

Maggie had been trying to avoid asking herself that very question. "It shouldn't." After all, she'd repeatedly told herself that she could separate work from the Den. "I mean, he's still the boss from hell."

"But you'll always see him with that sexy chest and those handcuffs attached to his waist."

Miserably she nodded.

In fact, she wasn't sure she'd ever be able to banish that image.

Shaking her head, she reached for her wine and studied her friend. "That's enough about me. I want to know what you did tonight."

Vanessa frowned. "Are you sure you don't need to talk some more?"

"Positive." The more distance she put between her and thoughts of David, the better.

"In that case, let me tell you about what happened to me…"

* * * *

Stark raving mad.

Thoughts of David Tomlinson were going to drive Maggie insane.

On Monday morning, after driving to the office, she stayed in her SUV, rather than walking the few blocks to the Market Street offices.

Her thoughts in turmoil, she stared at the Rocky Mountains in the distance. Even the stunning view of bright sunshine splashing on the distant peaks couldn't banish images of David from her mind.

Ever since her father had passed when she was ten, Maggie had prided herself on her predictable, responsible behavior. In addition to helping her mother with cooking and cleaning, she'd set an alarm clock each night and gotten herself to school every morning.

She'd secured a college scholarship and had worked as a server at a local restaurant, so she'd never have to ask her struggling mother for help.

Since she'd joined her mother in business, Maggie showed up to work on time to unlock the door. After all, she didn't trust her mother to do it. When her creative ideas were flowing, Gloria often stayed up all night. Even in the best of circumstances, time seemed to be a vague concept to her.

Now that David owned the company, several people had keys to the office, and he was almost always early. But still, in a show of solidarity with the employees who'd stayed with them, Maggie felt it was her responsibility to be there for the official start of business.

So why was she still in the vehicle at ten past eight, fingers curled around the steering wheel?

She blew out a frustrated breath. Then, in her typical fashion, she forced herself to face facts. *I'm stalling.*

Even though she'd spent all of yesterday torturing herself, visualizing dozens of ways she could deal with him, Maggie still hadn't figured out how to act.

Cool? Professional? Nonchalant? Or maybe warmer than normal? For certain, she would not behave like a submissive. She'd meet his gaze, talk to him as an equal.

Reminding herself she wasn't a coward, she determinedly unwrapped her hands from the death grip she had on the steering wheel.

Then she gathered her purse and briefcase, kept her sunglasses on her face to disguise the weekend's lack of sleep, then exited the vehicle.

Trying to pretend this was a day like any other, she purposefully walked toward the brick building that housed Elevated Edge.

Near the entrance, her shoulders slumped a little. She could be in denial all she wanted, but most Monday mornings she didn't arrive at the office bearing tiny marks that her boss had left on her ass and breasts.

She drew a breath, smoothed her skirt and hair, dropped her sunglasses in her purse, pulled her shoulders back, then opened the door and stepped inside.

The receptionist sat at the front desk, a huge mug of coffee in front of her.

"Morning, Mags," Barb greeted.

"Tell me there's more of that coffee?" she asked hopefully.

"Are you kidding? I just put on the second pot. Should be about done."

"How long have you been here?"

"Eleven minutes."

Maggie laughed. Good thing coffee went on the office supplies line item in the budget. David didn't have to know how much was actually spent on staples and paperclips as opposed to caffeine. "So…" She affected a breezy, conversational air. "What kind of mood is David in today?"

"No idea." The admin shrugged. "I haven't seen him yet."

"Meaning he's in his office with the door closed?"

She shook her head. "Meaning he hasn't shown up yet. I was the first one here today."

Maggie blinked. Elevated Edge had flexible and remote work hours, except for certain prescheduled meetings. But still, in the six months that he'd owned the company, he'd never shown up late.

"He didn't call in or anything."

She'd spent Sunday and all morning psyching herself up, and he wasn't even here? "Really?"

Barb shrugged. "Since he's not here, it's kind of a mini vacation for us. You should enjoy it."

Air left Maggie's lungs, leaving her feeling like a deflated balloon.

Still, hesitant to believe it, she glanced at his closed door.

"Enjoy the reprieve. I'm sure the Tyrant will be here soon enough."

More unnerved than relieved, Maggie grabbed a much-needed cup of coffee before heading into her office and sliding into the chair behind her desk.

She checked her email.

Though there was nothing from David, she had a response from a potential client she'd been trying to schedule a meeting with.

And she had a message from their preferred caterer. Maggie and her mother had decided to host an open house as a way to increase business and introduce David to their existing clients. It would keep her busy for the time being and, honestly, give her something to fixate on other than her boss spanking her again.

Frustrated, she sighed and sat back.

No matter how hard she tried to keep thoughts of him out of her mind, they lurked, waiting to pounce.

If only he hadn't been such a masterful Dominant and lover.

Damn it.

With determined focus, she confirmed a time to speak with the potential new customer, studied the catering menu, and jotted a few notes to go over with David, since he now had to approve her budget.

More than an hour later, her coffee was gone, she'd handled all the urgent tasks, and she still hadn't heard from her boss.

But her mother breezed into her office.

"Darling!"

Gloria was a sight in her long, flowing skirt and tank top, with jewelry dripping everywhere—necklaces, bracelets, earrings, even toe rings. Over the weekend, she'd dyed her hair—pink this time—and her fingernails sparkled.

Exuding the charisma of a movie star, she threw herself into a chair.

"What are you drinking?" Maggie asked, looking at the plastic cup her mother held. The liquid was deep green with chunks of something floating on the surface.

"Green tea latte. With soy."

"Lactose intolerant again?" she asked.

"Still," Gloria corrected.

She hadn't been on Friday when Barb had brought in flavored cappuccinos with whipped cream on top.

"Where's the Tyrant?"

"David?"

"Who else would I be talking about?" Gloria sipped through the straw and wrinkled her nose before schooling her features.

Maggie was betting the green tea phase wouldn't last past Wednesday. "He's not here yet."

"I need his signature on a contract."

With a sigh, Maggie nodded, understanding her mother's frustration. For as long as she'd been in business, Gloria had signed all the business documents.

She and her mother had made decisions together and handled all the negotiations.

Now David double-checked everything, verified the math, set deadlines, and reviewed every file. It was as time-consuming as it was annoying.

But, if Maggie were honest, she'd admit that his attention to detail was turning the business around. Last quarter, Elevated Edge had posted their first double-digit profit. Now they even boasted income projections for the current and future quarters.

On a daily basis, the staff who'd been with them for a long time complained about his interference, but the truth was, if David hadn't come along when he did, the business would have needed to downsize or relocate to a less expensive zip code—if they'd survived at all.

Though her mother chafed at answering to a man, and a much younger one at that, she was producing the best work of her career.

David Tomlinson believed in exploiting each person's talents. Sometimes that meant assigning them to a new position. In Gloria's case, it meant getting her entirely out of the bookkeeping. She no longer saw bills. Even better, someone else was tasked with handling collections. Removing the financial burden from her shoulders had given her a lot of mental and emotional freedom.

He'd been right to restructure the staff's responsibilities, but Maggie wished her mother's confidence hadn't been undermined by his high-handed ways. Then again, that was probably the only way he knew. The man was assured, directive. Domineering.

"I'd like this contract to go out today," Gloria said.

"Call him?" Maggie suggested, grateful her mother had interrupted her musings.

"Maybe Barb can."

"Mother, he's not an ogre."

"Are you defending the man?"

Had she really been so swept up in her disdain for the employment contract that she never said anything good about him? "Maybe I need more coffee."

"You do look tired." Gloria narrowed her eyes. "What did you do this weekend, anyway?"

"Went to the Den."

"That explains it. I may have to go with you sometime. Sounds like a kick."

"Why not? Maybe you can find someone to keep you in line, finally."

"On second thought..." With that Gloria stood, creating a cacophony with her clanging metal jewelry.

Just then, David appeared in the doorway.

Maggie's breath vaporized in a shocking rush.

His dove-gray suit hugged his broad shoulders, while his tailored pants snuggled his strong thighs. As usual, he had on a white shirt and a red tie with the knot high and tight. But today, she knew exactly what lay beneath the formal attire, and that made it impossible for her to think straight.

No matter how she wished it were otherwise, David Tomlinson now affected her on a deep, primal level.

"Ladies," he said, voice growly, sending shivers through her.

"Good afternoon," Gloria said, pointedly looking at her watch.

Since it wasn't even nine-thirty, Maggie winced.

For the first time, she wished her mother would at least pretend to be cordial. If they could all work as a team, perhaps the business could reach his lofty goals. Everyone, including her mother, would benefit from that.

"I've been waiting for you."

"Oh? Something urgent?"

"I need your signature," Gloria replied with great drama.

"Put it on my desk. I'll handle it before anything else."

"But—"

"Put it on my desk, Gloria," he reiterated with clipped finality. The same tone he'd used on Maggie at the Den.

Beneath her desk, she twisted her hands together.

David stepped aside as Gloria flounced past him.

Then without an invitation, gaze riveted on her, he entered Maggie's office and took the seat her mother had vacated.

"Morning, Maggie."

"David."

At the use of his first name, he angled his head.

Did anything escape his notice?

Until now, she'd addressed him as Mr. Tomlinson. But since that had been a requirement at the Den, there was no way she was calling him that ever again.

"Did you need something?" He was close, too close, enveloping her in his masculine, spicy scent, and she was desperate to get rid of him...before she gave in to the temptation of asking him to bend her over and give her the spanking she suddenly craved. "I have work to do before my boss accuses me of wasting time."

"I'm in negotiation to acquire another company."

She sat up straighter. With the solemn expression on his face, she'd expected him to mention what had happened on Saturday night. But he was talking business while she was obsessing about the time they'd spent together?

Obviously, what they'd shared meant nothing to him. She was a random sub that he'd spent some time with.

The realization was the jolt of reality that she needed, and she held on to it as if it were a lifeline.

"Maggie? Are you listening?"

She couldn't admit she'd barely heard a word. "You're acquiring another business?"

"They're a competitor of ours."

"Oh?" He had her complete attention.

"If the deal goes through, it will impact you."

"How so?"

"Your role will grow. I'll need more time from you."

"Good God, no. You've got all you're ever going to get from me." She stiffened her spine.

He propped an ankle on the opposite knee. He looked so corporate, so unconcerned by her response.

"Hear me out."

"There's not much reason for that. If you want to go around buying up businesses in your free time, go right ahead. You and I have a written agreement in place. I have eighteen more months that I'm tied to you. You won't get a day more."

"Everyone has a price, Maggie."

She wanted to think she didn't.

"I'll do whatever it takes to keep you and your talents on the payroll. Of course, I'm hoping you'll stay with me because you want to, since we —"

"Excuse me?" Embarrassment blazed through her. "Was that what Saturday night was about? Part of your plan to manipulate me?"

He dropped his leg to the floor, stood, strode to the door, shut it then returned to plant both hands on her desktop.

Eyes lethal, he leaned forward.

When he spoke, his tone was clipped with anger. "Don't fucking going there. If you think that our scene was about anything other than my desire for you as a woman, as a submissive, you're wrong."

His flat statement defused her emotion.

She squeezed her eyes shut.

"Let's keep things straight, Maggie," he went on, tone much softer, but every bit as intense. "When I noticed you at the Den in that skirt and those shoes with your hair all around your shoulders, I was intrigued. I would have wanted you even if we'd never met. Then with the perfect way you responded to my commands, the way you begged for my touch —"

"That can't happen again."

"It will." His voice held a note of certainty. "And we'll be clear that fucking, spanking, and sceneing with you has no bearing on our work relationship." He lowered his voice. "That's what you want, isn't it?"

She shook her head, and he chuckled softly in response. "Little liar. You can't even look me in the eye."

Maggie hated that he was right.

"We will discuss that in a few minutes. But back to business. I have a proposition I think you might be interested in."

Chapter Seven

"I've got your attention?"

One hundred percent. "I'm listening."

"I very much want you to be involved in the acquisition of Peak Imaginings."

Her mouth dropped.

That company was Elevated Edge's biggest rival — the only competitor she and her mother routinely lost business to.

For years Maggie had dreamed of putting them out of business. And David was offering her the chance to be part of that. She couldn't let him know how much the idea appealed to her. "That's ambitious."

"When I see something I want, I go after it." He looked at her pointedly. "And as you know, I don't fail."

She tried to keep her mind on his new proposition, rather than allowing images of his naked body to fill her mind. "How will this affect my employment contract?"

"As I said, it will take a lot of work to get the deal done. We want to go through their books, assess their sales projections and year-to-date results. We have to perform our due diligence. Of course, both sides have signed non-disclosures."

She nodded. "This business must operate at an optimal level while you're distracted."

"Precisely."

"That's where I come in?"

"Negotiating the deal is only the beginning."

How well she remembered from the way he'd taken over her mother's company.

"The first six months will be the most complicated. We may need to adjust the number of employees. I need someone who understands strategy and tactics. I need your cooperation and your brain."

"I'm already working enough hours for you as it is, David."

"And that's a hardship, is it, Maggie?"

Her entire body vibrated with the awareness of him.

"As for your employment contract, it stays in place under the original terms. Unless you agree to my new proposal."

Was he willing to let her go in less than eighteen months?

As if reading her mind, he flatly stated, "The time remaining is unchanged."

She exhaled. In frustration? Or relief?

Purposefully she shoved that second thought aside. The sooner she got away from him, the better.

"Your mother's pay-out remains the same."

She scowled.

"But you'll walk away with a hundred-thousand-dollar bonus, after taxes."

Mouth open with shock, she stared at him.

"Along with ten percent of all profits of the combined companies."

The offer was beyond anything she might have asked for.

Still, if this worked, he would be the big winner. The combined entity would be the Mile High City's largest advertising agency. "Gross profit," she countered.

"In that case, five percent."

"Ten."

He sat back. "That's not how negotiation works, Maggie. You give a little."

Like you did? "I learned from the best." Trying not to betray how hard her heart was racing, she placed her hands on top of the desk and folded them primly. "Look, David, we both know there are a dozen ways that the financials could be presented in a way beneficial to you."

"That's insulting."

"It's business." She steadily met his gaze. "And you're the consummate player of the game." The bonus he offered was tantalizing, but she had only one shot to make this deal. "If you want my help, knowing that it may take months to acquire Peak Imaginings — time that I will not be paid for — then I need a cut of gross."

"The bonus covers that." His face offered no glimpse of his internal thoughts.

Ignoring the butterflies unfurling in her stomach, she leaned forward, taking a gamble. She'd planned to apply for a job at Peak Imaginings, and if he bought it, she'd have nowhere to go once she was free of her golden handcuffs. "No deal."

He regarded her with those chilling blue eyes.

Since she was accustomed to it, the look shouldn't have unnerved her as much as it did. But now that she'd been the focus of his complete attention on multiple levels, she knew the depths of his intent. He missed nothing, and he considered all angles before acting.

"Seven percent."

Potentially, that was a lot of money for a year and a half's worth of work. She should take it. "Nine. Final offer."

"Eight."

"Done. And I'll expect this to be added to the contract by tomorrow."

"*Fuck.*"

She blinked. Until this morning, she'd only seen him be controlled, every reaction hidden. But this was twice, in less than ten minutes. "You were serious that you don't like to lose."

"I don't. I'll just have to make sure we both work hard enough to make it a win for each of us." He crossed his leg over his knee again. "You're going to be putting in a lot of time, Maggie."

With you.

"As for the other—your submission—I will have you again, Maggie." He leaned forward, bringing them inches apart.

Though her entire body heated, she refused to shrink back.

No matter how insane the idea was, she very much wanted it, too.

"Have a glass of wine with me tonight. We'll celebrate our new arrangement."

"No."

"No?"

"Let me be honest with you."

"Please."

Ridiculously, as if someone might be watching, she glanced around. "Having a relationship with the boss is a stupid idea. Fraternizing is against company rules. Even if it weren't, I still wouldn't do it. I refuse to be accused of sleeping with the enemy."

Damnably, a smile teased the corners of his lips, making him more approachable and cutting through her defenses. "Coworkers often have after-hours meetings."

It was so much more than that. If she met him for a glass of wine, her inhibitions would be loosened and she'd end up naked, begging him to fuck her.

It wasn't so much his control she worried about — it was hers.

"The scene worked for you."

"Is that a question or a statement?"

"You climaxed for me, Maggie, repeatedly."

Her response was swift and prim. "We're not mixing business and sceneing, Mr. Tomlinson."

As he raised an eyebrow, she cursed herself for being a fool. By using his last name, she'd instinctively retreated to the familiar in an attempt to keep distance between them. But all it did was remind them both of their time together.

"I see." With a crisp nod, he exited the room, leaving the door open.

Unnerved, slack-jawed, she stared at the empty threshold.

Had she won two battles in a row against David Tomlinson?

She tapped her fingers on the desktop. That was as unlikely as the earth tilting off its axis.

Which meant he was changing his strategy. She just had to be prepared for it.

She spent the morning on edge, waiting for his next move. But he didn't show up for the eleven o'clock staff meeting, the first he'd missed since becoming the new owner.

Around one, he left for lunch and never returned. To her knowledge, he'd told no one where he was going or when he'd be back.

All afternoon, she'd looked over her shoulder, expecting to see him. She'd told herself she wasn't hoping to see him, but a small, constant voice whispered that she was lying.

Feeling somewhat ridiculous, she stayed late on the off chance he might return.

At twenty minutes after five, she exhaled deeply, wondering — again — what was wrong with her. He wasn't coming back to the office. Even if he did, being alone with him would be disastrous. Neediness was crawling through her, and that would lower her defenses. Not putting herself into a dangerous situation was the only thing that made sense.

Still, logic conflicted with her emotions.

While she didn't necessarily want to live a twenty-four-seven BDSM lifestyle, she loved everything about the power exchange — giving up control, being subject to a strong Dom's will.

Sceneing with David had given her satisfaction. Resisting him when he was near would be all but impossible. So, she told herself, it was better for her that he hadn't been in the office.

She powered down her computer, turned off her office light then went home.

An hour later after answering some emails and having a quick dinner, she was restless. Because the evening was still relatively mild for the time of year, she poured a glass of wine and went outside to sit on the deck of her apartment building.

She was relieved when the phone rang.

Vanessa.

"I need to know how things went," she demanded.

Maggie spent a few minutes outlining the events of the day, including the fact they'd be together a lot in the coming months and his determination to scene again in the future.

"That man is not going to leave you alone. I promise you."

"He needs to. We've got a lot of work to do."

"Ten dollars says he'll be spanking your butt in under a week."

"No!" She shook her head. "Absolutely not." Though she protested, a naughty, unwelcome part of her hoped to lose.

After they ended the call, she had a small sip of her wine. In the distance, shadows hovered over the Rockies, making them look dark and moody.

Absently she wondered where David would have taken her if she'd accepted the invitation to join him for a drink. His house? A nice restaurant? Or the new speakeasy that had recently opened to rave reviews on Larimer Street, just a block over from Elevated Edge's building?

Then, her wayward thoughts strayed to what might have happened afterward.

Where would the evening have ended?

Her place? His?

And then what would happen?

With a sigh, she finished her wine, then headed back inside to take a shower.

She set the temperature to hot, hoping it would banish the tension gnawing at her.

While she stood there, water rushing over her, the memories she'd been shoving away caught her. The harder she tried to fight them, the deeper their grip became.

For a moment, she remembered the way she'd been tied to the medical table at the Den, spread for David — her Dom — as he'd explored every inch of her. Memories of his touch returned...the skillful way he'd toyed with her clit before taking her deeply, completely.

Maggie reached for the showerhead and detached it from its hook.

After adjusting the setting to pulse, she directed the water over her body, letting it tease her nipples before guiding the spray lower.

Then she spread her legs and closed her eyes, allowing her imagination free rein.

Suddenly, David consumed her imagination.

His rich voice seemed to resonate in her ears, as he urged her to fight off her orgasm.

She moved her hips, seeking more sensation on her swollen clit. She was ready to come, desperate to come.

Fantasizing that he was urging her on, she screamed and climaxed, dropping the showerhead and grabbing hold of a bar for support.

It took a full minute of gulping in deep breaths for her to regain control.

Then slowly, she forced herself to uncurl her clenched fingers and finish her shower.

No man had ever gotten in her head like he had.

Generally, when she had this kind of experience, the Dom was nameless and faceless. But this time, it had been so much more real, as if he'd been there with her.

Her limbs heavy, she dried off and changed into her pajamas, finished her nighttime routine, then went to bed only to toss and turn.

Powerful orgasms almost always relaxed her, but tonight she'd been left feeling restless, maybe because David's presence seemed so real.

After tossing and turning for over an hour, she finally drifted off.

In her dreams, she was being chased. No matter how hard or fast she ran, she couldn't escape.

Finally, firm hands clamped on her shoulders, and she was spun to face David with his stunning, electric blue eyes and devilish, all-knowing grin.

Then he laughed, a diabolical sound that scraped her nerves raw.

Screaming, drenched in sweat, she woke up disoriented.

Minutes later, still trying to drag in full breaths, she threw back the covers, climbed from her bed and wrapped herself in a robe, cinching it tight with her shaking hands. After turning on every light in the house, she grabbed a bottle of water and headed outside.

The change of location didn't calm her.

David Tomlinson was consuming every part of her.

And she was powerless to stop it.

A few minutes later, she leaned against the railing and glanced at the sky. The moon was obscured by some clouds, but the normality helped stop her hands from trembling.

Determined to relegate him to the position of boss and nothing larger in her life, she went back to bed.

Her sleep was broken, and the alarm rang way too early.

Exhausted, she dressed all in black, donning it as if it were armor. Her relationship with David did feel a bit like a battle. He was a master strategist, and she was always a step behind.

"Morning, Mags," Barb greeted when Maggie entered. Then she leaned forward and whispered, "The Tyrant is here."

Maggie's heart lurched. "Oh?"

"He's brewing coffee. I asked if he needed help, but he said he thinks he can handle it." Barb shrugged. "I'm not sure I believe he's capable of menial tasks. Maybe one of us should make sure he's not screwing up."

At one time, Maggie might have added a disparaging comment of her own. Though she was far from becoming the president of the David Tomlinson Fan Club, maybe she'd judged him a little harshly. Maybe. "I'm on it," Maggie said.

He was wiping down the counter when Maggie entered the break room.

Though she'd watched him organize his toys at the Den, here, in a suit and tie, he looked out of place.

As if sensing her, he turned.

In a single, approving glance, he took her in, turning her inside out.

Determinedly she reminded herself of last night's dream. He was the predator — she was the prey.

After clearing her throat, pretending he didn't affect her, she breezily said, "The productivity of the entire business rests on your shoulders."

"I gathered that from Barb's reaction, so I dumped as much coffee in the filter as it would hold, and I filled the tank to the top."

She glanced at the pot then back at him. "We should be okay," she said. "As long as you used a new filter? Sometimes people put new grounds on top of old ones."

"Good coffee is essential to happiness. Has to be made fresh."

"Good call."

This was perhaps the first time they'd exchanged anything close to pleasantries. Which meant she was lowering her guard.

Which was the one thing she dared not do.

When their gazes met, she shuddered. His eyes were the same startling blue as in her nightmare.

"I spent all of last night thinking about holding you down."

"No." Frantically she shook her head. "I told you we weren't doing this."

"We'll see about that." His voice held the same terrible, mocking tone as it had in her dreams. "My office? Fifteen minutes? We need to talk about Peak Imaginings."

How does he do that? Flip from sex to business in three seconds?

"Uhm… Yes."

"Yes, Sir, would sound even better." With a tight nod, he moved past her.

He flustered her so completely she couldn't respond.

When she was alone, she exhaled.

Damn him.

Did he spend all of his free time thinking up ways to keep her off-kilter?

After depositing her purse and briefcase in her office and checking messages, she returned to the breakroom and poured herself a cup of coffee. Then she paused. David's mug was on the counter, waiting to be filled. She waged an internal debate before getting one for him.

She carried both to his office. Seeing he was on a call, she stopped in the doorway, but he waved her in.

He continued his conversation while keeping his gaze on her.

Self-consciously, she placed his mug on a coaster bearing the company's logo. Then she balanced her cup as she sat.

She started to fidget then, realizing what she was doing, she crossed her legs and sat still.

His attention never left her, just like that night at the Den.

Needing a distraction, she took a drink, then looked everywhere but at him.

Behind him, on a credenza, were several stress balls, each in a different primary color. Other than that, there were no personal effects in the office. He'd repainted after her mother had moved out—evidently bright yellow didn't suit him.

Now the walls were a calm taupe. The furnishings were sleek and functional, with no space wasted and nothing cluttered.

For the first time, she wondered how he lived his life away from the office.

From her observations at the Den, she knew he was meticulous. Other than that, she knew next to nothing about him.

Once he ended his call, he picked up his mug. "Thank you for this." His voice held the same appreciative tone that he'd used with her on Saturday night. "Thoughtful. Appreciated."

His words of approval fired a response in her. "Of course..." *Sir* hovered at the edge of her tongue, and she bit it back.

"You wanted to say it as much as I wanted to hear it."

He missed nothing. "I have no idea what you're talking about."

"Who are you fighting? Me? Or yourself?"

Because the question was too perceptive and made her squirm, she made a show of checking her watch. "You wanted to discuss Peak Imaginings?"

"I had meetings with the owner and a key manager yesterday and went over financials."

"And?"

"They are not as big as we are."

"Are you serious? I was sure they did more revenue."

"They have more accounts," he clarified. "But they've underbid some of their bigger projects."

"So that should put you"—she stopped and corrected herself—"I mean *us*, in a better position."

"When the acquisition closes, we should get an immediate lift in profits, yes. But raising prices could mean losing some accounts."

"You don't sound worried about it."

"I'm not. I focus on results and the things I can control." He put down his coffee. "Where are we on the open house?"

"Do you still want to move forward or put it on hold?"

"I still want an event with our current clients. And we can have another event when we own Peak Imaginings. Maybe around the holidays," he added.

"I like that. The open house could be here, and the holiday party could be at a client site. We recently signed a winery. They have beautiful grounds, including a gazebo, and they give tours of their cellar. I think hosting an event there would be elegant, and it would give them some exposure."

He nodded thoughtfully. "Is the space big enough?"

"They have an events center, yes."

"And it's in Denver?"

She leaned forward, gaining enthusiasm. "Surprisingly yes."

"I'll trust you. Give me some available dates."

"Are we keeping our company name, or are you changing it?"

"We'll stay with our name. But I figure we'd incorporate their logo."

She nodded. "We may want to freshen it. I'll come up with a few ideas, but since this is still quiet, I won't have our graphics people work on it yet." The Peak Imaginings logo had a mountain on it that was so uninspired that she couldn't wait to get to work on it. "Good. What do you think of the idea of getting a privately labeled wine for the occasion? Could serve as the debut of the new marketing package and maybe a take-home gift for attendees."

"We have a lot of details to plow through before we're close enough to have that discussion," he cautioned.

"You're not the only one who can move fast, David."

He sat back. "Glad we're on the same side."

"It's temporary." Her response was as quick as it was prim.

He sat back and pressed his index fingers together. "I see you, Maggie. Deeper than you imagine. Everything you try to hide. Your beautiful lying lips say one thing. Your eyes betray the truth."

Her tummy plummeted.

"You can't hide from me. And soon you'll be honest enough to admit that to both of us."

* * * *

For the next few weeks, his terrible statement haunted her.

At work, Maggie managed to keep her distance, sending emails and text messages to keep him updated on her projects and deals in progress. When they met, other people were generally in the conference room with them.

On the rare occasions they were alone, he didn't mention anything about a personal relationship. Frustrating her, that bothered her more than anything.

By honoring her wishes, the man had tied her in emotional knots.

Almost every time she went to sleep, she had the same nightmare – the heavy hand on her shoulder, and the shock of blue when she was spun around.

Lack of sleep was making her an emotional mess.

Masturbating no longer helped, and neither did the visits to the gym that she forced herself to make.

Finally, almost a month after the Ladies' Night at the Den, she and Vanessa met for dinner. Sushi and sake could fix nearly anything, or at least it had been able to until now.

"Color me shocked," Vanessa said as she used a chopstick to smear wasabi on a tuna roll. "You're working with one of the world's sexiest Doms, and he's hot for your ass. So tell me again why you can't sleep with him?"

"Hello? He's the enemy, remember?"

"Right. Terrible, very bad, awful boss."

Maggie rolled her eyes. "Even though he's gorgeous, he's still the bastard who has my future mapped out for the next seventeen months."

"I don't get it." Vanessa studied her. "Aren't you capable of sleeping with a guy without it interfering with your job performance?"

Clearly not, if the way she felt was any indication. "He has a no fraternizing rule."

"So break it and give him something to punish you for." She popped a sushi roll into her mouth.

"Could you be serious here?" Maggie demanded.

After putting down her chopsticks, Vanessa met Maggie's gaze. Softly she said, "I want you to be happy, and you're not. You're totally on edge. So, fine. He has a policy. Is it in writing in the employee handbook?"

"No."

"Not all companies have those kinds of policies in place, but when they are, it's generally to protect morale, avoid conflicts of interest, or to protect subordinates from feeling like they might be harassed. But a lot of coworkers have relationships. I mean, we spend so much time at work and the people we're around. It only makes sense. And plenty of CEOs marry their admins. You're an executive at the firm. You're more of an equal than an actual employee. Right?"

Because Vanessa was offering Maggie a way to justify having her boss spank her, she wasn't sure the conversation was helping.

"Your situation is unique," Vanessa continued. "But I'd say that a relationship between the two of you is just that. Unless one of you is going to file a lawsuit, then it's really just personal preference. A lot of small firms employ family members, and this is no worse than you working for your mom, right?"

Vanessa had a point.

"David is the one who made the rules, and he's made it clear he's interested in you. He's clearly aware of the risks. So if you want him to dominate you, and he's not using his position of authority to unduly manipulate you, then let him paddle your rear." Vanessa poured a small amount of soy sauce over the top of her next lobster roll then slammed down the bottle and scowled. "*Is* he pressuring you?"

"No." Maggie shook her head. "He hasn't mentioned it in a while." Long enough for her to wonder if he truly had lost interest. "And he's offered me more incentive to stay."

"Have you considered he's just as constrained by that damned contract as you are?"

Maggie took a drink of her cooling sake. "What do you mean?"

"He's got a lot of capital invested in your mother's company. He can't go hire a hotshot salesperson who's loyal to him while he's agreed to pay your salary and put money aside for Gloria. Something's gotta give." Vanessa popped the bite into her mouth then blinked furiously.

"Too much wasabi?" Maggie asked with a laugh. The way Vanessa's eyebrows had shot up ruined her lecture and the moment.

"Shit." Vanessa reached for the sake and took a massive gulp. "I need to take it easy here." She fanned herself furiously.

A minute later, after dabbing her eyes with a napkin and shaking her head several times, she went on. "Let me tell you how I see it. I love you, but you look like hell. You're not sleeping, and I'm guessing you're still having those nightmares?"

Maggie nodded. "Unfortunately true."

"What do you think they mean?"

"That I should be very wary of him?"

"What if it's your own feelings that you're scared of?"

She shifted. That was uncomfortably close to what David had previously asked her.

"You've never been one to let life pass you by. Why start now?"

Maggie thought about that for the rest of the night.

Saturday morning, she'd finished her laundry and workout by nine o'clock, leaving a yawning gap in her calendar. Vanessa had a date that evening, and her mother was going to a friend's retirement party. Finally, Maggie sat down in front of her computer and visited the Den's website.

The online calendar showed that tonight's event was geared toward first-time attendees. Maybe she'd find an experienced Dominant there, but the long drive, by herself, made her think twice.

And if David showed up... What then?

Would he be with someone else?

If not, was she up to sceneing with someone else when she craved his lash?

Shaking her head, she raked her hair back.

Annoyed with herself, she flipped her laptop lid closed, then ended up doing a ton of work from home and streaming an entire season's worth of a police drama.

Too often, her thoughts returned to her boss.

By Sunday, and after another broken night's sleep, she knew Vanessa had been right.

She wasn't running from him as much as she was trying to protect herself.

That left only one course of action.

Maggie had to talk to him, whether she wanted to or not.

All day Monday, tension nipped at her.

Because she didn't want to mix work and sex, she decided to talk to him after everyone else had gone home.

Finally, later than normal, her mother waved goodnight, saying she was heading to her first belly dancing lesson.

Once the door had closed behind her, Maggie squared her shoulders and walked down the hallway to David's office.

She knocked on the doorframe and waited until he looked up from the stack of papers before him.

"Maggie."

She cleared her throat and smoothed the front of her skirt. Then realizing she was betraying her nerves, she dropped her hands and asked, "May I come in?"

"Please." He nodded toward the chair across the desk from him.

Her stomach plunged as she took a seat.

Now that she was here, the object of his scrutiny, looking at his disturbingly beautiful eyes, inhaling his ultra-masculine scent, words failed her.

For long moments, he allowed the silence to grow and the tension to stretch. "Something on your mind, Maggie?"

"Yes." She tipped back her head as she twisted her hands together in her lap. "I was wondering..." *I can't do this.*

As he waited, he reached for the yellow stress ball that was sitting on his desktop.

After swallowing her nerves, she seized all her courage and met his intense gaze. "What does a girl have to do to get a spanking around here?"

Chapter Eight

David had wondered how long it would take for her to break.

For weeks, he'd honored her wishes, and it had demanded every damn bit of patience he possessed.

But he'd refused to push her.

If Maggie wanted to confine their personal experience to a one-night stand... Well, that wasn't the way he wanted it. For any relationship with a sub to be successful, she had to offer herself freely.

So he'd kept his own counsel, never revealing how many times he'd jacked off as he replayed their evening together and picturing others in the future.

Since that night at the Den, concentrating on business had been almost impossible. Every waking moment was consumed with thoughts of Maggie and her unrehearsed responses, her whimpers, the way she moved her body, sometimes with sensuous grace, sometimes with an exaggerated tease.

A smarter man might not have played with her at all.

But when it came to her, he was fucking smitten.

A single taste of her response had whetted his appetite. Seeing her every day, tight skirt clinging to her rounded derrière, made it worse. Now he spent his nights and morning workouts fantasizing about having her in his cuffs, over his knee, begging for his attention.

With deliberate mastery, he reined in his thoughts.

Maggie had kept her tone light and teasing, maybe so that she could be flippant if he turned her down. But shakiness made her words wobble, betraying how much his reaction mattered.

If that hadn't given her away, the way her shoulders were held back in a rigid line might have. Her false smile would have sealed the deal.

But he admired how much courage it had taken for her to walk into his office.

And now that she was here…

He would never let her go.

Choosing his response with great care, he said, "She'd have to ask for it, and she'd have to be specific about her intent." Leaning back in his chair, he watched and waited.

Maggie unclasped her hands and scooted back in the chair, crossing one leg over the other in a sexy slide of silk.

A tendril of hair had escaped its confines to tease her cheekbone. He wanted to stroke it back as he grabbed her chin and held it hostage. "She would also be frank about her expectations and what she was willing to give in return. She'd have to be honest with herself as well as me." He released the ball and let it fall to the desktop.

"That's why I'm here."

He didn't press, giving her the opportunity to sort through this at her own speed.

"I...uhm...haven't slept well in weeks. I think that hooking up with you will relieve some of my angst."

"You just caused permanent injury to my ego, Maggie." He placed his hand over his heart in mock affront. "I was hoping you were going to flatter me, throw yourself on your knees at my feet, telling me I'm a fabulous Dom as you prettily beg for my attention."

She grinned. "That, too."

For a moment, he was silent. This was one of the rare moments of lightness between them, and he appreciated it. "The last time we spoke about this, you were clear that you don't want to feel as if I'm manipulating you. Or that you're sleeping with the enemy."

She ran her thumb across a cuticle and didn't seem to know what to say next. "If we agree to keep our business and private lives separate, it should work."

"Go on."

"I thought we could scene on occasion. No strings. Just when it's convenient for both of us. If it suited you, we could meet at the Den and keep it less complicated."

"I can understand if you need that for security."

Boldly she brought her chin up and met his gaze. "I trust you."

Those words humbled him. "In that case, it's easier if we use one of our places."

She nodded.

"When were you wanting to get together?"

"I was hoping we could do it tonight," she confessed. "So that I can sleep. I understand if—"

"Would you like me to take you to dinner first?"

"No. I don't need anything else from you."

"Only my flogger and my dick?"

She blew out a breath. "You asked for honesty."

Any more ways you'd like to destroy my ego?

"So, what do you say?" she asked breezily, as if his answer didn't matter. "My place or yours?"

"I'll give you a ten-minute head start while I finish up a few things here. When I arrive at your place, I want you naked, lying on your back on the floor, your knees raised and held apart by your hands."

She blinked.

"Any questions?"

"Where in the house? My bedroom?"

"You tell me."

"Ah..." She shifted. "Right inside the doorway."

"Good answer. I'll need your address." He slid a piece of paper across to her.

Maggie scooted forward on her chair and wrote down her information.

"Make good use of your time."

She met his eyes. Her luminous eyes were wide, unblinking, and her lips were slightly parted.

He'd yet to touch her, but because of the things he'd said, she clearly understood that their scene was already in progress.

His cock hardened as she stood and fidgeted, much like she'd done at the Den. The betrayal of her nerves was utterly feminine and enchanting.

At the door, she paused and looked back over her shoulder.

For a moment, he expected her to say something, but after a few seconds, she left.

David finished his work, shut down his computer, turned off the lights, and walked through the offices, giving her the allotted amount of time.

His car was the last one in the parking garage. As he climbed behind the wheel of the SUV, the overhead light bounced off the handcuffs he'd left on the console.

Before the night was out, he'd have her in them.

He navigated out of the maze of one-way streets and merged onto the crowded interstate. Restlessness and anticipation collided.

Tightening his grip on the steering wheel, he reminded himself he'd be at her home soon enough. The more time he gave her to get ready for him, the better. As a bonus, it would stretch her nerves tighter.

He hoped she understood how much he, too, wanted this. It had been years since he'd had a regular playmate. And he missed that.

The pleasure that came with exploring a new woman was gratifying, but to him, getting to know a sub—figuring out her likes, catering to them, finding her limits, and shattering them—was even more sublime. Control.

The mindfuck.

He exited the highway on the south end of the metro area, and as he drove west, the traffic thinned out. It was a bonus that she lived in the same general direction as his house in Castle Pines.

Her condo complex had nicely tended gardens and an inviting-looking swimming pool. As for the hot tub, the one in his backyard was much more private.

He attached the cuffs to his belt loop and took the steps up to the second floor to find her place.

After knocking once, he tried the knob and found it unlocked.

He let himself in and secured the deadbolt behind him.

As he'd instructed, she was lying on her back on the living room floor, legs spread, knees held apart. Her chest rose and fell rapidly. Maggie was stunning in her nudity and compliance. The weeks of waiting for her capitulation had been worth it.

"Beautiful," he murmured as he walked around her, taking her in from every angle. She'd closed the blinds and, he presumed, moved a coffee table up against a wall.

Her space was what he'd expected — comfortable, lived in. She had a few knickknacks, and the two paintings on the walls were slashes of bold, abstract color.

But it was difficult to look at anything other than her. "I love the way your pussy is on such perfect display for me. Since you're so well behaved, I may go a little easier on you than planned." That was a lie. He'd give her everything she asked for, and more. "Would you like me to start by pulling your nipples until you whimper?"

She exhaled a shaky breath.

He crouched next to her and kept her gaze hostage as he flicked her right nipple several times until it became a hard peak. "Hmm?"

"Yes, please, Mr. Tomlinson."

"That's what you like, isn't it, sub?"

"Oh yes. It is."

He stood long enough to shrug out of his suit jacket and drape it over the back of the couch. Then he rolled back his cuffs before squatting again.

Since he knew she was expecting more nipple play, he smacked her gorgeous cunt.

Arching her back, she cried out.

"Do you need a gag?" He didn't wait for a response. Instead, he loosened his tie, pulled it from around his neck then wadded it and said, "Open your mouth."

When she did, he shoved the material between her teeth. "That's meant to give you a bit more freedom to scream, but your hands are free. Remove it if you need to use your slow word. Eclipse, right?" He waited for her assent before continuing. "Halt will stop the action right away, and I'll be watching you and your reactions. Since we haven't played together enough for me to know your true limits, I don't want to push you too far."

She nodded.

Next time, he'd arrange for her to visit his house — there were no neighbors nearby, so she could be as loud as she liked. The higher her volume, the more he'd enjoy the experience. "I want you to do your best to keep your legs apart."

She mumbled something that sounded like agreement.

"Release your knees and keep your hands flat against the floor unless you need to signal me." Then he stroked between her legs, where he'd blazed her with the harsh spank.

Maggie held herself rigid, as if expecting more of the same.

Which he absolutely wouldn't deliver.

Keeping her off balance was part of his diabolical strategy to keep her coming back to him.

He made soothing sounds while he slid his fingers on the inside of her labia. She drew a deep breath and exhaled. As she relaxed, she seemed to allow the floor to take more of her weight, and her body's response coated his fingers with dampness. "That's it." He continued until he knew she was almost orgasmic, then he smacked her again, hard, three times in rapid succession.

"Fuck, Sir!"

Though her words were muffled by the fabric in her mouth, he understood perfectly.

To her credit, she stayed in position. "Do you like that, Maggie?"

She nodded.

"Perfect." It was a treat to be with a woman whose desires matched his. "I want you to come from this."

She tightened her buttocks but didn't protest or use a safe signal.

"Ready?" Before she could respond, he cupped his hand and slapped her damp pussy several times.

Whimpering, she thrashed her head back and forth.

He paused to allow her to catch her breath, then he licked two of his fingers and tenderly stroked her again.

She moaned.

"That's it," he soothed. "Give me your responses." David tormented her until she dug her heels into the floor and lifted her hips. He responded by slapping her several more times.

Behind the makeshift gag, she screamed.

He watched her carefully to ensure his repeated blows weren't more torturous than enjoyable.

Deliberately he alternated the pleasure and the pain.

She held nothing back, arching to meet his hand.

He smacked her swollen pussy hard.

She took a shuddering breath and lowered her buttocks to the floor. He caressed her, sliding a finger into her pussy.

Then she lifted her pelvis again, signaling her need to continue. "Brave sub." Slowly, he resumed his smacks.

Her pussy became redder.

"Such a beautiful sight," he told her approvingly. "I'm imagining it will still look like this when you're getting ready for work tomorrow. Skip the panties," he commanded.

Eyes wide, she stared at him.

He wouldn't know if she'd taken his suggestion. But the idea of her labia being plump and tender would distract him all day.

He continued on, bringing her to the edge of a climax. "Show me you want it."

With tiny whimpers, she rubbed herself against his hand, grinding, seeking.

"That's it." He made tiny, encouraging sounds, meeting her next thrust by plunging two fingers inside her to find her G-spot and press against it.

She cried out and dug her heels into the carpet. Her lovely thighs quivered as he continued. Then she convulsed around his fingers as the orgasm finally claimed her.

"Ride it," he encouraged.

Obediently, she wriggled her hips, groaning.

He grinned, delighted she'd sought him out. This beat the hell out of a cold beer and spending the night wondering what the hell she was doing.

When she settled again, he stood to admire her.

Covered with a fine sheen of dampness, her curvy body lay open for him.

Her responses intoxicated him.

Not quite finished with her, he asked, "Where are your nipple clamps?"

She inclined her head to indicate a room down the hallway.

"Show me." He crouched to help her up.

As she slid her palm against his, an unfamiliar, but not unwelcome, urge to protect her struck him.

Where the hell did that come from?

Maggie was the last woman who would appreciate that thought.

In her bare feet, she only reached his chest and had to tip her head back to look at him. The tie remained in place. In her submission, she was exquisite.

The reminder of her trust humbled him, making him even more determined to please her.

The musk of her arousal smelled sharp on the evening air.

It was a good thing he was still dressed, otherwise he would have pinned her to the floor and fucked her hard. "Hands behind you."

Her gaze was riveted to him as she watched him detach the formidable-looking metal from his belt loop.

"I've kept them in the car for you." He moved around to secure them at the small of her back. He checked the position of her shoulders. "Comfortable enough?"

After she nodded, he ratcheted the cuffs one notch tighter. "Turn your thumbs down if you need to signal me. I will be watching you." The sight of the glinting metal against her creamy skin appealed to him on a very carnal level. "You were meant for these, Maggie."

She gave him a small nod.

Absently David wondered if he could gag her when they were at work. It would make his life much more pleasant. But, he had to admit, less productive, as well.

He'd spent a lot of days fantasizing about filling her mouth with other things. "After you," he invited.

She hesitated, so he pinched her right buttock, urging her forward. He followed a couple steps behind, admiring the way her body swayed seductively as she walked. Her gait was much more feminine than it was at work, as if being naked, cuffed, and gagged changed not only her frame of mind but also how she moved.

This woman was a natural submissive.

And at least for now, *his* submissive.

Inside the bedroom, she stopped.

He appreciated that the room was large and uncluttered. There was an en suite bathroom, and he took a moment to close the blinds and turn on the overhead fan.

She led him toward the closet.

Unsurprisingly, all of her items were well organized. Work clothing was on the far left, grouped by color. Next, she had casual clothing.

Then came the sexy stuff that made his jaw drop.

Though he tried to concentrate, the sight of her short skirts, skimpy V-necked blouses, and a corset nearly brought him to his knees. "The clamps?" he asked, voice hoarse as he struggled to harness his thoughts.

She nodded toward a set of drawers.

The first one he opened contained lingerie. He picked up a lacy shelf bra and held it as he looked over his shoulder at her. "Is this what you wear to work?"

She nodded.

"And this?" he asked, scooping up a garter belt.

Even with the tie in her mouth, she managed a grin.

"Every day?" When she nodded, he slammed the drawer closed, knowing he'd never again get any work done. His fingers would be itching to trace the seductive straps that attached to her silky hose. Now that he'd discovered this secret, keeping their work and private lives separate was going to be far more difficult than he'd imagined, especially once he factored in her reddened pussy and soon-to-be tormented buttocks. "I'm going to buy you some granny panties," he said. "And all-day support bras. There's nothing wrong with cotton."

She drew her eyebrows together.

"Maybe a chastity belt."

He found her toys in the next drawer down.

As he now expected, everything was in perfect order. Clamps were on the far left. Two floggers were laid lengthwise across the back. Beneath them was a paddle with holes in it. She also had a hairbrush and a tawse stamped with an eagle. "A Master Marcus creation, if I'm not mistaken?"

Her response was muffled, but her nod was clear.

"You do like your spankings."

Tipping her head back, she met his gaze.

In every way, she was perfect for him.

Returning to the toys, he made a mental inventory of her selection of butt plugs, vibrators, and dildos. "Good God, woman." Her treasure trove rivaled his. It would take days to explore how she liked to have them used on her delectable body. He intended to do just that. "We're spending the weekend together."

Her response was unintelligible, but her eyes were wide open.

"If you have plans, you'll be rescheduling them."

Chapter Nine

As much as David liked having her gagged, this conversation mattered too much, and they needed to be able to communicate. He removed the tie from her mouth, but he laid it on her shoulder for easy access. "I meant it. We're spending the weekend together. Any questions?"

"That's..."

Out of bounds? Impossible? Suddenly he didn't care. "You want it as much as I do."

She glanced away, as if wanting to hide her truth, but it was there, revealed in her eyes. Maybe she needed to be cautious, but he wouldn't be denied. "Maggie?"

"Maybe we can work something out."

Something? They'd be having a whole lot more than that. He had four full days to convince her of it. But he was betting he didn't need more than the next hour or two.

He picked up a pair of clamps and held them in his palm. "Too lightweight," he surmised, glancing at her.

Her nod confirmed his guess.

The second set was a bit more intense. "You have them laid out by pressure?"

She glanced away as if embarrassed.

"Smart," he said. "Makes it easier to find exactly what you want. Do you want the hardest ones?"

In response, she wrinkled her nose.

She licked her lips, and he was gripped by the image of that tongue pressed against his dick.

With determination, he focused on her.

"I almost never play with the hardest ones," she told him. "I have to work up to them or be really deep into a scene."

"Understood." He selected those and the pair next to them. "These?"

"My favorites," she said.

He tested the pressure. To him, the bite felt vicious. Then he recalled he'd added weights when he'd clamped her at the Den. "Do you need anything before we continue? A drink of water? To stretch your muscles?"

She waited a moment. He expected her to ask for another orgasm or to get on with the spanking, but her silence made it clear she was going to let him set the pace.

"No, Mr. Tomlinson. I'm fine. Thank you."

He didn't wait any longer. He picked up the tie and guided her back into the middle of the bedroom.

After depositing the clamps and tie on the nightstand, he captured her right breast and held it while he teased her nipple with his tongue. When it started to lengthen and thicken, he sucked on it.

Maggie moaned and leaned toward him. Again, he was struck by the lack of inhibition in her reactions.

When she was naked, she didn't attempt to hide anything from him.

Her little sounds of approval drove him on, and he moved to her left breast and coaxed the same response from her body before pulling back to look at her pert, pink nipples.

He adored the way both stood so erect, waiting for his further attention.

Pulling on each in turn, elongating them, he held them distended while he placed the clamps.

For a moment, she exhaled deeply and closed her eyes. *Adjusting to the pain?*

When she opened them, she looked at him and said, "Thank you."

Her words were appreciative, so beautifully submissive.

She seemed like a puzzle, each piece unique and complex. To him, she was no longer a woman who worked with him, alternately helpful and confounding, or a sub he enjoyed playing with. She was much more complicated.

He stood and curved his hands around her upper arms. "This is more than a desire for an occasional kick for you, isn't it?"

She drew a few, shuddering breaths.

The silence stretched for so long he began to wonder if she would answer.

"Yes, Mr. Tomlinson, it is."

As it was for him. Suddenly he was hungry to know much, much more about her.

Studying her, he fisted the chain that draped between her breasts and dragged her nipples together.

Though she gasped, she didn't protest.

No anguish painted her face, only serenity.

"So pleasing." Ever so slightly, he eased the pressure.

"Thank you, Mr. Tomlinson."

"I do love your manners. How would you like your spanking?"

"Well done," she replied, her tone full of sass.

With a grin, he tugged on her clamps, making her sigh in response. "Impossible wench," he observed with an exaggerated huff.

"I liked that, Sir," she said softly. "It's so different than when I play with myself. Not knowing what you're going to do, how it's going to feel, being unable to brace myself. So honestly, however you want to spank me is fine. I just..." Her voice cracked. "Need it."

How could he not give her everything she wanted?

Since he'd had her across his lap at the Den, he opted for something else, though if he were honest, he'd admit that he loved the feel and the sight of her body as she squirmed against his skin. "I'm going to remove your cuffs temporarily." He released the lock and freed one wrist. He rubbed her skin because he wanted the connection he got from touching her. "They don't seem as if they were too tight."

"Not at all."

He repeated the process with the other. Then he massaged her shoulders before instructing, "I want you to kneel on the bed, but then scoot back so you're close to the edge of the mattress, facedown with your rear in the air."

Her motions were deliberate, slow, and feminine, and he helped her up and into position. "That's it. I want your breasts smashed against the mattress, Maggie. I want you to feel that burn from the clamps."

"Yes, Sir." She did as he instructed, then hissed when he pressed down on her back, forcing her down even farther.

"That's better. Now show me your gorgeous butt." It took several seconds for her to get in the exact position he wanted.

"Are you comfortable enough?"

"Yes, Mr. Tomlinson."

Next, he walked around to the far side of the bed. "Please stretch out your arms toward me."

When she had, he cuffed her again. "How's that?"

Since she obviously didn't want to break position, she could only lift her head a few inches to look at him. Her eyelids were lowered a bit, and he was recognizing the look as one that came over her when she was getting deeper and deeper into a submissive headspace. "So good, Sir."

As he checked the fit of his restraints, he held her gaze. "I'm going to spank you. And I'm not telling you with what."

"*Oh.*"

"And if you behave, you'll earn another orgasm."

"Thank you, Mr. Tomlinson."

"Are you comfortable enough?"

"Not at all."

He grinned. "Perfect."

"I figured that might be your response, Mr. Tomlinson."

"Do you really want it otherwise?"

"No, Sir," she said clearly.

"As I thought." He moved behind her.

He trailed his fingers down her back until he was between her buttocks. She parted her legs to give him greater access.

Her muscles tensed from the strain of fighting to remain in place while he fondled her. As she squirmed slightly, he lazily continued to touch and explore.

"Please, please, please," she begged, shamelessly pressing against his hand.

The tang of her arousal rent the air and urged him on in a primal need for possession. "How do you keep this side of yourself hidden at work?" He gave her a few light slaps.

"Oh, Mr. Tomlinson. That's... It's too..." she half protested as she gyrated, keeping her butt high.

"You're a bit sensitive from earlier?"

"Yes. It won't take much for me to come. I thought I should let you know."

"I'm glad you did." He changed the tempo to give her momentary respite. "Will the spanking be more memorable to you if you don't orgasm?"

"Probably," she admitted.

"Better not take the chance, hmm?"

"As you wish, Mr. Tomlinson."

"I could listen to you say that all day long." After another stroke—because he could—he removed his hand.

She exhaled, settling deeper into the mattress and—it seemed—into herself.

At some point, the only thing he wanted her to wear was his handprint.

He unbuckled his belt and pulled it free from the loops with a snap. She moved in response to the sound, perhaps trying to prepare herself.

David folded the leather over and gripped the buckle. She swayed as he spread his legs and turned sideways to her so that he could stroke her with good, precise swings.

He caught her ass with a smack, and the sound echoed satisfyingly.

Her approving purr flowed over him in a satisfying wave.

She stayed in position, and he continued in earnest, catching her ass cheeks one at a time, then placing a powerful one beneath the curve of her buttocks.

Unlike earlier, she kept quiet, not requiring anything to muffle her sounds.

"You're made for this."

"Yes, Sir."

He fell into rhythm, bringing back his arm and laying the leather to her tender skin.

The longer he went on, the more she seemed to relax.

He kissed her with the belt again, just above the backs of her knees.

Hissing out a breath, she lifted her head a little. Moments later, she whispered, "Thank you, Mr. Tomlinson."

Her appreciation reached somewhere deep inside him that hadn't been touched in years.

"More, please."

David changed his stance and flicked out the belt so it was more of a single tail. Now he could use the end to catch her skin with the harsher licks she'd asked for.

She whimpered when he marked her, filling him with the masculine urge to give his woman everything she desired.

"Please spread your knees farther apart." Once she had, he continued, able to reach more of her unmarred and tender places.

Her noises became a little more pronounced, especially when he lighted across her pussy. "Such a good little pet," he whispered approvingly.

"Oh, Mr. Tomlinson."

"Is that a request for me to slow down?"

"*No.*"

"Or the gag?"

"If it pleases you, Sir. But it's not necessary. I just want more, please."

He resumed, landing most licks across her buttocks punctuated by an occasional and careful tease of her pussy.

She grabbed the bedding, bunching the comforter in her fingers.

Driven by her greed, he measured his spanks, delivering them at the same interval until her sounds all but ceased, and she relaxed her grip. He knew she was getting lost in the endorphins flooding her system, but she had the presence of mind to keep her body in the position he required.

Though his arm was tired, he stayed with her a few more minutes. "I'm going to bring you back," he said, his words a whisper so as not to shatter her reverie. He continued to let the belt fall, but with less and less force. "Take your time," he said. "I won't hurry you."

He touched her shoulder, then stroked down her spine.

It took at least a full minute for her to begin to move. "That's it," he soothed, tossing the belt on the nightstand. The buckle hit with a thud that made her inhale sharply and look up.

"I'm going to release your cuffs," he said with some reluctance. After all, at the Den, she'd run the moment he'd released her restraints.

At least at her house, she couldn't physically leave him, but she could build an emotional wall that he didn't know how to summit.

He'd do anything to prevent that from happening.

After opening the cuffs and removing them, he rubbed her wrists like he had earlier.

This time, her skin was slightly chafed from the metal, so he spent another full minute soothing her skin. "Remain in position, please. I'll be back in a few seconds. Is that okay?"

When she nodded her assent, he crossed to the bathroom and washed his hands. He found towels in a cupboard, and he dampened one before carrying it back to her.

Her body was heated and covered in a sheen of perspiration.

Gently he wiped her shoulders then lifted her hair to cleanse her nape before moving lower to give relief to the tiny marks on her buttocks and legs.

"That feels good. Thank you, Mr. Tomlinson."

He finished by dabbing her pussy and ass before tossing aside the towel and turning her over. With extreme care, he removed the clamps and immediately sucked each nipple to chase away the pain.

Then he toed off his shoes and moved her to the middle of the bed and lay beside her, pulling her against him. "Don't fight me."

Surprising him, she obeyed. She laid her head on his biceps, and her hair spilled across him.

Outside, night cast her shadows across the Rockies.

As she emerged from her place of pleasure-pain, her breaths became deeper. She curled against him, and he wrapped his arms around her to keep her warm.

"That was…"

He waited.

"One of the best scenes I ever remember."

One *of the best?* "I'll have to improve."

She scooted away so she could face him. "I meant it as a compliment, Sir."

He grinned and brushed hair back from her face. Her cheeks were still flushed. "Do you have bandages?"

"Mr. Tomlinson?"

"This time, I fear your words have caused my ego to sustain a mortal wound."

"Well, I'll volunteer my services so you can get more practice." She gave a long-suffering sigh.

Sexy and *sassy.* This was the Maggie he was beginning to know, buried beneath layers of professional clothes and a haughty demeanor. The more she revealed the real her, the deeper he wanted to excavate.

He pulled her tighter against him and held her while she dozed.

Minutes later, when she roused, he got a full-on erection.

"Your turn, I should say, Mr. Tomlinson."

"Just to be clear, Maggie, I have no expectation that you have to sleep with me because we played together."

"I was hoping you would fuck me."

He held her chin.

"It's part of it, for me," she admitted.

"I thought we had taken care of your restlessness."

"You did." Her big green eyes were wide, and she blinked a couple of times, and if the woman were someone other than Maggie, he would have said the look was flirtatious. "Okay, fine," she said. "Is this what you want to hear? I'm needy."

He chuckled.

"I could give you a dozen emotional reasons, but I want sex. If you choose not to allow me to come, I accept that, but I really want your enormous, gigantic cock in me."

"'Enormous, gigantic cock'?" he couldn't help but repeat, a smile playing around his lips. *Tempting wench knows how to get exactly what she wants.*

"I'm trying to repair the damage to your self-esteem, Mr. Tomlinson. Shall I go on? Gorgeous dick. Perfect penis. Throbbing—"

"Where's that gag?"

"Are you going to do me, or what?"

"Well, when you ask so nicely…" He let her go long enough to get out of bed. He removed a condom from his wallet before placing it on the nightstand. Then he undressed and hung his clothes from a bedpost.

She turned on her side and propped her head on her upturned hand and watched as he put the condom on his dick.

"What *was* I thinking? That's a gargantuan cock," she said.

"Maggie… I think you're forgetting yourself."

She grinned and rolled to her back, spreading her legs in invitation. "Sorry, Mr. Tomlinson."

"I'd give you a paddling, but you'd like it." He was as aroused as she was.

Maggie wrinkled her nose. "I could be brattier."

"In which case, I'll put you in a corner with your nose against the wall," he warned as he joined her on the bed.

Color drained from her face. "I'll behave," she said.

"Maggie, mine..." He captured her chin between his thumb and forefinger. "You couldn't be any more wonderful."

He guided his cockhead toward her entrance. He intended to enter her with short strokes so that her body could accommodate him. "You weren't kidding about being ready."

"I'm wet for you, Sir."

"So hot," she said softly.

They were good together. He slid inside her in a single surge.

"That's what I need. Hard, Mr. Tomlinson." She bit her lower lip. "I mean, if that's all right?"

"I'll fuck you however you want it." He released his grip on her and said, "Put your legs around my waist." That forced her to lift her hips and gave him a different angle. "Keep some of your weight on your arms or elbows so you can keep yourself open for me." If she wanted a ride, he'd give it to her.

She looked at him, nothing but trust in her unblinking eyes.

It took all his mental control not to lose himself in her feminine warmth.

Again and again, he drove into her.

"This is... Damn. You're so deep in me."

Holding nothing back, he pounded her until she trembled, struggling to meet each of his surges. Her brow furrowed, and she dug her heels into his back for purchase.

"Mr. Tomlinson, I'm going to come," she frantically said.

Maggie's words were as much a question as a warning. "Do it."

Almost instantly, her pussy clenched, and the constriction of her muscles milked his cock. He gritted his teeth, determined to satisfy her first.

He moved to put his hands beneath her buttocks, giving her extra support as she rode her orgasm.

She whimpered, and her body convulsed as she reached for it.

David spread her buttocks apart slightly and pressed his thumb against her anus.

Her scream rent the air.

Maggie broke position and grabbed his shoulders. She held on to him as she bucked and cried out.

For long seconds, she didn't breathe. Then eventually her internal pressure eased.

She feathered her fingers into his hair. "Thank you."

"Pleasuring you is an honor, Maggie."

"Now your turn," she said. "Before your big cock explodes."

He'd have glanced pointedly at his makeshift gag, but he didn't have the energy. If he were honest, he'd admit he didn't want to look away. All he wanted was to fuck her.

David removed his thumb and adjusted their positions a bit. "Put your buttocks on the mattress and grab the headboard." Once she had, he nodded his approval. "That's it." He had her where he wanted her, unable to move. He slid his hands beneath her and dug his fingers into the buttocks he'd reddened earlier.

With short, then lengthening strokes, he took her.

Her muttered sounds of pleasure fed him.

"You fill me," she told him. "So, so full."

Knowing she was getting off was enough for him. It took less than thirty seconds for the orgasm to erupt from him — and that was what it felt like. It came from deep inside, hot and pulsing, joining them together.

He gritted his teeth as he ejaculated.

His nerve endings electrified, he collapsed on her. God, this woman with her wayward hair and wild abandon did it for him. He hadn't had this sense of connection in a long time, if ever.

When he'd worked out on his rowing machine this morning, he hadn't anticipated the day ending like this. She wasn't the only one who would sleep well.

He disposed of the condom then returned to her and scooped her up. "We need a shower."

"We?"

"I'm not done with you yet. A shower will restore you for what I have in mind next."

Chapter Ten

First, though, he ordered dinner for them. "You'll need your strength."

Food was the last thing on her mind. But when David made a decision, there was no arguing with him.

Because the delivery wasn't expected for an hour, he joined her in the bathroom where he turned on the shower water. Within a minute, steam billowed, fogging the mirror. "There's room for two."

His invitation was irresistible. She took a few seconds to pin up her hair then paused to look at him.

The man made her mouth water.

Because they'd been sceneing when he'd been naked before, she hadn't fully appreciated his sculpted, masculine form until now.

His biceps could have been chiseled from marble, and his abs were honed, without an excess ounce of fat anywhere.

And more shockingly, his enormous cock was already — or still? — semihard.

"Come here, Maggie." He extended his hand toward her.

After shrugging off her robe, she joined him.

Tenderly, over her protests, he lathered her body then rinsed off the floral-scented soap. He took his time bathing her between her legs, leaving no part untouched and sending heat crashing through her again.

Then he set her away from him just a little. "I want to look at your bruises." Gently, he trailed his fingers down her spine, then he captured her buttocks and parted them.

After everything they'd shared, she shouldn't have been embarrassed, but she was.

"Relax, Maggie Mine."

How does he know me so well?

Determinedly he continued on, squatting behind her to inspect the backs of her thighs. "You have a couple of tiny marks. Hopefully they won't bruise."

Which meant she might not have anything to remember him by.

There was no reason for him to remain where he was, but he didn't immediately stand.

"If you find sitting at work to be a little uncomfortable, I won't mind."

She turned to face him. "Did you really just say that?"

"No apologies." Slowly he stood and cupped her breasts in his palms. "How are your nipples?" He captured them, and a simultaneous combination of pain and arousal gushed through her.

"Wow."

"Maybe you should wear clamps to work tomorrow."

"Mr. Tomlinson!" She wasn't sure whether she hated the idea or loved it.

"I'll buy you some nipple jewelry that's light enough to wear every day. It would be a turn on to know you were suffering a little for me."

They'd agreed to keep work and pleasure separate. *So why aren't I reminding you of that fact?* "It might be distracting."

"For both of us. But in the interim, I can have you come into my office, unhook your bra, open your shirt, and I can suck on them until your knees weaken."

Suddenly needing support, she reached for him.

"You like the idea."

A damp tendril of her hair had curled against her cheek, and he brushed it back. "Shall we have a standing appointment? After your coffee, perhaps?"

The image was so powerful and compelling that she couldn't force it away.

"Sometimes you could just stand there, prim and proper, while I lowered my head."

Her pussy throbbed with need.

"Others I might be seated, and you could feed your nipple into my mouth."

"*Sir!*"

"In fact, that might be the preparation to properly affix the jewelry."

The idea—even if it never happened—was enough to drive her out of her mind.

"Your nipples are so hard, Maggie. And I'm betting your pussy is wet. Shall I see for myself?"

Without waiting for a response, he parted her labia to slide a finger back and forth across her clit, then he thrust it inside her.

Gasping, she raised up onto her toes.

"You're so responsive, even to my voice." He angled his finger to find her G-spot.

It would take moments for her to climax.

"I want you to wait."

As he removed his finger and stepped back, she squeezed her eyes shut in frustration.

"Edging you is something I should do more often."

"No!" Her objection escaped before she could stop it.

"That wasn't very submissive."

Not even a little bit.

He delivered a quick smack to her pussy that pushed her even closer.

"Lucky for you I enjoy watching you come."

"So..."

Towering over her, fully Dominant, he folded his arms. "Not this time."

"But, Mr. Tomlinson..."

"I'm a generous Dom. I'm giving you a chance to maybe earn another one tonight."

She blew out a breath. "Anything you say, Sir."

"And?" he prompted.

"Thank you for..." *Leaving me totally unfulfilled.* "Edging me."

As if he'd read her mind, he chuckled. "You're very welcome." He tipped his head to one side. "I advise you to use your pretty manners more."

"Of course, Sir." She forced the words through gritted teeth.

"Do you have arnica?"

What?

The previous conversation apparently over with, he'd switched the subject, leaving her off balance. "I do," she replied.

"Good. I'll want to rub some of that into your buttocks."

While he finished up, she exited the shower, dried off, dressed in her robe again, then found the tube of arnica. As far as she was concerned, it didn't get nearly enough use. But maybe now that she'd agreed to play with David, that would change.

Eventually he joined her in the bedroom, a towel wrapped around his waist and a droplet of water meandering down the center of his chest.

"Bend over the bed for me."

When she did, he bared her butt and massaged some of the white cream onto her marks. While it acted as a pain reliever, it also helped minimize bruising.

If this was his version of aftercare, she was sorry she'd missed out that night at the Den.

Once he was satisfied, he helped her to stand, then pulled on his slacks and shrugged into his dress shirt, leaving it unbuttoned.

Because they were still expecting dinner, she changed into a cozy top and yoga pants, and not a moment too soon.

The food arrived before they'd moved to the kitchen area.

David had ordered a ridiculous number of selections.

"Let me get you a tip," she said to the woman.

"Already handled." She pointed to the bottom of the receipt.

Not only had he covered it, the amount was more than generous. "In that case, thank you. Have a good evening." But the woman was already halfway down the first flight of stairs.

"Wow," she said, joining him with the enormous brown paper bags. "This is a feast."

"You won't need to worry about cooking for a few days."

Or a week.

He'd already made himself comfortable in her space, finding plates, silverware, napkins and organizing them on the dining room table.

Though he hadn't been here before and it had been years since she'd had anyone sharing her space, she was comfortable.

During the meal, they talked, avoiding discussion about work.

"I meant it that I want to spend the weekend together."

She met his gaze. When they'd been in the bedroom, part of her had wondered if he'd been speaking from the heat of the moment. That he was reiterating it now meant something.

"My place is in Castle Pines."

While she was more comfortable here, if things became too much at his home, she could always walk out the front door.

"Can you clear your calendar?"

Her sense of self-preservation warned that it wasn't smart to indulge in something more than a casual hookup. But when it came to David Tomlinson, especially with him sitting here, so handsome and intriguing, she was willing to ignore the alarm bells that clamored in her brain.

Instead of shaking her head, she nodded. "If you're okay with me coming over on Saturday afternoon. I'd like to work a little and go to my yoga class in the morning. And I have my usual chores."

"Perfectly fine."

Why was he not always this accommodating?

After they finished eating, he loaded the dishwasher while she put away the leftovers.

She was seeing a totally different side of him, one that was difficult to resist.

When he was finished, he turned toward her, eyes darkening.

In response, her heart rate slowed.

"How's your energy level?" His voice was gruff with Dominant demand.

"I…" When he looked at her that way, addressed her in that tone, she would give him anything he wanted. "What did you have in mind, Sir?" The honorific slipped out in automatic, submissive response.

"I want to take you."

She glanced down.

"Perfect." His voice held an approving husk. "Please remove your clothes."

Because of the implacable note in the command, she didn't dare argue.

Instead, she immediately stripped, even though she stood in the middle of her kitchen.

"I'd like you to crawl to the bedroom so I can watch your ass move and maybe catch a glimpse of your cunt."

At his raw words, she sucked in a shallow breath.

"But first…"

Before lowering herself to all fours, she looked up. "Sir?"

"So you know what to expect tomorrow…" He lowered his head to take one of her nipples in his mouth.

Then he sucked hard. Because he'd already tormented her, her slight pain instantly crashed heat through her. "God! *Sir!*"

"Don't tell me you hate it," he said softly, "because I can already smell your arousal. And I'd hate to have to punish you for lying."

Frantically she shook her head.

"Shall I leave you feeling lopsided?"

"Please suck the other one, Sir!" Already he had her on the verge of coming—probably because he'd been edging her. If he touched her pussy, she'd orgasm in an instant. "Please."

"Are you uncomfortable?"

"Yes." She ached for his attention.

He stepped back. "Good."

Her mouth fell open. Did he mean to leave her like this?

"I'll follow you to the bedroom." Purposefully he glanced at the tile floor.

Frustrated but knowing better than to argue, she lowered herself to her hands and knees.

"You don't want me to think you're stalling."

Wrinkling her nose, she began to make her way down the hallway, her hips moving from side to side, her breasts swaying.

She was horribly aware of the way the breast he hadn't given attention to felt heavier than the other.

Had she ever been with a more evil or wonderful Dominant?

Once they reached her bedroom, he instructed her to bend over the bed. After rolling on a condom, he dug his strong fingers into her hips and claimed her from behind.

"Come as often as you like. And take advantage of the opportunity because you may not be allowed another until you're across my lap at my house."

You can't mean that.

But then she realized he probably did.

He did her hard, giving her three orgasms before claiming his own.

When they were replete, exhaustion claimed her.

After disposing of the condom, he bathed her pussy like he had earlier, then he turned back the covers and climbed into bed alongside her.

Snuggled into his hard, comforting embrace, she fell asleep.

Hours later, when her alarm shattered the silence, he was gone, and her body was chilled.

After finding her robe, she slipped into it, the material abrading her nipples. Impossibly, her left breast still seemed to ache from the lack of attention he'd given it when he'd sucked her right nipple in the kitchen.

With a sigh, she wandered into the main part of her condo.

David hadn't left a note.

Other than the residual tenderness in her body and the fact her discarded clothes were neatly folded and placed on the back of the couch in the living room, there was no sign he'd been here at all.

And she wasn't sure how she felt about that.

Relieved?

Lonely?

In a desperate attempt to sort through the emotions of the past twelve hours, she brewed a cup of coffee.

As she rested her hips against the counter, the first sips of caffeine waking her up, her eyes opened wide.

Physically, she felt better than she had in weeks, then she realized she'd slept soundly all night.

Had Vanessa been right about her nightmares? That Maggie needed to face herself and not just David?

As the warmth from the cup soothed her, her thoughts spun backward.

Being with him had been everything she'd needed. The spanking from his belt had been masterful, allowing her to surrender to it, to him. And because he'd been so thorough, he'd sent her to subspace and allowed her to linger in that amazing, magical space that she'd only achieved once and never thought she'd reach again.

When he'd blazed into her life months ago, his confidence had irritated her. She'd wanted to label it as overconfidence, but during the previous months, he'd backed up everything he'd said.

Now, rather than chafing under his control, she was accepting it. As a result, all her inner tension had been soothed.

Conscious of the time ticking away, she hurried through her shower then walked into her closet.

As she stood there trying to decide what to wear, some of his comments from last night flitted through her mind.

Almost every day, she wore stockings and a garter belt to work because she liked the feeling. Today, though, David would know what was beneath her skirt.

Until him, she'd been able to separate her BDSM play from the rest of her life, compartmentalizing each piece. Of course, until now, she'd never had to face her Dom at the office the next day. Well, not that she'd ever had a true Dom before, either.

Maggie shuddered. She had been certain she could manage to work with him. After all, the contract wasn't forever, and they had an agreement in place.

Suddenly that didn't seem to help.

After selecting her lingerie, she shoved the drawer closed.

She winced a little when she slipped her bra into place. Her nipples were more tender than she'd realized.

In the mirror, she caught a reflection of a red mark—a single welt—above the back of her knees. She fingered it the best she could with the awkward angle. Breath evaporated from her lungs.

Even if she tried to forget last night, she'd have constant reminders.

Once she'd dressed, she added a blazer for professionalism and took extra time with her hair.

By the time she entered the office, she was a competent businesswoman, rather than a sub.

"The Tyrant hasn't shown up yet," her mother announced.

Agreeing with Gloria would feel disloyal to David.

Gloria huffed. "It's becoming a bad habit."

"He was the first one here yesterday," Maggie pointed out. She refused to add that she had no idea what time he'd made the drive from her place back to Castle Pines.

Gloria had one elbow propped on the reception desk. A maxi skirt flowed over her hips and ended at her ankles. She wore sandals that showed off her bright blue toenail polish. Specks of white seemed dropped on the tops.

Maggie wondered if the abstract blobs were supposed to be flowers, but she decided not to ask. Her mother would launch into a long explanation about art and how even her body was a canvas.

Barb was leaning back in her chair, cup of coffee in one hand, as if enjoying the show.

"Is there more of that?" Maggie asked, pointing at the coffee.

"Knew you were coming in," Barb responded. "So it's extra strong." She made no attempt to go get a cup for Maggie.

Gloria tapped the side of her drink, and her numerous bracelets jangled. "It's a tropical smoothie," she explained without prompting. "Coconut water, pineapple juice, orange juice, with whey protein, and an energy booster."

"Is that whipped cream on the top?"

"Non-dairy."

"Uh-huh," Maggie said.

"That's what I told the girl I wanted. Anyway, when the Tyrant can be bothered to drag his carcass in for the day, I wanted to have a talk about the Tyler account."

"Isn't the meeting scheduled for ten o'clock?"

"No sense waiting."

"Which means you stayed up all night so you're already exhausted and want to go home?"

"Creative genius knows no time constraints."

"Of course not." Had Gloria always been this eccentric? Or had David allowed her full artistic personality to blossom? Some might label her a nut, but she was turning out some of the best work Maggie had ever seen.

Their musings were interrupted when David walked through the door.

"Ladies."

Maggie's pulse jumped.

Barb rolled her chair forward and pretended to be working on the computer.

"*There* you are," Gloria said.

Though she tried to look away, Maggie couldn't help but stare at David.

Did he have to be so devilishly handsome?

Today he wore a navy-colored suit with a crisp white shirt, accented with a midnight-blue tie.

As she looked at him, her mouth dried as she imagined him unknotting the tie and stuffing the silk in her mouth to muffle her screams.

Until him, she hadn't fantasized about gags. But now that David had introduced her to one that he wore, she couldn't focus on anything else.

"Do I have something on me?" With a grin he brushed his fingers across his lapel.

No one looking at him right now would suspect he could swing his belt with such precision that he left almost no bruises behind.

"Maggie?" he prompted.

She shook her head. "Sorry. I was lost in thought."

"Did you not sleep well?"

She met his gaze. The blue he wore made the color of his eyes more startling than usual. Heat crept up her neck and seemed to settle on her face. "I slept all the way through."

"Good to hear."

"If it's okay with you, can we cut the chitchat and start the meeting early?" Gloria said.

"Am I allowed a cup of coffee first?"

Gloria made a dismissing signal with her free hand, jangling her requisite bracelets together.

"Half an hour?" David suggested. "As long as the conference room isn't booked?"

"It's free," Barb said after checking a calendar.

"I need to speak privately with Maggie first."

As he skimmed his gaze over her, no mistaking his intention, she froze.

"My office." To others, his voice might sound conversational, but she heard the steel beneath it. "Five minutes." It wasn't a question.

With that, he strode off.

"He's a hot man. I wonder if he works out. He has to, right?" Barb mused.

"He's a tyrant," Gloria said around a long-suffering sigh.

"I heard that," he called out from down the hall.

Humiliation crawled through Maggie, and in that moment she was torn between loyalty to her boss and to her mother. "Strike that word from your vocabulary."

"Whose side are you on?"

"*You* are the artistic talent, Mother," Maggie said. "And he's giving you freedom to explore that."

"By having him look over my shoulder at every turn? Submitting my work for his approval? Checking up on me to be sure I got everything turned into his bookkeeper the moment I finish each step? He's suffocating me." She broke the word into four distinct syllables.

"Then why are you producing more than you ever have before?"

Gloria flounced away, and Maggie shook her head.

"Any idea what he wants to talk to you about?" Barb asked.

She shook her head.

"Sounds serious," she observed.

"I'm sure it's just a question or two." Maggie was lying to them both. She'd recognized the gleam in his

eyes, and what he wanted from her had nothing at all
to do with business...

Chapter Eleven

When Maggie approached David's office, he was standing behind his desk, a hip propped against the credenza, a cup of coffee in hand. His focus was on the entrance, as if he'd been waiting for her.

With a wave, he beckoned her inside. "Close the door behind you. And lock it."

Her heart thundered, echoing in her ears so loudly that she barely heard what he said.

As she neared, he put down his drink and folded his arms across his chest.

"Any bruises?"

She shook her head. "A tiny red mark on the back of my leg, above my knee."

He nodded.

"I think the arnica helped." Even to her, the comments sounded ridiculous, as if she were making conversation without really saying anything.

"You know what I'm expecting."

"I…" This couldn't be happening. But there was no mistaking the tone in his voice. "We were going to keep work and BDSM separate."

"Is that what you want?"

"I need to be able to do a good job."

"And spending private time with me will prevent that?"

Needing a spanking had caused her a much bigger distraction. Sceneing settled her down, helping her to concentrate.

"You're welcome to leave."

Meeting his gaze, she remained in place.

"Very good."

She'd endure almost anything to hear the approving purr he wound through his words.

"Now be a good girl and do what you're supposed to."

Swallowing hard, she untucked her shirt before reaching beneath it to unhook her bra. Then she unfastened a few buttons to bare her breasts.

"Say it."

Nerveless, she glanced over her shoulder at the door.

"Focus on me, Maggie."

With a nod, she did as she was told.

"How are your nipples this morning?"

"A little tender, Sir." Scandalized, she wondered where that had come from. How easy it was to slip into a submissive mindset when he was near.

"Your jewelry should be delivered this afternoon."

"You meant it?"

"When it comes to this kind of thing, I don't joke around."

Feeling a little awkward standing before him, half undressed, she waited for him to give her another instruction, then she realized he already had, and he was simply waiting for her obedience. "Please, Mr. Tomlinson. Suck on my nipples."

He smiled, filling her with joy.

Pleasing him sustained her.

"Of course, Ms. Carpenter. It would be my pleasure. I think perhaps you should tug on them a little first, being certain they're already hard for me."

Her knees weakened as she did what he said.

When she finally released them, wincing a little from the pain, he considered her. "Are they ready?"

"I believe so, Sir?" Her response lacked confidence, so she cleared her throat and tried again. "I mean, yes, Sir."

After standing up straight, he bent to suck one of the sensitive tips into his mouth.

She expected him to be gentle, but he wasn't, and that made her gasp. Then confoundingly, her pussy flooded with warmth.

When he finally released her, the air caressed her damp skin.

"How was it last night, when I only sampled one of them?"

"Awful." He wasn't considering doing that to her again, was he? "I'd appreciate it if you didn't leave me lopsided all day today, Mr. Tomlinson."

The annoying man lowered her bra to cover her breasts.

Gaping, she shook her head. "You're really going to do this?"

"Oh yes. I want you in the meeting wondering when—*if*—I'll give you any relief."

"That's…" She tried for a word that conveyed her feelings but remained inside the boundaries of respect. "Diabolical."

"It is, isn't it?"

Her hands shook as she struggled to re-hook the strap behind her.

That, he took pity on. Capturing her shoulders, he gently turned her, then he brushed aside her hands and handled the task himself. Then he brought her back around to face him.

With deft movements, he fastened her buttons. "I believe our five minutes are up, Ms. Carpenter. I'm sure you need to do some preparation before our meeting."

She blinked.

Are you serious? He'd sucked on one nipple, made her dizzy with desire, then was sending her on her way.

He reached over to grab a stress ball and tossed it in the air.

Wordlessly she pivoted and strode toward the door to unlock it.

As she turned the knob, he spoke. "Maggie?"

She paused.

"You look beautiful today."

Her pulse slamming into high gear again, she left.

David Tomlinson was a law unto himself.

Trying to get her head back in the game, she grabbed a cup of coffee before going to her office to organize her notes and get some work done, or rather, try.

Her biggest priority today was finalizing plans for the open house. A save-the-date email blast had been sent a week ago and formal invitations were almost ready to drop in the mail.

And once David finalized acquisition of their rival, Maggie would begin work with the PR firm she'd just hired.

Unfortunately answering her emails took longer than expected, and she reached the conference room a few minutes late, and everyone was waiting for her.

David swept his gaze over her, as if ensuring she was okay...which meant she had to do a much better job of managing her emotional reactions if she was going to have any kind of outside relationship with him.

Gloria tapped one of her green-colored fingernails on the outside of her smoothie. "Now can we get started?"

Maggie slid into her chair and picked up her cup.

"You've got the final draft for approval, don't you, Gloria?" he asked, taking charge of the meeting from his place at the head of the table.

"I do." She handed out copies and then gave an overview.

David sought Maggie's opinion, and when they'd reached consensus on all points, he jotted his signature at the bottom of his copy and slid it back to Gloria. "Nice job," he told her.

"I was up all night," Gloria said with a heavy, exaggerated sigh. "I'm going home to rest."

"You've earned it."

The aura of her drama still wafting on the air, Gloria breezed from the room, leaving Maggie alone with David. He sat back and perused her, his attention making her body tingle.

She had a couple of things on her mind. First up was apologizing for her mother's behavior. Next was updating him on the plans for the open house. At some point, she wanted an update on the merger. "David —"

The moment she broke the silence, his cell phone rang.

Excusing himself, he grabbed his belongings from the table and left the room as he answered his phone.

She collapsed against the chair, exhaling a heated breath.

Until now she would have never considered excusing her mom's behavior.

God, this is getting complicated.

Being with him had changed how she felt. And she wasn't sure that was a good thing.

Determined to banish thoughts of him from her mind, she gathered her belongings then returned to her office and typed out a couple of emails to him. And she decided not to say anything about her mother. Their relationship was between them.

He responded to one of her messages right away, the other took several confounding hours.

When she left at the end of the day, his office door was closed, and she tried to fight back her disappointment.

The next morning, she was the first one to arrive at work.

She entered her office, flipped on the light, and found a piece of paper in the middle of her desk.

Her hand shaking a little, she drew the page toward her.

Though there were few words, his bold scrawl filled the entire space. He'd given her his home address and added that he expected to see her as soon as was convenient on Saturday.

She gripped the note to her chest.

From anyone else, she might have found the instructions and assumptions off-putting. For her, after not hearing from him last night, this was like much-needed oxygen. For the first time since she'd fallen asleep in his arms on Monday night, she truly relaxed.

He didn't show up at the office the entire day, but on Thursday morning, she found another note on her desk, but this time, it was accompanied by nipple jewelry.

Scandalized, she hurried back to close and lock her office door before walking back to look at the gift — if it could be called that.

Each looked like a tiny, pink flower.

Since she wasn't sure how to affix them, she picked them up and quickly realized they were magnets. She pulled apart the first one and practiced putting it in place on the tip of her pinkie.

The pressure was slightly more intense than she'd imagined.

Then she picked up his note.

Wear them.

Because the words had been underlined, his commanding voice seemed to echo in her head.

Feeling more than a little self-conscious, she lowered her bra cups to expose her breasts.

Playing with her own nipples at work scandalized her, so she hurried through the process of placing the first.

She gasped at the shock of pain as the magnets sought each other.

Quickly realizing she'd put the pieces too close to the tip of her nipple, she pried them apart and tried again.

Now that they were in place properly, they weren't all that uncomfortable, but the sensation wasn't pleasant, either.

Around ten, he sent her a text message telling her she could remove them if she wanted.

Whispering a silent prayer of gratitude, she did.

But at four, he instructed her to put them back in place until she went home at the end of the day.

The man was impossible.

Friday, morning, he was in her office, sitting in the chair behind her desk when she walked in, and her knees wobbled. "Mr. Tomlinson."

"Maggie."

She couldn't get a read on his attitude.

Though he wore a suit, his tie was loose. A lock of hair hung over his forehead, and stubble darkened his jaw. Had he stayed up all night? "What can I do for you?"

"I've missed you."

Trying to hide her reaction, she clutched the handle of her purse.

"I'm heading home for some shut-eye and a workout."

So he hadn't yet been to sleep.

"We're close to finalizing the deal."

"Congratulations."

He lifted one shoulder in a shrug. "By this time next week, we may be celebrating. A final draft is in legal hands."

She nodded.

"I wasn't going home without seeing you." His eyes darkened. "You've missed me tormenting your nipples."

"No, Sir," she protested, shaking her head. "That jewelry is wicked."

A slow smile sauntered across his beautiful lips. "It was advertised as lightweight."

"Doesn't feel like it to me," she fired back.

"Mmm." With a tip of his head, he indicated the door. "Close it and get over here."

She squeezed her eyes shut. How was it possible that she already lived for his attention?

Moments later, he swiveled his chair, signaling his intent.

Anticipation made her reactions sluggish.

"You know what to do."

At her house, he'd made his requirements clear.

After placing her purse on the desk, she fumbled with her buttons, then her bra strap. Seeming to enjoy her struggles, he watched without offering assistance.

Then, with nerves stretched tight, she cupped one of her breasts and walked toward him.

"That's it."

As she leaned toward him, he opened his mouth slightly, and she slipped her nipple inside.

Instantly he closed around it, sucking it in deep, pressing it against the top of his mouth and holding it in place, exerting exquisite pressure that made her whimper.

On and on he went until she grabbed hold of his shoulders for support.

She was whimpering, on the verge of uttering a slow word when he stopped.

When he'd said he'd be paying attention to her, he meant it.

"You *are* sensitive," he said.

And aroused beyond belief. "Yes, Sir."

"Good." He trailed a fingertip over the dampened tip. "Now show me how it looks with my jewelry on it."

"But you've already tormented it," she protested.

"Safe word or do it."

With a small nod, she pressed her lips together then went back to her purse to remove the little flowers from a zippered compartment. "You know," she suggested. "You could try them yourself to see what they feel like."

He chuckled with no mirth. "You're the sub, Maggie."

Which meant she'd suffer while he blissfully slept.

"But I did try them on the web of my hand. So I know they're not pleasant. But they're far from the clovers you love. And when I see you tomorrow, I want you to be able to come from me barely touching your nipples. There's a method to my requests, Maggie."

"I should have known."

"Your sass will earn you a spanking."

How desperately she was starting to need one of them.

"Tomorrow."

Are you trying to ruin my life?

"Get on with it before others start to arrive and wonder what we're doing behind closed doors."

"Yes, Sir," she replied miserably.

Because he was studying her so intently, she fumbled as she tried to place the flowers properly. Unfortunately, the attraction of the magnets was so strong that they clamped anyway, pinching her skin and making her yelp.

"I'm sure that makes it more uncomfortable."

The annoying man didn't help, not that she wanted him to.

Within seconds, she had the thing properly placed.

"Your nipple looks gorgeous. That color of the flower catches the overhead light."

She'd been too busy hating them to notice how pretty they were.

"Since I'm a kind and thoughtful Dom whom you'd be well-advised to be a little more appreciative of, I'll give each of your nipples equal attention."

Where have my manners gone? It wasn't like her to forget the basics. "Thank you, Sir," she said hastily, hating that he'd had to remind her.

For at least a minute, but seemingly forever, he tormented her second nipple. But this time, he took pity on her and placed the second flower himself. His motions were quick and efficient, but that didn't diminish the magnetic bite in the least.

"They are more beautiful than I imagined." He captured her gaze and didn't let her glance away. "And I imagined plenty."

His words vanquished her pain. When he looked at her like that, spoke to her in that approving, gruff tone, she'd endure anything.

He stood to refasten her bra and help her button up her blouse.

"I want you to wear them until I text you."

Would that be in an hour? More? Less?

"Thinking of you suffering for me will keep me hard the entire way home."

Her thoughts swam.

Through the layers of fabric, he sought and effortlessly found her nipples. Then he squeezed mercilessly.

Though the pressure was unbearable, she dug her fingers into his wrists and softly cried out.

Ruthlessly, he kept his grip tight, and shocking sexual response pulsed through her.

Desire spiked in his eyes as he slowly released her.

Once she had exhaled and found her footing again, she uncurled her grip and dropped her hands to her side.

After gently soothing a finger across her forehead, he walked toward the door.

He paused and looked back as she sank into the chair he'd just vacated.

"Maggie?"

She might have responded, but she couldn't find her voice.

"Think of me."

How can I do anything else?

"And tomorrow I'll be sending instructions that I'll expect you to follow before you arrive at my house."

Slowly, she nodded.

"And know this… They'll be worse than you expect."

He left, clicking the door closed behind him.

The man was an expert at turning her world upside down.

Worse…?

How is that even possible?

Chapter Twelve

On Saturday morning, Maggie was awake several hours before her alarm.

Yesterday, he'd only made her wear the jewelry for a little while, but then he hadn't contacted her again.

He kept her off-kilter, and she wasn't sure she knew which way was up.

Filled with restless energy, she made coffee, filled a to-go cup, then headed to the fitness center.

The sun hadn't been up for long by the time she'd tossed in a load of laundry and taken a quick trip to the grocery store.

No matter how long she stayed at his place, she'd be ready for the upcoming work week.

Even after a shower and drying her hair, it was barely nine o'clock.

Dressed in a robe, she was standing in front of her closet, trying to decide what to take in her overnight bag when her phone dinged, signaling an incoming message.

She snatched up the device.
David.

Looking forward to seeing you. Please be sure that your nipples are bare.

At least he hadn't required her to wear clamps. Relieved, she sent back a simple acknowledgment.

Then she remembered her gratitude and typed out a quick thank you.

Your slow response has been noted.

Her tummy plunged.

Frustrated with herself and vowing to be more cautious in future, she waited for further instructions.

When none came, she busied herself with packing her toiletries before returning to her bedroom.

Within moments, her phone chimed.

Bring one toy of your choice.

She immediately acknowledged his words and added her thanks for allowing her that luxury.

Well done, Maggie Mine.

No one other than him had ever called her that, and every time he did, part of her melted.

Crossing to her closet, she opened her toy drawer and studied her spanking implements. The brush? A flogger?

He'd used one of those on her previously, along with his belt.

But that night at the Den, she remembered he'd also laid out a tawse, but hadn't used it.

She traced the logo that Master Marcus — the Den's resident BDSM artisan — had stamped on the one she'd brought at a holiday festival.

It was no doubt considerably more wicked than any of her other implements, and she was feeling daring enough to experiment. After all, she did have a slow word.

Once more, her phone sounded.

Send me a picture of your selection.

Immediately she did.

My brave pet.

His words of approval — even in writing — reinforced her decision.

You'll feel that one. And it may leave some bruises.

She hoped.

After adding the implement to her bag, alongside a couple of outfits and a set of pajamas, she zipped the top closed.

Which left only one other decision: what to wear to his house.

After discarding several choices, she selected a shelf bra that would leave her exposed nipples bare, along with a thong, stockings, and a garter belt.

Next, she pulled out a short, figure-hugging skirt that was barely long enough to cover the tops of her stockings. To the pile, she added a white blouse that was borderline too small.

Unsure what to do next as she had another hour or so before she had to get ready, she double-checked that she had everything she needed for a night away from home.

Feeling satisfied, she zipped her bag closed only to have him send a message telling her to select her favorite butt plug and to send a photograph of it.

Butt plug?

Wrinkling her nose, she snapped an image of the only one she enjoyed, which was stainless steel with a pink, blingy base. Interesting that the color was almost a perfect match for the jewelry he'd bought her.

Wondering what he had in mind, she waited for his response, which came swiftly.

Nice try, pet. Put it back and select a larger size. Let me know when you've inserted it.

Blinking, she re-read the message, hoping against hope that the words would magically rearrange themselves and that he didn't really mean what he said.

You're running out of time. I guarantee you that you don't want to be late, Maggie. So quit stalling.

How did he know her so well?

And if you dare show up without it being stuffed up your ass to the point you're uncomfortably full, I'll be shoving my biggest one up there. Be warned that the stem on my preferred plug is thicker around than my dick is.

She gawked at her phone.

Last night, when he'd said his instructions were going to be worse than she expected, she hadn't believed him. But now...

Time's ticking.

Maggie dashed to the bathroom and spent long minutes getting the thing in place.

Even though she hated wearing something this large, the metal piece that spread her anus wasn't nearly the size of his cock. For that she was grateful, and she made sure to tell him so when she sent her response letting him know it was in place.

That's my pet. Now use that tawse on your ass and the backs of your legs twelve times. I'll be pleased if you arrive with marks on your delicate skin.

Startled, she dropped her phone.

Being warmed up is a good thing. We'll be able to play longer that way.

Are you serious right now?

In that moment she realized that he hadn't waited for her arrival to start their scene. With his carefully worded comments last night, he'd begun the mindfuck then.

By the time she entered his home, she'd already be in a compliant, submissive mindset.

After disrobing, she bent over the bed.

Maggie had never done anything like this before, and getting the angle right was both awkward and challenging.

Her first couple of spanks were weak, and the next few didn't land close to where she wanted them.

But eventually, she managed to administer all twelve and even warm her skin a little.

When she was finished, she let him know and was surprised to realize she was more than a little turned on. No doubt that was his intent.

Still, she'd much rather receive them from a Dom. Or, if she were honest with herself, from David.

Now that she was almost out of time, she hurriedly dressed.

The fabric from her shirt abraded her bare nipples, hardening them.

Her diabolical Dominant had known what he was doing when he'd issued that order.

She completed her outfit with stiletto heels and hoped she didn't regret the selection. If the terrain around his house was uneven, she might end up sprawled at his feet.

After a critical glance in the mirror, she straightened her shoulders, grabbed her bag, her purse, and her laptop computer tote, then walked outside for the car.

Since she'd previously entered his address into her phone, she simply plugged in the device and headed for the highway.

As she drove farther south, the traffic thinned, and her map program showed she'd arrive a little early.

When she neared his home, a message displayed on her car's large screen — a single word from David.

Soon.

Her speedometer read ten miles an hour over the posted limit.

Since getting stopped by a police officer while dressed like this wasn't on her to-do list, she eased her foot off the accelerator, cranked up an oldies song on her app, and sang along. She couldn't carry a tune, but the noise drowned out the nervous thoughts skittering through her mind.

After she exited the highway, she turned down the radio so she could hear the directions to follow.

As she drove west for several miles, houses became farther apart and civilization seemed to disappear.

She left the main road and still had to meander for a while to reach his place.

Though she'd lived in Colorado almost her entire life, she'd had no idea that these houses on acres of verdant, rolling land existed.

As the map showed she was nearing her destination, her pulse picked up.

Suddenly she was cognizant of her exposed nipples and the way her asshole was held apart for him.

She and David had scened together before and had engaged in sensual play all week, which should have made her less nervous about their upcoming time together. *Should.* But if anything, she was more wound up than she'd ever been.

Clenching the steering wheel, Maggie stopped in front of his gate.

Moments later, it swung open, and she turned the car into his driveway, braking to a stop on the steep concrete.

The setting was idyllic, remote, and quiet, a contrast to the high-density area where she lived. In the distance, a red-tailed hawk screeched.

Nerves a jangled mess, she pushed the button to turn off the engine and reached for the belongings she'd placed on the passenger seat.

As she exited the car and took a step back, she bumped into a hard, solid mass.

Startled, gasping, she lost her balance, and he instantly wrapped his arms around her to steady her.

Within seconds, he had her firmly on her feet, and she turned to face him.

"I'll get those for you."

Without giving her a chance to argue, he effortlessly plucked the bags from her grip.

He stood impossibly close, consuming her personal space, and his spicy masculine scent filled her senses.

She'd seen him dressed in business suits and wearing jeans with an armband when he'd been serving as House Monitor.

Today, a black T-shirt hugged his muscular frame and blue jeans snuggled around his hips and thighs. Though he'd skipped a belt, his motorcycle boots gave him a rakish air.

Whether he was bare-chested or had rolled back his shirtsleeves and exposed his forearms before he spanked her, the sight of him always overwhelmed her.

Here on his own turf, he seemed somehow even more potent and in control than he ever had. The Den was Master Damien's territory. At her condominium, she felt comfortable. This sprawling house and grounds was his domain. He didn't just own it, he dominated it.

Butterflies skittered around inside her tummy, in anticipation as much as anything.

"Shall we?" he asked.

After grabbing her purse, she closed the car door.

"I'll follow you."

Aware of his hot gaze on her, she walked up the path and stepped up onto the porch.

"Go on inside," he told her.

He'd left the enormous door open, and she stepped into a massive foyer that took her breath away.

In front of her, arched windows soared two stories high, and his place seemed to be an intriguing mix of modern and eclectic. Metal and wood. And stunningly, a waterfall flowed down the far living room wall.

Unable to help herself, she was drawn in.

Behind her, he closed the door.

Sectional furniture had been positioned for guests to take in the ambiance, and she could imagine sitting there, lost in creative thought.

Near the windows with their stunning mountain view, she looked at him. "If I lived here, I might never leave."

"Good plan."

Their gazes met.

She'd said her words with flippant disregard, like she did when she vacationed at a fancy resort. But he'd responded with a seriousness that resonated deep inside her.

For a moment, she considered what it might be like to have him come home to her and the expectations that went with that. She wasn't sure she could manage it.

He placed her overnight bag at the bottom of the stairs. "I assume your computer is in here?" He lifted her tote.

After she nodded, he carried it into the living room. "If you want to use it, you might be comfortable in here."

"Thank you."

"Can I get you something to drink? Mineral water? Soda? I'd offer you a glass of wine, but maybe later?"

She appreciated that he didn't want to mix BDSM and alcohol, even a small amount.

"Mineral water would be wonderful."

"Unless you'd like to go out — which is fine — I was planning to make dinner later. Steak and salad?"

"Sounds perfect."

"You'll need to keep your energy up for what I have in mind."

The last time he'd issued that warning, he'd meant it. A chill raced down her spine.

"Let me show you around so you feel comfortable. If you need anything, ask for it or help yourself. I don't stand on ceremony."

"I appreciate that." She followed him to the kitchen, and she marveled at the gorgeous marble countertops and chef-quality appliances.

"Hot tub outside," he said as he squeezed a lime into a glass then poured chilled mineral water over it. "I'll put you in it before bed to loosen your muscles."

"I didn't bring a swimsuit."

"You wouldn't be allowed to wear it even if you had."

When they were together, he exerted his dominance in dozens of subtle, thrilling ways.

After pouring a second glass, he lifted one and offered it to her.

"Join me?" he invited.

Anxious to see his place, she accepted the glass and followed him out the French doors and onto the deck.

Because of her earlier mishap, she was careful with her shoes as she followed him across the redwood planks.

"Another reason to keep you naked." He shrugged. "It's safer."

Like a gentleman, he cupped her elbow.

An automatic protest sprung to mind, but she bit it back. Even if it wasn't totally necessary, being protected was nice.

The tub was in a gazebo to the right of the deck. The area held numerous built-in benches, and several tables were placed in strategic locations. "This is amazing. You must entertain a lot."

"I used to."

She glanced at him, but he was gazing straight ahead.

The southern portion of the deck was shaded by a trellis covered with vines, while others were exposed to soak up the sun.

"Do you have your morning coffee out here?"

"Even when I have to shovel off the snow."

She laughed.

"And a soak in the tub. The colder it is, the better the water feels."

Steps at the far edge of the deck led to a manicured, grassy area, then beyond that, wilderness claimed the property.

Views were everywhere, and rails seemed to invite lounging, which was what they did, staring into the distance.

A few seconds later, a subtle movement followed by the sound of a faint crack—like breaking wood—caught her attention. "Is that a deer?" She pointed to the left.

"Very likely."

After he took a drink, he regarded her. "Ready to go back inside?"

"I could happily just stay right where I am." Hanging out on the patio at the Den was one of her favorite things.

"You'll get plenty of time. We can maybe even play out here."

She knew better than to ask if he was serious. As he'd said, there were things he didn't joke about.

Reluctantly, she followed him back inside. "Everything about your place is wonderful."

"I'm glad you like it." His smile was warm and genuine.

After he showed her the dining room, a bathroom, and an unused office that he invited her to enjoy if she wanted, he grabbed her bag and said he'd show her the upstairs.

A loft with large, comfortable furniture and enormous television overlooked the first floor and the mountains.

He had a home office, all black and chrome with a glass desk. Three gigantic flatscreen monitors formed a semi-circle around his keyboard. All the equipment left little space for personal effects.

"This looks like command central." *Only more sterile.*

"I spend most of my time here," he said.

Clearly, you need someone to jazz up your life.

Where had that insight come from?

And why did she want to be the one to do it?

Right away, she gave herself a serious mental shake.

This wasn't the first time she'd had a ridiculous thought about him that made her question her sanity.

He was her boss. This was a fling. Nothing more.

Forgetting that would only lead to heartache and devastation.

After showing her a couple of guest bedrooms, he led her to his suite.

A king-size bed dominated the space, and the headboard was crafted from slotted, beautiful pine.

Did he mean to secure her to it?

The thrill of possibility raced through her system.

David placed her bag in an empty closet and said, "This is yours to use. Feel free to leave anything you'd like. Not that I've forgotten that I want to go through your toy box and all your lingerie as well."

His words hinted at something more serious than she'd been anticipating. Since she didn't know how to respond, she remained silent.

She peeked inside the bathroom and didn't see a bathtub, not that he needed one. The massive shower unit had no door. Outside of designer magazines, she'd never seen anything this luxurious.

"I want you to feel comfortable here, Maggie."

"In that case, I may take several showers a day."

"I understand the temptation. And there is a soaking tub in one of the two other bathrooms, if you need one later." He raked his gaze over her.

Suddenly the energy shifted.

He was no longer the gracious host. He was her Dom.

"I'll be downstairs. Take as much time as you need. Towels are in the drawers beneath the vanity. I'll see you in the living room when you're ready." At the door, he paused and looked back at her. "Be naked, except for the shoes."

He left, and his footsteps reverberated from the open, wooden stairs.

She collapsed against the wall. So much for all the time and care she had taken with her clothes.

Mindful that he was waiting, she channeled her concentration into getting ready.

Her rear was stretched wide open. Every move made her aware of how full she was for him.

After taking a sip of the citrusy sparkling water, she kicked off her shoes then entered the closet — her closet — to remove everything else. Not only had he provided an assortment of hangers, but there was a built-in chest of drawers.

The man knew how to make her feel welcome.

Then, realizing she couldn't stall any more, she slipped the shoes back on and pulled back her chin, searching for confidence she didn't really feel.

With her hand curved around the banister, she drew a steadying breath then took the first step toward him.

Chapter Thirteen

Waiting for her, arms folded across his broad chest, David stood near the waterfall. Because her nerves were so shredded, the pounding of her pulse drowned out the sound of the splashing water.

His gaze was focused entirely on her, and a slow smile of approval curled his lips.

She'd never known a man as appreciative as him.

"Please stand over there," he instructed, pointing to a spot on the hardwood floor that was drenched in sunlight. Because cool air had pebbled her nipples, she welcomed the warmth.

"Place your hands behind your neck and arch your back."

Once she'd complied, she shifted uncomfortably.

"Nice. Now spread your legs wide."

Silently, she did as he said.

"As sexy as your outfit was, I like seeing your whole body." Dropping his arms, he closed the distance between them and circled her.

Fighting off embarrassment, she kept her gaze straight ahead.

"I'm tempted to keep you here, nude and restrained for my pleasure." When he went on, his voice was lower, inviting. "Would you like that, Maggie Mine?"

She met his gaze, unable to ascertain whether or not he was joking.

"Oh, yes. I'm serious."

He'd touched a dark, deep fantasy, but one that could never come true.

"Let me have a closer look at you."

As he cupped one of her breasts, she sucked in a sharp breath.

"You've been wearing your jewelry each day?"

"Of course, Sir." She wouldn't dare disobey that order. Truthfully, she liked him dominating her even when they weren't together.

"But you've missed my *personal* attentions?"

How did he turn every word into a seduction? "Yes," she admitted.

"Same."

On edge, she wondered if he'd touch her, but he didn't.

"Now bend over and hold on to your ankles. I want to be sure you've got the correct plug inserted."

A little humiliated, she did.

"Your asshole is spread nicely. Comfortable enough?"

"Not at all, Sir," Maggie snapped back. She'd answered so quickly that she hadn't been able to conceal her disbelief that he'd even asked the question.

"There are times I think you need to be reminded of certain things." He took hold of the base and tugged on it slightly.

She gasped as the biggest part of the toy spread her even wider. "I mean... It's fine, Sir. Thank you for not making me wear something bigger."

"That can be remedied. I have half a dozen or more upstairs, all bigger than this tiny thing."

She gulped hard.

Well and truly, we're into the scene now, and I'd do well to remember that. "Thank you, Sir."

"I'll be changing it out later, to reinforce my point."

So she didn't topple over, she grabbed hold of her ankles. She couldn't think of anything worse. "Could you just spank me, Sir?"

"Absolutely not." He chuckled—the sound totally terrifying. "You'd enjoy that."

Once more, she wondered if he could read her thoughts.

"You used the tawse on yourself?"

"I did, Sir."

"Tell me about it."

She should have expected the question. "Awkward at first. And a few of the spanks were really light."

"Which you redid, correct?"

Why hadn't she thought of that? "Uhm..." She took a breath, not wanting to fib, but also not wanting to confess her transgression.

"How many were too easy?"

"Two?" she guessed.

"Only two?"

From her upside-down position with her hair brushing the floor, she thought back. "Maybe three?"

"Your voice lacks confidence."

Maggie blew out a breath.

"We'll call it four, shall we?"

Hastily she added, "But the last ones were really hard."

"Were they?"

"Yes, Sir."

"I think you should show me."

She lifted her head slightly but couldn't see above his thighs. "Sir?"

"I'll wait while you fetch your toy."

In all her years of sceneing, she'd never had an experience like this one.

Slowly she righted herself.

Once again, totally male and overwhelming, he folded his arms. Then he made a show of studying his watch. "I want you to be careful on the stairs, but be aware that I'll be noticing if you stall."

So that she didn't show her annoyance, she clamped her mouth shut.

Damnable man.

She turned, only to have his voice stop her.

"Maggie? Before you go…?" He walked to the coffee table to pick up a pair of clamps.

They appeared to be lightweight, something that would either turn her on or annoy her to no end.

"Cradle your breasts."

When she did, he then instructed her to part her legs.

With her gaze on him, she did so.

Deliciously, he played with her pussy, making her gasp.

Craving an orgasm, she angled her pelvis toward him, offering more.

Then, shocking her, he tugged on her labia and attached the clamps. *"Oh my God."* Sensation, unlike anything she'd ever experienced before, rocked through her. "Holy crap," she protested around a gasp.

"My thoughts exactly," he said, stepping back.

On her most tender flesh, this set of clamps seared.

"Be careful as you go upstairs," he warned. "Too much movement will make the clamps sway."

If she had her way, she'd remain right where she was indefinitely.

"And you don't want them to rub together, I'm sure."

She blinked hard, trying to force away the awful image his words had conjured.

"I'm sorry? I didn't hear a response."

"You're right." She met his gaze and saw the terrible gleam there. "I appreciate your advice, Mr. Tomlinson."

"They are securely in place?"

If their nasty bite was any indication… "Yes."

"Would you like for me to be sure?"

No. Thank goodness she'd managed to restrain her annoyed response.

With respect, she primly replied, "Thank you. I'm sure they're fine, Sir."

"I'd hate for them to fall off while you were on the stairs. That would be painful."

A few minutes ago, she'd been aroused, on the verge of an orgasm. Now she'd be grateful if he didn't go anywhere near her pussy.

Deep down, she knew that was a hopeless wish.

Slowly, ensuring she was watching him, he lowered his massive hand.

Then before she was ready, he pulled on the chain.

Screaming, she pitched forward, and he captured her in his arms, soothing her, whispering reassurances in her ear.

When she could finally breathe again, he helped her to stand on her own two feet.

"They're fine," he told her.

Asshole.

"Perhaps you might want to show some gratitude for me looking out for you?"

Trying to be civil, she replied, *"Oodles* of gratitude, Sir."

He chuckled.

And that terrified her way more than a swift reaction would have.

"I'm waiting to have your toy in my hand."

"Of course, Sir."

She turned and the chain between her clamps swayed.

Hating everything about submission in that moment, she proceeded very slowly toward the stairs, her steps more of a shuffle than anything.

All the while, he watched her.

Maggie had no idea how long it took her to return to him, but he hadn't stayed exactly where he was.

The approval in his gaze almost made her anguish worthwhile. *Almost.*

In front of him, she extended her hands, palm up, offering him the implement as she cast her gaze to the floor.

"Beautiful sub."

She drank in his approval.

"Maggie *Mine.*"

The emphasis on the word thrilled her, erasing any other thought.

"Thank you." He accepted her offering. "Now bend yourself over the dining room table."

No doubt he'd decided on that, rather than any of the nearby furniture, just to prolong her suffering.

Because her labia were already much more tender than they had been even a few minutes ago, she took her time complying with his order.

"That's it."

He rubbed her rear, almost tenderly. "I don't see any traces from earlier. You're sure you spanked yourself?"

"Yes!" Desperately she brought up her head. "I did."

"And how many did you say were what I might have expected?"

Trying to remember what she said, she replied, "Eight?"

"And how many did I require?"

Why was it so difficult to string two thoughts together? "Twelve, Sir."

"So, if my math is correct, that means that four were rather weak?"

"Will you get this over with, Sir?" she demanded.

He fisted the chain, making her yelp.

"I mean yes, Sir. Four were weak."

"Since I know you are a perfectionist, I'm sure that is bothering you."

Not in the least. "Yes, Sir."

"Shall I remedy that situation?"

"Of course, Sir."

This was the most incredible playtime ever, simultaneously horrible and sexy, something she'd recall for years.

He spent a couple of minutes rubbing her hard to minimize marks, even though he'd said he wanted to see some.

Which—hopefully—meant that he had a lot of spankings in store for her over the next twenty-four hours.

"Count them down for me, backward."

He blazed the underneath of her left thigh, and she forced out a breath. *Damn.*

When she'd recovered, she said, "Four, Sir."

The next three were harder than any she'd given herself.

When he'd finished, she started to stand, but he pressed her back down. "Now you give yourself the twelve you should have earlier. Any that don't make you catch your breath will be repeated."

Humiliated, aware of her ass sticking out with the clamps tugging on her pussy, and the visible butt plug, she curled her hand around the tawse that he pressed into her palm.

"Is this how you did it?" he asked. "Bent over?"

She nodded.

"Get on with it. Unless you want me to think you're stalling?"

"No, Sir!" His little demonstration was still stinging her skin.

Like before, her spanks were awkward and lacked power.

He snatched the toy from her and showed her again what he meant.

Screaming, she cried out, "I understand, Sir."

"I think perhaps the position is part of the problem." With that, he scooped her from the floor and deposited her on her back on the table. "Raise your legs and pull them toward your chest, wrapping your hand around the backs of your knees to hold yourself in position."

Lord help me. This was even more lewd than before.

Her pussy was on full display to him. And if she wasn't careful with the tawse, she might catch the chain.

As if thinking that through, he captured the links and moved them up onto her belly.

But of course he didn't remove the torture device.

She spanked herself once, much harder than before.

"Good job, little pet."

Wanting it over with, she gave herself another three, all hard, making it difficult to breathe.

"Much, much better."

After dropping the toy, she started to lower her legs, but he captured her ankles and held her in position.

"I want you to really absorb them."

He kept her there for a few minutes, until her muscles began to tremble.

But still he didn't relent.

"Scoot back."

Before she could ask for clarification, he released her legs to capture her waist. In an easy move, he readjusted her so that she was in the middle of the table.

"Now put your feet flat on the table."

Which meant her knees would be upturned.

How many ways did this Dom want to display her?

Because her labia were already going numb from the clamps, she minimized her motions.

"So pretty. Now open your legs as wide as you can."

Her worst imaginings were no match for his plans.

When he had her where he wanted her, he sharply and repeatedly spanked her pussy.

Thrashing, heedless of everything except a need to escape, she screamed.

"Good. So beautiful. Be as loud as you want. No one will hear you. This is the music I've been wanting from you."

"Sir!" She sobbed as waves of anguish washed over her.

"Louder." He spanked harder.

The room began to swim, and suddenly she dropped into a spiral of bliss.

As he continued, she tipped back her head, lost in her internal haze.

Then she was...

Gone.

When reality nipped at the edges of her consciousness once more, David's head was between her legs, and he was sucking on her clit as he fingered her wet pussy.

Her eyes still closed, an orgasm overtook her, and she called out his name.

"Perfect."

She might have passed out right then, because the next thing she knew, she was in his lap on the living room couch.

Though she was confused, she couldn't rouse herself to ask any questions.

Aware of him holding her, arms tight, she rested her cheek on his chest. As she breathed with him, she inhaled his familiar, reassuring scent.

There was nowhere she'd rather be.

"How was it?" he asked sometime later.

"Amazing." Though she had no desire to wear pussy clamps ever again.

"It was for me, too."

She smiled.

Then she realized her labia throbbed but no longer burned. "Did you take off the clamps?"

"I did."

Thank goodness she hadn't been aware of that happening.

"Are you curious about what's next?"

"There's more?"

"We're barely getting started," he promised her.

"In that case, yes. Absolutely."

"Please lift the top of the coffee table."

"Oh?" Sliding from his lap, she reached for the edge of the wood.

On silent hinges, it raised, revealing an array of spanking implements resting on black velvet. *Wow.* "That's a clever toy box, Mr. Tomlinson."

"Another of Master Marcus's functional designs. He seems inspired these days."

"I'd say." Who needed a dungeon when you could keep all your naughty secrets hidden in plain sight?

David regarded her.

"This was why you checked me for bruises," she said.

"Since you've already been warmed up, shall we use a paddle? A cane? Or go for a lighter touch? A suede flogger, perhaps?"

She studied the dozen or so selections.

Some of them frightened her, a few captured her interest. "The leather paddle?" she suggested. It looked sturdy, but not awful, unlike the one crafted from Lexan, and another that was made from thick wood and had precise holes drilled in it.

"There are two." He shrugged. "Which do you prefer?"

Maggie started to reach for one, but then paused. Toys could be very personal. "May I?"

"Most certainly. They're yours."

"What do you mean?" She frowned.

"All of these are new. I haven't used them with anyone else and never will."

"You mean that."

David nodded. "Every word." Then he grinned. "Pick up the purple one and turn it over."

Curious, she did, then her eyes widened.

Pain slut was emblazoned in raised lettering.

"Does it suit you?"

Laughing, she shook her head, but then told him the truth, "When I'm with you, Sir, yes. It does." She took him in. "No one else has ever reached me in the way that you do."

"Now have a look at the other one."

A little nervous, she picked up the red one.

"It matches the color your ass and upper thighs will be when I'm done with you."

Carefully she picked it up and looked at the inscription. *David's Pet.*

Breathlessly, she pressed the toy to her chest. If she chose this one, his name would sear into her skin.

"Master Marcus made these for you. *For us.*"

They were both unbelievably personal.

"Have you made a decision yet?"

She nodded. "This one, Sir."

Eyes softening appreciatively, he nodded.

Then, as he took the paddle from her, he grinned wolfishly. "You never asked which I preferred, Maggie."

Oh no. He'd created a submissive trap, and she'd blindly walked straight in. "I'm sorry, Sir." She spoke so fast that her words were a mashed-up jumble. "Forgive me?"

"Don't apologize, my pet. I was going to give you a pleasure paddling." He slapped the paddle against his open palm. "But now you've given me something to punish you for."

Chapter Fourteen

She froze.

What did he have in store for her now? For sure, it wouldn't be an ordinary spanking.

He stood to lower his jeans, revealing his enormous erection.

Though they'd had sex before, it was as if she'd forgotten how large his cock really was. "Do you want me to suck it, Sir?"

"Did I ask you to?"

Frantically, Maggie shook her head. "No, Sir."

With a stern expression, he said, "You are the sub. I am the Dom."

Her mouth dry, she was unable to look away from his magnificent cock and its glistening drop of pre-cum on the tip.

"Maggie? Are you clear?" He caught her chin and forced her to meet his eyes.

After clearing her throat, she nodded and dutifully repeated, "You are the Dom, and I am the sub."

"Any questions?" His voice held no hint of a tease.

"None." Her gaze drifted once more.

"You seem to be having difficulty concentrating, my pet."

That was an understatement. She wasn't sure she'd been functioning at one hundred percent in days.

"There's a condom in my front pocket. Lower yourself to your knees and get it for me."

Not knowing what to expect made every bit of this experience all the more thrilling.

Kneeling between his booted feet, she fished into his pocket and pulled out the packet.

"Kneel up and put it on me."

The request was simple enough and should have taken about two seconds, except for the fact she was a nervous wreck. Because of that, she required several attempts to get the magnum-size latex rolled into place.

"I enjoy it when you do that."

She adored touching him.

"There are clover nipple clamps on the table. Please get them for me."

His words alone were enough to make her tingle.

Once she had them in hand, he said, "Drape the chain around the back of your neck so I can grab them when I'm ready."

"Yes, David," she replied, lifting her hair and doing as he said, the metal cool against her skin.

Then, instead of trying to guess what he wanted, she remained where she was.

"Excellent behavior, Maggie Mine."

His comment helped tamp down her natural impatience.

"Now, I'll expect you to follow my instructions. Carefully." He raised an eyebrow, as if in question.

She nodded.

"No more, no less."

What wicked thing did he have in mind that he needed to issue that warning?

"You're going to slide your cunt down my cock."

Stunned, she opened her mouth to protest. With that massive plug inside her, the fit would be impossible.

Realizing he was studying her, she swallowed her unspoken words.

"You told me your nipples have been wanting more of my attention."

Demanding is more like it.

"When I say, you will straddle me. Then, like we have done at the office, you're going to put your nipple in my mouth." He held her gaze. "And then you're going to tell me to torment it."

Shock held her immobilized.

"As I do, you are going to keep hold of your breast. You're not going to attempt to pull away. In fact, no matter what I give you, you're going to lean forward and beg for more. All the while, you're going to ride my dick." He paused meaningfully. "Without coming."

Gobsmacked, she gaped.

Ignoring her reaction, he continued, "This is about me sucking you off. Making you ache. Any questions?"

A million of them. But she was so delirious with desire that she couldn't even remember her own name.

"You know what to do?"

Shakily, she nodded.

"Take it from here." He sat on the couch and relaxed, allowing his head to press into the seat back where he would have more leverage.

Awkwardly she rose to kneel on the couch beside him. Then, fighting for balance, she parted her thighs and raised herself up until his cock was at her entrance.

Shockingly, even though he hadn't played with her, her pussy was wet.

"You have a hungry little cunt."

His filthy words turned her on.

"You want me to fill it, don't you?"

"Yes," she whispered, wishing she could hide her reaction.

To stabilize herself, she put one hand on his shoulder and then held his cock with the other as she stroked herself down his shaft.

Their bodies pulsed together with each tiny bit that she took.

As she went lower, she gasped because the plug took up so much space. If she hadn't been so aroused, there was no way she could have fit him inside her.

Finally, after a seeming eternity, he was balls-deep.

A little nervously she leaned forward and cupped her right breast and teased his lips with her hard nipple.

She couldn't believe the words she was about to utter. "Please, Sir... Fuck up my nipple."

"Little pet, I'd enjoy that very much." Gently he took the sensitive flesh in her mouth.

The exquisite movement of his tongue made her sigh.

As if taking that as encouragement, he sucked it deeper.

Eyes closed, she attempted to pull back, but he clamped his teeth around her nipple. The harder she tried to escape, the more he persisted.

His earlier instructions reverberating in her head, she forced more of her breast between his lips. This was impossible. And sublime. She craved more. "Torment me, Sir," she demanded, pressing forward, seeking to be the sub he wanted and take everything her body demanded.

A harsh swat on her ass jolted her.

Yelping, she drew away only to have him press a strong palm to the middle of her back and forced her forward again.

When he gave her ass another spank, she remembered his demand that she ride him.

Frantically, desperately she moved up and down rocking back and forth, so full, so overwhelmed with sensory stimulation that she could focus on nothing.

She almost didn't notice when he moved on to her other nipple.

"Aren't you supposed to say something?" he prompted.

"Torment it, Sir. Do it." Shocking herself, she meant it.

He elongated her nipple with his tongue, worrying the nub between his teeth, giving her everything she'd ever dreamed of and more.

On and on, it went, and an orgasm uncoiled its demand, the need so powerful she wasn't sure she could resist it.

Shaking, she froze and looked at him. "Oh, Sir!"

Shocking her, he released her to grab her hands and hold them behind her back. "Don't move." He grabbed her waist and picked her up to deposit her next to him.

Sweat drenched her, and she struggled to blink reality back into focus. Her entire body was desperate for his possession.

"I think maybe they're ready for the clamps."

How could she have forgotten about that?

"Put them on, please."

Because she was shaking so hard, she struggled to comply and yelped as she affixed each one in place.

"They look perfect on your reddened nipples. Now get the paddle and drape yourself across my knee."

How was it possible that the moment she thought a scene was over because he was out of ideas, he came up with something else to surprise her?

As she stood, he kept a hand on her for assistance.

Once she picked up the red paddle, she placed it on one of the cushions next to him, then she lowered herself into position.

Her ass stuck up in the air, but even that was obviously not good enough for her Dom.

Instead, he jostled his knee, upending her so that she pressed her fingers into the hardwood floor for stability.

Then he trapped her legs with his much stronger ones.

"How many spanks?"

Since answering a question like that was the thing that got her into trouble in the first place, she primly replied, "As many as you say, Sir. I'll be grateful for each one."

"Ah." His voice curled around the word appreciatively. "You're a quick study, Maggie."

"Thank you, Sir."

"In that case, the answer is, as many as it takes."

Rather than covering her in a blaze of swats, he methodically moved up her thighs, starting just above her knees, taking his time, allowing her to absorb each stroke.

"I like reading my name."

She had no idea how many times the word seared into her like a brand, but it had to be a dozen or two, perhaps even three. But his precision and exquisite handling, combined with the way her clamps swung, made it the best paddling she'd ever received.

"And now, Maggie, you may finish what you started."

Her body was on fire for him.

Gently, he helped her up back into his lap.

"Ride me until you come."

He unclamped her and soothed her nipples with his tongue as she took him deep inside her.

"Find your rhythm."

The physical and emotional shock of going from a paddling back to sex took a minute, but when he claimed her mouth with a tender, loving kiss, she came undone.

He'd reached a place inside her that no one else ever had.

Within moments, she orgasmed, crying his name.

Moments after she climaxed, he found his own satisfaction.

For a seeming eternity, she remained where she was, in his arms.

Eventually, he soothed a finger down her jawline. "Are you doing okay?"

"I just…"

Patiently, he didn't press, giving her time to sort through her emotions.

This was different for her.

Generally, after a scene, she behaved like she had that night at the Den, adopting a breezy air and putting space between her and her Dom.

But things were different with David.

Though words were inadequate to express her tumultuous emotions, she tried, "That was everything I could have hoped. And more." Her body would be sore for days to come. And her feelings would take at least that long to sort through.

David slid his hand into her hair and pulled back her head.

"My name is on your skin."

A shudder rippled through her.

"You are mine, Maggie. The world will know that." He paused, his expression serious, his tone allowing no argument. "And so will you."

Chapter Fifteen

Maggie had never met anyone like David. And even though she'd told herself she could play with her boss and separate BDSM from her normal life, just like she always did, she realized she couldn't.

This experience with him wasn't just physical. David—with the way he pushed her and alternately cared for her—had affected her on a deeply emotional level.

It would have been smarter to confine her scenes with him to the Den where she could thank him, skip the aftercare, savor the wonderful relief that a good spanking gave her, and not be burdened by any troublesome feelings.

Instead, she was in her enemy's arms, snuggled against him, seeking comfort, and never wanting to pull away.

How had he upended her life so completely in such a small amount of time?

She should run now, while she still could.

Still, she couldn't force herself to push herself away from him.

A few minutes later, David stood. After removing the condom, pulling up his jeans and fastening them, he walked to the powder room, then returned to scoop her from the couch.

"What are you doing?" she protested with a squeal, grabbing his shirt tightly.

"Taking you upstairs for a shower."

"But... You can't do this!"

He grinned down at her. "Why not?"

"I'm..." *Mortified.* "Too heavy. You'll hurt yourself."

Eyes intense, David looked at her. When he spoke, his voice was firm, as if he would tolerate no argument. "I want you to be clear on this, Maggie, I've got you. In all ways."

The hard edge in his tone was more frightening than reassuring.

Upstairs, he placed her on the edge of the bed while he turned on the shower. Appreciatively, she watched him, admiring his strength and the power in his stride.

When he came back, he was naked, his cock glorious in its arousal.

God, she wanted him inside her again with a desperation she'd never had before.

When he reached for her, she put up a hand in protest. "I can walk on my own." Hastily she added, "But thank you."

"You'll do as I say."

"Beast."

Ignoring her, he continued what he was doing, and she wrapped an arm around his neck while he carried her into the bathroom where steam billowed in the air.

Once they were in the shower, he slid her down his body, then he held on to her shoulders for a few seconds to ensure she was steady.

"Oh. My hair's going to be a mess."

"If you have something with you, I'll grab it."

"I can—"

"Don't, Maggie." He leveled a hard glare at her. "Don't fucking argue."

Exhaling, she nodded. Having anyone do anything for her was so far out of her experience that she wasn't sure how to act. "There's one in my toiletry bag, which is…"

Since he'd already exited the shower, she didn't bother finishing.

After tucking her hair behind her shoulders, she allowed the hot water from the overhead waterfall attachment to wash over her.

He also had a separate, detachable showerhead.

Less than a minute later, he rejoined her, offering her the thick banana clip.

Instead of handing it over, he scooped up her tresses and pinned them on top of her head.

"Thank you."

"Honestly, Maggie, I enjoy taking care of you. Relax a little."

"You don't ask for much."

He grinned, then it faded fast as he leaned toward her. "Everything you have to offer. And then more."

This wasn't the first time he'd said something like that. And this time, she couldn't pass it off as words of passion during a scene.

"Warm enough?"

"I'm afraid I'm going to drain your water heater."

"It's an on-demand system, with a second installed as a backup. Enjoy to your heart's content."

That was a luxury she wasn't accustomed to.

"I want to look at you." He backed her against the far wall, a little outside the spray. "How are your nipples?" He eased a thumbnail across one.

She winced even as the flesh instantly tightened. "A little tender."

"I'll give you a break."

Even though that would be smart, she wasn't sure that was what she wanted.

"Now turn around and place your palms on the tiles."

Without giving her the opportunity to argue, he guided her into the position he wanted.

Leaning in closer, he crouched behind her. "A few letters are visible." He traced his thumbnail over a few. "Most are not."

Glancing over her shoulder, she said, "You can change that anytime you want." After hesitating for a moment, she added, "Sir."

Desire flared in his eyes. "Careful what you wish for."

Maggie faced the wall again so he couldn't see her secret smile. She wanted exactly the same thing he did.

"Keep your hands on the wall."

He tugged on the plug, and she inhaled sharply. "I, uhm —"

"Be quiet." He pulled again. "That's not a request."

Miserably she replied, "Yes, Sir."

"Stick out your ass for me."

Though she obeyed, she squeezed her eyes shut, as if that could save her from any of the embarrassment she was feeling.

"Bear down."

Even as he spoke, he pulled it straight out, and she exhaled a huge breath of relief. "Whew."

"Is that better?"

"About a million times. Or more." Now that it was gone, she realized how uncomfortable it had been— even if it had made sex spectacular. "I'm not sure I will ever be okay with you doing that."

"Mmm. As if you have any say in the matter." After setting the thing aside on a built-in shelf, he washed his hands and turned her back toward him.

"Relax."

He spent the next few minutes lathering her body, gently soothing her nipples, caressing every inch of her, more of a lover than any Dom she knew.

Then he took down the handheld attachment to rinse her with warm water. "Spread your legs for me."

When she did, he directed the spray there, rinsing her pussy.

Even as it soothed, she was so sensitized that the first pulses of arousal began to unfurl. "Mmm." Gently, she rolled her head from side to side.

Had she ever had a more perfect day?

When he was finally satisfied, he turned off the faucets and wrapped her in an oversize, fluffy towel. Then he carried her back to the bedroom where he instructed her to lie on the mattress on her belly.

She turned her head to one side to watch what he was doing. "Arnica?" she asked when he picked up a white tube. "I thought you liked the sight of your name on me."

"I have a lot more in store for you, so I'd prefer you not be too sore to play."

"Clever, Sir."

"Glad you approve. The weekend is still young," he said.

And she was happy to know their playtime wasn't entirely over.

"Ready for dinner?" He went into his closet and returned wearing a pair of black lounge pants, a clean T-shirt, and running shoes.

"I'm ravenous."

"In that case, I'll get the grill going."

At some point, she should force herself to move.

He sat next to her and plucked the clip from her hair. "Take all the time you need."

Despite her best intentions, the warm shower and physical exertion overtook her, and she drifted off, only awakening about twenty minutes later, much more refreshed.

Taking him up on his offer, she leisurely padded to the closet and dressed in yoga pants. Because of all the amazing attention he'd given her breasts, she donned a sports bra then pulled a soft sweatshirt over her head.

Downstairs, he had rock music blasting and all kinds of veggies on the kitchen island, along with a bottle of wine.

As if sensing her presence, he looked up, perused her, then instructed the whole-house computer to turn down the volume of the music. "You look beautiful."

Still unaccustomed to that kind of compliment, she blushed.

"No worse for wear?"

"I feel amazing," she admitted. "This is better than any vacation I've ever been on."

"How long has it been since you've taken one of those?"

Frowning, she tried to remember.

Ever since she'd joined her mom at Elevated Edge, her every waking moment had been consumed with making the business a success. "I honestly have no idea."

"Maybe you should plan one."

"We have too much going on." And she didn't want to spend too much time away from him. "With your acquisition, the open house, maybe a holiday party." Not to mention regular business and the ongoing challenge of landing new accounts.

"If you need the break, just get it scheduled. We'll work around it."

"Says the man who works twenty hours a day."

He grinned.

"I forget you're not mortal." And his sexual staying power proved he was some sort of superhuman.

"Wine?"

"Are we playing some more?"

"Later this evening. For now, one glass with food should be okay."

"I think I'll skip it until afterward. If I don't, I'm afraid I'll fall asleep on you."

He shot her a quick grin. "No fear of that, I promise you."

"Anything I can do to help?" she asked, not because she wanted to, but because a good guest—and sub—would make the offer.

At this moment, the only thing she felt capable of doing was relaxing.

She'd been under so much stress for so long, and now it seemed to have caught up with her.

"Just have a seat." He indicated the barstools on the far side of the island. "Sparkling water?"

"That would be wonderful." She took a seat, then shifted to make herself more comfortable. There might not be any real marks on her skin, but her muscles were a little achy. "Thank you."

Within seconds, he'd pulled two glasses from a cupboard and grabbed a lime from the refrigerator.

Wielding the knife with deliberate precision, he quickly sliced it, then squeezed a wedge into her glass and then poured the effervescent water on top.

Then he slid the glass toward her.

"You're spoiling me. If you're not careful, I might get used to this."

"After the first night at the Den, I wondered."

Maybe because of everything they'd shared and the level of trust they'd established — or perhaps just because she was exhausted and her defenses weren't up as high as she normally kept them — she admitted, "I avoid entanglements."

"Bad experience?"

"I've been told I'm impossible to please."

"Perhaps others were too lazy to figure out what you enjoyed?"

She sucked in a sharp breath.

"I think you're very easy to pleasure, and the way you scream and whimper make it rewarding for the person you're with."

"I don't—"

"Oh, yes, Maggie Mine, you most certainly do." He grinned. "And I'll prove it to you later."

She shivered. From his promise? His threat?

Either way, she looked forward to it.

After he'd finished preparing the salad, he opened a drawer and pulled out silverware.

Jolted into action, she said, "Let me help."

With a nod, he told her where to find everything she needed.

Less than two minutes later, she'd set the table and placed the salad bowl in the middle, next to a pair of tongs.

"I'm going to grill the steaks outside. Care to join me?"

"That sounds wonderful."

There was a bite in the late afternoon air, and he thoughtfully turned on an overhead heater.

"There's a blanket in that storage bin."

That sounded cozy, so she selected a fuzzy blue one and draped it across her knees.

As she enjoyed the surroundings, a hiss and sizzle filled the air.

A few minutes later, they were back inside, and he transferred one of the steaks from the platter to her plate.

Because it smelled so enticing, she immediately cut a piece and popped it in her mouth. "Delicious." Momentarily she closed her eyes so she could savor it fully. "I mean, this is really good."

"I'm glad you like it."

"You cook for yourself often?"

"Always have. I'm particular about what I eat."

She studied him. "It's obvious."

"Like you, I need to keep my energy up."

The reminder that their evening wasn't over made her catch her breath.

After dinner, she helped him clean the kitchen.

"We make a good team."

"We do," she agreed.

For a moment, the atmosphere sizzled, as if electricity hung there, ready to strike. How would the business do if they cooperated this much all the time?

But still, to what end?

At the end of their contract, she'd need to find a new place of employment. No matter how hard she worked, the company would always belong to him, and her income would be limited.

Even if she poured her heart and soul into it, Elevated Edge would always be the firm her mother had started, and Maggie had bought into.

It was difficult to go from owner to employee when she'd been accustomed to making all the decisions.

Neither of them spoke for long moments before he shattered the silence by inviting her to spend a few minutes outside.

She'd much rather do that than curl up in front of the television.

He refreshed their drinks, then, when they were on the deck, he invited her to sit next to him at a short, round table with a firepit in the middle.

After she had tucked herself beneath a blanket on an oversize chair, he sat next to her.

David leaned forward to flip a switch that ignited the flames, and they instantly danced to life in a blaze of blue, reflecting off the beautiful azure-colored stones lining the pit. She was reminded once more of his eyes...the same ones that still haunted her nights.

Shaking her head, she leaned forward to hold her hands over the heat. "I meant it earlier when I said I'd never leave this place if I lived here. All of your surroundings are comfortable. You really have thought of everything."

"All the credit goes to my decorator."

"Oh?" Before today, she honestly couldn't say she'd had many glimpses into his personal life, and there was surprisingly little office gossip about him.

"After my divorce—"

"Divorce?" She tipped her head to the side. "I didn't know you'd ever been married."

"It didn't last long." He shrugged. "Her name was Sandra, and she deserved a better husband than I was."

"After spending time with you, I'm not sure I believe that."

"I work too damn many hours."

Don't we all?

"She was ready for children, and I never slowed down long enough to consider it. She didn't want to work—which I was fine with—but she wanted me at home in the evenings. Preferably by five." Shadows from the evening and the dim light played on his features. "On the rare occasions I managed that, I never put away my laptop. She'd find me in my office at all hours of the night. She accused me of having an affair— with my work." He shrugged. "In a way, she was right."

"You're still that way?"

"Probably." He raked a hand through his hair. "It's no way to live."

How well she understood.

"I let her keep the house. I figured she deserved it. When I started looking for a new place, I wanted something that wasn't too far from town, but was remote enough that it felt like a world away from the office." He quirked a smile. "The only thing I had input on was the mattress. I wouldn't compromise on that, nor would I let anyone else make that choice for me."

"Sensible." She took a drink of her water. "Any regrets?"

"That I wasted so much of her time." He drew his eyebrows   together   as   if   he   were   seriously contemplating her question. "Getting married seemed like the right thing to do. We'd known each other since college and had dated off and on. I thought she was the perfect wife material—whatever the hell that really means. I approached the proposal with less thought than I give a business deal."

The admission shocked her.

"She had no interest in BDSM. I thought that was fine." He pressed his palms together.

"It wasn't?" she guessed.

"I told myself I could live without it."

"But when it's part of who you are…"

He nodded.

"And the stress relief."

"That's part of it for you?"

She hadn't meant for this conversation to get turned back around on her. "To be honest, that's one of the biggest factors for me. In a good scene, I stop thinking entirely. The endorphins, the mindfuck. Even the pain. It just"—she picked a piece of fuzz from the blanket—"takes me somewhere else."

"Subspace?"

You had to ask about that. "I wasn't going to admit this…"

He leaned forward. In the dim, flickering light, the expression in his eyes was unreadable. "Go on."

"Before you, I'd only gotten there once. But now…" She exhaled, seeking courage to be vulnerable. "You seemed to have figured out the right combination of things that will send me there quickly."

"You're welcome to feed my ego as often as you want." He shot her a quick grin.

It was the truth, though.

"Let's see if I can take you on that journey once more." He stood. "I have a basement you haven't seen. And I think you should lead the way."

Her eyes widened.

"After you." He turned off the fire, then and picked up both of their glasses.

As intrigued as she was apprehensive, she folded the blanket then made her way back inside.

He stopped long enough to place their unfinished drinks on the kitchen island before saying, "It's the door beyond the powder room."

With a nod, she walked down the hallway, and he reached around her to turn on the light switch. "I'll follow you."

Do you have a full-on dungeon like the Den? Curiosity getting the better of her, her heart began to race.

She stepped off the final stair and entered a large entertainment room, with a big-screen television, comfortable furniture, and a small kitchenette area.

"What do you think?" He grinned.

"It's nice." She frowned a little. "Not what I expected, maybe."

"It doesn't look like a dungeon?"

"Not even a little bit."

"Pull that tapestry off the wall."

When she did, she took a step back to study the pieces of wood attached to the wall. "Interesting." She placed the tapestry on the floor and rolled it up.

"It serves the same purpose as a Saint Andrew's cross."

Maggie looked again, closer. "Oh! Clever. Like your coffee table that's a toy box. Your BDSM equipment is hiding in plain sight."

"Master Marcus, again."

"It's impressive."

He nodded. "About seven and a half feet in width and height."

Holes were drilled at strategic intervals, for placement of hooks, she imagined. Which meant he could secure her wherever and however he desired.

"The structure doesn't have an official name, so I call it the Cavendish."

"You could have a party, and no one would ever know it's down here."

He opened the top of a bench.

"Let me guess, another of Master Marcus's designs?"

"It is indeed."

"And toys inside?"

"I've been planning for your arrival."

A fresh shudder rocked through her.

"Your personality is like this room, isn't it?" she observed, studying him. "You'd never expect what's beneath the exterior."

"I'm the same on the inside and the outside."

"I'm not sure about that. You are much deeper, more concerned about things and people—me—than you let on."

He shrugged. "I can tell you this..." He crossed to her and pressed a finger beneath her chin. "Your wellbeing matters a great deal to me."

Intensity pulsed between them, and in this minute, she believed him wholeheartedly.

"Because of that, I want to set your expectations." His voice turned growly and Dominant. "Our earlier scene was intense, so this will be more about pleasure."

She knew him well enough to realize that didn't mean it would be boring.

"I'm going to start with a flogger that has broad straps so I can play with you for a good, long time."

"I'd like that," she admitted. When he spoke to her in that tone, she instantly slipped into a compliant, submissive mindset. A few minutes ago, they'd been having a serious discussion about his past relationship, yet with a few words, he became her entire reality. "Thank you, Sir."

He laid the implement aside and took out hooks and restraints then flicked his glance in her direction. "Come to me, Maggie Mine."

When she did, he scooped her sweatshirt off. "Now remove the bra."

Taking a steadying breath, she became his to command.

"How are your nipples feeling?"

"A little sore," she admitted.

"I imagine so." Taking great care with her, he laved each with his tongue before looking at her again. "You may need to take a break from your jewelry for the first few days next week."

"Really?" She met his gaze.

"I'll let you be the judge of that."

"Thank you, Sir."

"And I'll trust you to not take advantage of my good nature."

"I promise that if they're healed and I can bear it, I will."

His approving smile did funny things to her insides—enough so that she'd do anything to please him.

He was focused on his next task, fastening her into his fabric cuffs and checking that the fit wasn't too tight.

"I prefer the metal ones, but they'd chafe your skin too much and potentially leave bruises."

Then he picked up a collar, and she slowly blinked, going cold.

"Will you wear this?"

It was pretty, delicate, a thin strip of soft black leather. Unlike the one she'd bought for herself on a whim, it didn't have a ring for her to attach a leash or anything else.

"It's up to you."

Even though it was rather benign, to her — and she was sure to him — it held significance. "I've never worn one for a Dom before."

"I'd be honored to be the first."

She considered the implications. "You'll take it off when we're done?"

"If that's your wish."

Which meant it might not be his. "Yes."

In silent response, she lifted her hair and turned her back to him.

"My perfect pet."

Moments later, it was in place. In reality, the thing was lightweight, but in her mind and heart, it felt like a heavy obligation.

"It's beautiful. Like you."

Searching his gaze, Maggie found nothing but pure sincerity. "Thank you, Sir."

"Are you ready to be secured to the Cavendish?"

"Yes, Sir."

With deft motions, he secured her in place, facing forward, her arms raised and spread as far apart as possible. Then he repeated the process with her ankles.

He pressed his body against hers, forcing her into the structure.

His cock was as hard as his body, and already she yearned for his possession.

"Surrender to the experience. You don't need to be on edge."

"Which isn't what I prefer."

He moved back just a little to lift her hair and place a gentle kiss on her nape, near his collar. "It's what you need."

"I think I hate that you're right."

Since she had little freedom of movement, she had no choice but to surrender to his wishes.

He began by rubbing her entire body, starting with her calves and methodically working his way up.

Then the flogging began, very gently, the strands a soft dance of pleasure on her skin.

"How are you doing?"

"Relaxed." Which surprised her. Something like this would generally annoy her. But he had mad skills that lit up her responses.

"A little more?"

"Please."

Though she could tell he was nowhere close to using his full power, he swung the implement with a little more force.

Sighing and giving him the surrender he'd asked for, she went slack, allowing her bonds to take more of her weight.

As he continued, she began to drift into her favorite place, this time of swirling colors and shooting stars. It was like a meditation or a dream, somewhere she never wanted to leave.

Without her consciously realizing it, the sensual sensations had stopped.

"Take your time. I've got you."

He was crouched behind her, releasing her ankles, then, moments later, he stood to unfasten her wrists.

After rubbing her shoulders, he helped her to lower her arms.

"That's it."

Though she was free, she made no attempt to move.

He scooped her against him and carried her back up the stairs to the living room, where he sat on the couch without ever letting her go.

Maggie had no idea how long she'd been in there, but when she opened her eyes, her head was on his chest, and she was snuggled beneath a blanket.

How it got there, she had no idea. "That…" She shook her head as memories tumbled through her brain. "Wow." Even to herself, she sounded incoherent.

He leaned forward to grab a bottle of water. After uncapping it, he offered it to her.

Because her mouth was so dry, she accepted, then she blew out a breath as she returned it.

"Are you okay?"

She thought for a minute. How to put that experience into words? "That was spectacular. In fact, my body feels like it's glowing." For a few moments, she was silent as she processed what she'd been through. Until now — until him — she'd had no idea she could reach that sublime space from a scene that she'd label tame.

Looking up at him, she whispered, "Thank you for the experience."

"Pleasing you matters to me, Maggie Mine."

His tone was so earnest, she had no choice but to believe him. *Which leaves me… Where?* Already she was beginning to wonder how she would go back to her normal life tomorrow.

"I think I should buy stock in a company that manufactures arnica."

With a quick grin she fired back, "I think we could skip it entirely."

"The marks are nice," he agreed. "But keeping away the pain would allow us to play more often."

"An excellent point, Sir." As always.

"Along those lines…"

"Sir?"

"How about a glass of wine and a soak in the hot tub?"

"Mmm." Both sounded wonderful.

"Let me take off your collar."

Since the leather probably wouldn't do well in the water, it was a good idea. Yet its presence hadn't chafed the way she expected it to, either mentally or physically.

Turning slightly, she lifted her hair.

His fingertip on the fastening, he hesitated. "I'd rather leave it in place."

Startled by his words, she glanced at him. "David?"

"I'm claiming you as mine, Maggie. And I want the world to know it. And I want you to acknowledge it."

Previously he'd said something like that, but she'd dismissed his comment. Words of possession uttered during a scene didn't always hold weight afterward.

But now, his eyes held a gleam of deadly intent, and the way he dropped his hand, as if wanting to leave the collar in place, told her he was serious.

David Tomlinson wasn't satisfied with an occasional scene. He wanted her submissive surrender.

His words terrified her.

The one thing he demanded was the only thing she would never give.

Chapter Sixteen

Hell and damnation.

Maggie's sharp, startled breath and wide, terrified eyes told David he'd severely miscalculated. *Miscalculated? No.* More like he'd fucked up. Big time.

He'd spent his life weighing options, examining issues from all sides.

But when it came to Maggie, he became a blundering idiot.

What the goddamn fuck was I thinking?

Clearly, he hadn't been.

Even with Sandra, he'd never been this possessive, and he'd been planning to spend the rest of his life with her.

"David..." Blinking, her chest frantically rising and falling, she shook her head.

Words of reassurance failed him.

Instead, he forced a tight smile and tamped down his unfamiliar, unwelcome emotions as he removed the collar.

But he didn't put it down. Instead, he curled the meaningful strip of leather around his hand.

"I..."

Part of him wishing he could take back his words, and another part of him refusing to add lying to his list of sins, he pressed his finger to her lips. "I'll pour the wine."

Tension hung heavily in the evening air, and he needed to defuse it. "There's an extra robe in my closet, if you'd like to grab it."

"Thank you." As if grateful for the excuse to get away, she slid from the couch and hurried toward the stairs.

"White wine okay?" he asked.

"Whatever you have is fine."

Contemplatively, he watched her go.

When she was no longer in view, he stood.

He still held the collar that fit her perfectly.

Not questioning his own actions, he slid it into his pocket.

Faint sounds of Maggie moving around reached him as he busied himself filling two insulated, covered tumblers.

Since his divorce, David hadn't had the inclination to share his space. But he enjoyed having this dark-haired beauty nearby.

Their time together hadn't satiated his need for her. It had magnified it.

When she returned, she was wearing his robe. The size dwarfed her small frame and alluring curves, and she'd knotted it around her waist. Despite that, she clutched the lapels tight. *Trying to protect yourself?*

Attempting to lighten the atmosphere so that he didn't send her fleeing from him the way she had after their first scene at the Den, he picked up their drinks.

After turning on the dim, atmospheric outdoor lighting, he led the way to the gazebo.

"It's so clear tonight."

It was.

"Hardly any clouds and only a quarter moon." She pointed skyward. "I think that's Mars."

"I'm sure you're right. Astronomy wasn't my strong suit in school."

He removed the hot tub lid and turned on the jets.

A loud bubbling sound filled the air.

"That's inviting."

While he removed his clothes, she shucked off the robe and climbed the couple of stairs and lowered herself into the tub, ensuring she was covered up to the chest.

Fortunately, he knew all of her delights and had memorized them all.

His cock was hard and ready.

Despite the way she'd emotionally retreated, she stared at him and touched the tip of her tongue to her lip.

Though he'd screwed up, perhaps he hadn't committed an unrecoverable error.

After placing the cups nearby, he joined her.

"This is magical," she said, accepting her wine.

"I try to soak at least once a day, sometimes two. It's a great way to wake up and to recover after a workout."

"Which you do a lot."

There was appreciation in her tone.

"I run, yeah. And use free weights." He tipped his cup in her direction, and she touched the rim of hers to it.

Progress. Small, but he'd take it.

After taking a small sip, she tipped her head back.

"Helping your muscles?"

"Every part of me feels wonderful," she admitted, maybe finding courage in the fact she wasn't looking at him.

"Sceneing restores you?"

Slowly she brought her head back to center. "I know it sounds ridiculous, but I really can't live without it."

"You've tried?"

"Yes."

"I'm curious why you're not in a permanent BDSM relationship?"

She was silent for so long that he wasn't sure she was going to answer. "It's complicated."

He waited, and after she took a second drink, she put down her wine and looked at him and went on, "Most of the men I've dated are scandalized by any suggestion that I want to be spanked."

"Not everyone is."

She exhaled. "I tried with one guy." She shrugged. "But he lost his temper because I was too demanding."

For another moment, she fell silent again before shaking her head. "I decided then and there I was done with relationships. It costs me too much inner peace."

He had his work cut out for him.

"My friend Vanessa told me about the Den and invited me to go. I'd been to munches before, but I really felt at home at Master Damien's. It's safe, you know."

His friend worked hard to ensure it stayed that way.

"I took some classes, learned what Dominants want from a scene, and I look forward to getting my kink on there."

"And you can leave the moment your needs are met."

She met his gaze. Even in the darkness, he read the mutinous set of her chin and the seriousness in her eyes. "And the best thing of all? I'm not judged for it."

Her direct arrow stung.

"Since the Top gets what he wants, everyone is happy."

Until her, he had been, too. "Are you planning to attend again?"

When she spoke, her words seemed to be chosen with deliberate care. "Vanessa and I almost always go on Ladies' Night. I circle the date on my calendar as soon as Gregorio sends out the announcement. And I mark off the days."

Her nonanswer revealed a lot, leaving him no choice but to press forward. "I prefer you didn't attend."

She hugged herself, cupping her hands around her shoulders. "That wasn't part of our arrangement."

Things had changed for him, and he was damn well betting they had for her, too.

"It is now."

"Did your report cards in school have notes that you don't play well with others?" On the surface, her words seemed light, but they were stretched tight with emotion.

"Don't tempt fate, Maggie." He meant every tightly formed word. Being sure she understood him, he said, "I'll make sure you get every one of your needs met."

"I'm just wanting someone to spank me from time to time."

"When you walked into my office, you offered me that position."

"I—"

"I accepted your offer." Ruthlessly he interrupted her. He was done listening. Even though he was being an ass, he was beyond caring. "Be clear about this." He leaned toward her. "I don't share."

Maggie gaped at him.

Who was this man sitting so close to her?

The David Tomlinson she knew wasn't possessive or demanding.

But this fierce stranger was issuing orders and expecting her to follow them.

Not waiting for her argument, he stood and exited the tub, then turned and offered his hand to her.

Though she wasn't sure she wanted to accept, she slid her palm against his.

"I want to fuck you, Maggie."

Yes.

Familiar ground where they connected without tension. Hoping it would get rid of some of the awkwardness between them and reestablish the amazing connection they'd shared less than half an hour ago before he'd messed it up with his dictates, she quietly agreed. "I'd like that."

"The bedroom, now," he urged, "before I take you here."

When she was standing in front of him, he released her to grab their unfinished drinks.

Mindless of his nakedness or the water dripping from his gloriously muscular body, he followed her into the house.

After putting down the tumblers, he went to the powder room to grab a towel that he wrapped around his hips.

Despite the fact he'd been in hot water, his hard cock pressed against the fluffy cotton.

"In the bedroom?" he asked. "Or here?"

"I..." She couldn't believe the thought that went through her mind. When he looked at her with his eyebrows drawn together, she hurried through her suggestion. "The stairs might be interesting."

"Interesting."

"I mean, we don't have to. Never mind. That was a strange idea."

"I should have thought of it myself," he disagreed.

Being around him made rational thought impossible.

A bed made much more sense. But the nearby staircase intrigued her. Because the treads were open, she'd be able to curl her hands around the backs.

The potential positions he could put her in were endless.

"Let me grab a condom."

After this trip to the powder room, he returned with a small, square packet and a small bottle of lube. She could only guess what that was for.

"Can we start with your dick in my mouth, Sir?"

He dropped his towel to the floor in front of her. "On your knees, sub."

This dynamic was as familiar as it was welcome, banishing her anxiety.

Though she'd sucked his cock before, she had almost always considered it something she was required to do. But since she'd tasted him that night at the Den, she had a real desire to have him in her mouth again.

Following his order, she lowered herself into position.

"Get to work, Maggie." Commandingly, he fisted her hair.

She inhaled his masculine scent before leaning in to lick his sac then suck each ball, one at a time, into her mouth.

Groaning, he gripped her shoulder, and the slight squeeze let her know how much he appreciated her efforts.

Emboldened, she reached for his cock and licked her way up the shaft to close her mouth around the head and press her tongue against his sensitive spot.

In response, he jerked his hips.

Pleased, she moved her hand as well as her mouth, working him, wringing a guttural moan from deep inside him.

In response, her pussy flooded with arousal, and it stunned her that she could become so turned on just from this connection.

"You're doing great, my pet." David imprisoned her head and held her so that he controlled how deep she took him.

Of course, it didn't surprise her that he'd wrested control from her. He was too much of a Dom not to.

"Excellent," he approved.

She continued trying to take him all the way to his root, but when she choked a little, he pulled back and released his grip on her hair.

"We can try that again another time," he said as her eyes watered.

"That wasn't what I meant to have happen," she said, wiping her face with the back of her hand.

"I appreciate your trying," he assured her, stroking a damp cheekbone. "As for now, I want to see your ass."

"Yes, Sir." Since she was already kneeling, it didn't take much to get on all fours and raise her rear end as high as she could. Without being instructed, she knew to reach back and part her buttocks.

"That is a nice view, Maggie."

She felt a slight pressure against her anal whorl. She was tender from the plug he'd used earlier, but as he fingered her hole, he used plenty of lubricant and she began to relax, giving him access.

"What a pretty pet. Breathe deep as I finger-fuck you." He went deeper, stretching her as he did.

When he slid in a second digit, she grunted, a very unladylike sound that made him laugh.

"Now a third."

Even though she hated this, struggling would make it worse. Without his coaching, she swayed backward, easing his way.

"That should about do it," he said. "Put your head down."

The position left her more vulnerable to him.

Fully in charge, he stretched her, fucked her anally, even as he played with her pussy.

"Sir! Sir, Sir, *Sir*!" Desperately she moved against him. The pain/pleasure threshold was so high she was unraveling from her core.

"Come for me, Maggie." It was more than permission — it was a demand.

Ruthlessly he continued to prove who was Master and who was submissive.

She might fight him outside the bedroom, but in a scene, he would always triumph.

As she teetered on the edge, he gave her more, overwhelming her with sensation until she pitched forward, shattering, unable to support her body weight.

Instantly, he gathered her up from the cold, hard floor, and she sat in his lap until the last aftershock receded.

"That's good for starters."

This kind of mind-blowing sex was what she'd always wanted. Unfortunately, his attentions came with strings attached.

"When you're ready, crawl over to the staircase."

The longer she was with him, the less self-conscious she felt. Her long-term exposure to the BDSM lifestyle had left her without too many body-image issues. If she wanted her ample bottom to get spanked, there wasn't much point in hiding it. But under his constant attention mixed with approval, her confidence had blossomed. That he found her sexy thrilled her, and that gave her the courage to use her body to entice him.

Exaggerating the sway of her hips, she sashayed across the hardwood floors. She started up the stairs and stopped when he told her to.

"Stay right where you are while I wash my hands."

Hungrily she tracked him, admiring his glorious nakedness.

It was a good thing he kept his clothes on for the most part. Seeing him with an insistent erection turned her into a needy, greedy sub.

Her mouth dried when he walked toward her, his jaw set, his deep blue eyes pulsing with electric energy.

She shook her head. *No,* she corrected herself. David wasn't walking. He stalked her as if she were prey.

When he stood right behind her, he rolled the condom down his length. "Who does this pussy belong to?"

In the throes of desire, she couldn't argue with him. "You, Sir."

"Who?" he demanded again, coming up behind her, grabbing her hip bones and pulling her ass back against his hard cock.

"You, Sir."

"Say the words. *Every single one of them.*"

"This pussy belongs to you, Sir."

"Tell me to prove it."

A wayward part of her longed for this to be real. "This pussy belongs to you, Master David. Take it. Own it. Prove it."

"I'm going to fucking destroy you, Maggie."

"Goddamn it, Sir. Do it."

"Spread your legs."

When she did, he slid his hand between her thighs to tease her pussy, finger-fucking her while pressing against her clitoris.

He tantalized and thrilled until she cried out for more. "In me," she said between pants. "I want you in me."

In a single, shocking stroke, he impaled her.

"Hold on," he warned her. "I'm going to fuck you harder than anything you've ever experienced."

She braced herself, holding on to two different stairs, which gave her greater stability, allowing her to thrust her hips backward.

"Your pussy is so damn tight." His tone was rough around the edges, emboldening her.

Exhaling, she pushed back when he surged forward. "Harder."

Repeatedly, maybe expressing all the frustration and emotion they were both enduring, he pounded her.

His actions and her responses overwhelmed her, and she was lost deep inside.

Hot tears poured down her cheeks as she cried out her orgasm.

On and on he went, his grip potentially bruising her hips as he fulfilled his earlier promise, possessing her in a way no one else ever had.

When he was done, shouting her name to the rafters as his hot seed spilled from his cock, she shattered again.

From the force of his physical strength, she was exhausted and weak, and he moved a forearm in front of her to support her limp body as he withdrew from her.

"Oh, Sir."

In a swift, sudden move, she was in his arms, and he stalked up the stairs and into his suite.

Once he'd pulled back the covers, he laid her on the bed, and brushed her hair aside. "Was I too rough?"

The concern knitted between his eyebrows touched her heart. "No, Sir."

Worn out from all the delicious sex, the incredible BDSM, great food, wonderful wine, a soak in the hot tub under the stars, and dancing through an emotional landmine, she turned on her side.

When he left the bed, she barely stirred.

Moments later, he came back to bathe her between her legs. Then when he was finished, he tucked the covers beneath her chin.

She wiggled, making herself cozy.

Later, when he pulled her against him, holding her tight and kissing the top of her head, she smiled and fell asleep, only to wake in the middle of the night because she was cold.

Instinctively, she scooted to his side of the bed, seeking warmth, and he wrapped his arm around her.

"Take me?" she asked. Probably because the night was timeless, her defenses had slipped.

"Anything for you, Maggie Mine."

This time, they made slow, gentle love, and the experience left her so satiated that she was back asleep mere seconds after she came.

When she blinked her eyes open the next morning, she realized that David had once again kept her bad dreams at bay.

Realizing she was alone in the bed, she flipped over to see him pulling on dark gray lounge pants.

The thinness of fabric allowed her to see that he was already semi-interested.

Even though her entire body throbbed from his use, she couldn't wait for him to take her again. "Is there coffee in my future?" she asked, striving for lightness.

"Even a latte if you want it."

"Wait. Did I die and go to heaven?"

"I'll hope you think so. And you can enjoy it in the hot tub. Your muscles will appreciate it after yesterday's acrobatics."

"Limbering me up for today's shenanigans?"

"Ah." He pantomimed twirling a mustache. "You're onto my nefarious plot."

Laughing at him, she pulled a pillow against her chest. It had been a long time since she'd enjoyed waking up with a man this much.

"You're welcome to stay in bed while I make your drink."

"I'll freshen up then be down."

"Your robe is in your closet." He nodded. "Take your time but hurry every chance you get."

She grinned.

With a quick nod, he left the room.

By the time she entered the kitchen, her latte was in an unbreakable mug on the counter. He was outside, in the tub, waiting.

Because the sun had barely crested the horizon, the air was still cool and crisp. Steam rose from the water, and jets created big, popping bubbles.

Like last night, she placed her beverage on the edge before shrugging out of the robe. But this time, she couldn't quickly hide herself from him.

Aware of her nudity, she accepted his hand for balance as she descended the stairs into the tub.

"Like a goddess," he approved.

"I…" She snapped her mouth shut. "Thank you." Would she ever get accustomed to hearing his compliments?

When she was settled, she took in the view. "It's so pretty. I really can't get over it." And she would never take it for granted.

"It's better when there's someone to share it."

"I would have thought you'd prefer peace and quiet."

"Certain sounds beat the hell out of silence. Your whimpers for one. Your screams for another. And yes, you do scream so don't bother denying it."

"Well then." She sat back and took a sip of her latte. "Damn. You could bring one to the office for me every day."

"You have to come and get them." His eyes were as serious as his tone.

For a moment, she allowed the fantasy to tantalize her.

What will it be like…?

And then she realized the truth. *Difficult.* He was all Dominant, all the time, and she liked confining her scenes to a small portion of her life.

Besides, he was still her boss.

Remembering her boundaries was essential for her survival.

If she couldn't do that, she needed to stop playing with him entirely.

Not liking that realization, she took a sip and kept her response noncommittal and her tone light, not wanting to reopen the painful discussion from the night before. "You're a tempting man, Mr. Tomlinson."

She held on to her cup tightly so she didn't give in to the temptation of trying to soothe the frown that was buried between his eyebrows.

From there, she tipped back her head, enjoying her latte, and not inviting further conversation.

In the distance, his phone rang. "If you'll excuse me?"

"Of course." She watched him climb out of the tub and pull his pants over his damp skin.

More than ten minutes later, he still hadn't returned, so she wrapped herself in the robe and headed back inside.

His voice, deep but edged with irritation, came from somewhere in the distance.

Deciding not to seek him out, she busied herself with washing their empty cups. Then she popped a pod into the coffeemaker and brewed a cup of French roast.

Since he was still on the phone, she decided to take a shower to wash off the chlorine.

And while she was there, she decided she should probably leave.

Around him, she was weak, and she'd even asked him to sex her up in the middle of the night.

If she stayed, they would scene again, and she'd become more attached.

When she turned off the faucet, he was lounging nearby, watching her.

"I like having you here, Maggie."

"You're a great host. Thank you. It's been wonderful."

He held a towel for her.

Quickly she took it and wrapped herself in it.

"You're leaving." It wasn't a question. It was a flat statement of facts.

"I have...uhm...a lot to do."

He folded his arms. "I hadn't figured you for a coward."

Damn. She sucked in a breath. "That arrow was a little pointed." Sharp, and intentionally aimed.

"Maggie..."

His phone rang again, and he cursed. "It's the CEO of Peak Imaginings."

"Problems?" she asked, genuinely concerned.

"Something came up on the due diligence, and he's trying to save the deal."

"You'd better answer."

"Look..." He raked back his hair. "Give me ten minutes. I'll make breakfast. We can talk."

The phone stopped ringing, only to start again almost instantly.

"You'd better answer that. It's important."

Cursing, he pivoted and walked out.

The reprieve might only be temporary, so she quickly dressed and packed her bag, then she headed for her car without saying goodbye.

The gates automatically parted, and she left David far, far behind her.

It wasn't until she was back on the highway that she gave into her emotions and allowed the tears she'd been holding back to fall.

Once they started, she wasn't sure they'd ever stop.

Her phone lit up and David's name appeared on the car's control panel.

Afraid of breaking, she pushed the red Refuse button.

She just wished thoughts of him were equally as easy to get away from.

Chapter Seventeen

That night, the bad dreams found Maggie again. When she summoned up her inner warrior and turned toward the blue-eyed monster, he vanished, leaving her alone.

Chilled, shaking, she sat up with a start.

Unable to shake the aftereffects, she got up earlier than normal and took her coffee onto her small patio to watch the sunrise.

She shifted in her chair, her body a little tender from the weekend of play.

The harder she tried to shove thoughts of David away, the more persistent they became.

In such a short amount of time, he'd demolished the blocks she had in place to keep him at bay.

This morning she had no remaining doubts.

Sceneing with him had been disastrous to her equilibrium.

She put down the cup before she sloshed her coffee over the rim. Her worst fear was realized. The more she got, the more she wanted.

Which meant she couldn't continue to see him.

Resolved, she stood, only to have her knees refuse to support her. She collapsed back into her seat and then tried again.

She was a strong, competent businessperson, and she'd deal with this in a straightforward manner.

In her bedroom, her nipple jewelry sat on the dresser. As she'd unpacked and put things away yesterday, she'd placed them there so she wouldn't forget them later in the week.

He'd told her to skip wearing them for a couple of days, but she decided she'd never again put them on.

So she didn't have to look at them, she opened her toy drawer and scooped them into it.

Determinedly, she shut it again.

She left for the office early, in time to stop by a coffee shop and grab their largest latte — with an extra shot — and a breakfast sandwich.

Her insides had been in such a knot last night that she'd ended up skipping dinner in favor of watching mindless television for hours in the hopes of distracting herself.

By the time she entered the office, she was no closer to figuring out how she'd behave when she saw him today.

"Did you have a good weekend, Mags?" Barb asked.

"It was uneventful." She almost choked on the lie. "How was yours?"

"Saw a play for my mom's birthday. Strolled the Sixteenth Street Mall and had too many drinks at a rooftop bar in LoDo."

"With your mother?"

She nodded. "And my God can she put away the vodka."

"You should introduce her to my mom."

Who, evidently having heard voices, breezed out of her office. Today she had on a turquoise pantsuit with a multicolored blouse topped with a contrasting scarf that should have clashed but somehow didn't. The drink in her cup was a shade of purple not found in nature.

"You're here early, Mother."

"We're meeting with the Arctic Fox people today. Did you forget?"

She had.

Maggie shook her head.

This was the first time something this important had slipped her mind. More proof that she couldn't continue to allow David to derail her focus.

"I sent you an email last week with all the information about the company."

"I remember." At least now that her memory had been jogged, she did.

Arctic Fox designed cold-weather gear for the least habitable places on earth. But whereas other brands focused mainly on functionality, Arctic Fox's pieces were ultrawarm, but stylish as well.

They were doing well overseas and were planning to open their first US store in the trendy Larimer Square area. Elevated Edge was competing with several other companies—including Peak Imaginings—to promote their launch.

This morning, she and her mom, along with David, had an informal sit-down with some of their higher-ups to get a better feel for the messaging the company hoped to convey. "Anything I can do to help?"

"Make sure the Tyrant is here. They want to meet him."

"I'm putting my foot down. Unless David is out of line, no more calling him names behind his back. He heard us the other day, and it's unfair. Agreed?"

It appeared Gloria tried to frown, but apart from the pursed lips, it was hard to tell. "You got more injections in your face," Maggie said. "Didn't you do that last month?"

"It's been six weeks." She waved a hand, and her bracelets jangled. "You should both go with me. Dr. Smythe knows all the tricks to keeping us looking young. Maggie, you scowl entirely too much. At some point, those lines will become permanent. I'll see if we can get a group discount."

Barb choked on her coffee. "Not for me, thanks."

"Let's get back to my point," Maggie said. "I'm serious. There will be no more bad-mouthing the boss. We have to set the example around here."

"You should have a cup of coffee," Gloria advised. "Your brain doesn't seem to be fully awake yet." After another sip of her purple something or other, she walked off.

Maggie sighed. "It's going to be a long day."

"Look, Mags," Barb began. "Sorry about calling David names. It's totally embarrassing that he overheard."

"You know, he might not be as bad as I thought."

"Skip the coffee," Barb said. "I'll call an ambulance. Obviously, you're not feeling well."

With a smile, she shook her head and went to her office to finalize details for the upcoming open house.

David arrived minutes before the scheduled meet and greet and impressed the VP of Marketing—a tall, willowy blonde.

After the meeting, the two of them moved to the far end of the conference room while Maggie and her mother chatted with two members of the creative team.

A few minutes later, David and the female VP excused themselves, saying they were going out to lunch. She frowned, and David inclined his head, letting her know he'd noticed her displeasure.

What the hell is wrong with me? He could eat meals with whomever he wanted. And besides, she'd decided a few hours ago that she was done with him.

So where had the unwanted feelings come from?

And worse, why was it so difficult to push them away?

She didn't see him for the rest of the day, which should have made her happy, but didn't.

Maggie had another restless night and arrived at the office late.

Her mother was wringing her hands near the reception desk, and Barb had a hand on Gloria's shoulder. "What's going on?"

"I screwed up," Gloria said. Her shoulders started to shake.

"Whatever it is, we can fix it. We always have," Maggie said, trying to keep calm and not disturb the rest of the staff.

"That's what I've been telling her," Barb added.

"Let's go in my office." Where they could close the door. "Is David in yet?" she asked Barb.

"He's at an offsite meeting. I think he'll be in around eleven."

"Thanks." He didn't need to see this side of her mother, either. After nodding her thanks to Barb, Maggie drew Gloria down the hall. "Have a seat," she said when they were in her office with the door closed.

Maggie sat on the edge of her desk while Gloria sank into a chair and dropped her head into her hands.

Maggie waited for a minute before gently saying, "I can only help if I know what's wrong."

"I got so caught up with Arctic Fox that I forgot to send the paperwork through on the Hoskins Group deal."

Maggie reeled.

When her mother looked up, Maggie blinked, trying not to betray her panic.

Cindy Hoskins owned six different businesses, and Elevated Edge handled four of the accounts. For years, they'd been trying to land all six, offering screaming discounts for the additional business.

But Cindy was a pragmatist who didn't believe in a single vendor approach. But losing the four accounts existing would be costly.

Maggie forced herself to breathe. "Surely, it's not that bad. When was it due?"

"Last Thursday."

"Why wasn't it on the company calendar?"

Her mother dropped her head again.

"Okay, never mind that. We'll remedy it in future."

"I took them the preliminary bid two weeks ago and..."

Forgot to follow up. And since she knew her mother didn't pay attention to details, Maggie should have been paying better attention. "Let me see what I can do." She picked up the phone and dialed Cindy's office direct and threw herself on the other woman's mercy.

Cindy agreed to consider their proposal, as long as she had the signed deal in hand before noon — with no price increase from last year.

Maggie summoned Barb to bring up the executed copy of last year's contract. Together, the three of them poured over it.

Since Cindy wouldn't consider a price increase, there wasn't much to do other than change the dates, have it digitally signed, and send it over.

David would be livid when he learned he'd been left out of the decision process.

Reluctant to confess their collective failure, but knowing she didn't have a choice, she called his cell phone. Instantly it went to voicemail. Frustrated, she hung up. *"Crap."*

With a sigh, seeing no other options, she told Barb to send the new contract for her digital signature.

When the copy was sent through to Cindy, she returned to the reception area, where Gloria uncorked a bottle of very expensive bubbly.

After creating buckets of drama, she liked to treat the survivors.

Nerves shredded, Maggie skipped the champagne in favor of a fresh cup of coffee so she could stay focused while she looked over the company calendar to ensure she didn't miss any other details.

Maggie didn't see David until the next day. She considered mentioning the Hoskins Group fiasco but couldn't find the words.

The deal had cost them nothing, except additional revenue they might have earned, and they'd saved the business. In addition, she'd met with her mother and Barb at the end of the day to ensure nothing like this ever happened again.

David was a big believer in systems, and they'd refined theirs as a result. Even as Maggie went through the calendar to be sure all key people were in the loop on all projects, Barb reviewed client files and entered all contract renewal dates in the scheduling program and set several reminders beginning two months in advance.

Other than pissing him off, nothing good could come of telling him about their colossal fuck-up.

"Come home with me Friday night after the open house," he said.

Startled, she looked up from her keyboard. "David."

He lazed against the doorjamb as if he owned the place. Which, really, he did.

"Don't tell me you don't need a spanking."

"I..." Beneath her desk, she wrung her hands together. "Sorry. I have plans this weekend," she lied.

"I see."

"If anything changes, I have a hot tub, a Cavendish, fine wine, and custom-made lattes."

Every part of her yearned to shout yes.

But his casual invitation had undone her determination to keep her personal feelings for him separate from the workplace.

Thursday, she worked late, double-checking RSVPs, and responding to a few last-minute stragglers.

One person asked for directions, even though she'd given them twice. She sent an updated head count to the caterer and glanced at her handwritten to-do list. Everyone else used a computer program, but there was nothing she liked better than the tactile sensation of marking through a task she'd completed. It was much the same high that she got when she crossed through dates on a calendar, like when she was going to the Den.

The phone rang, and since Barb had already left, she went to answer it. She frowned when she saw David's line light up. It wasn't unusual for him to take a call, she just hadn't realized he was still in the office.

She was cleaning off her desk when he entered her office.

Energy crackled in the air as he commanded her attention. "David?" A storm was gathered in his blue eyes, darkening them by several shades.

"That was Cindy Hoskins RSVP'ing for our open house."

Her heart stuttered. "Oh?"

"We had an interesting conversation."

Her stomach plunged.

"Something you'd like to tell me?"

She wondered how much he knew. Then she exhaled shakily. Did it matter? Even if he didn't know everything yet, he'd no doubt ask questions until he'd uncovered every last detail. "We had an issue with a contract not being delivered on time. I chatted with Cindy, asked for an extension, and we offered them the same terms as last year. I got the contract over to her, and she countersigned it." She picked up a pen and toyed with it, even though it betrayed her inner turmoil.

"At what point were you going to tell me?"

She tried to deflect away from answering. "I called you, but I got your voicemail."

"And you didn't leave a message?"

"No."

He held her gaze. "I'll repeat my question. At what point were you going to tell me?"

Dropping the pen, she softly admitted, "I wasn't."

"I see." He didn't ask for explanations or lose his temper.

In fact, his lethal control terrified her, sending goose bumps chasing up her arms. "David, wait, I can explain."

"Is there anything more to say, Maggie?" He shook his head. "I'm finally listening to you. You tried to tell me a hundred times, a dozen ways. I'm the enemy, the boss you can't wait to get away from. The Tyrant. I asked you to wear my collar and to admit you were mine, and you refused." He shoved one hand into his pocket. "I invited you over this weekend, and you refused, even though you need to scene as badly as I do."

"I..." *Can't think. Don't know what to say.*

"I'm giving you everything you want."

Confused, she frowned.

"You're fired."

Chapter Eighteen

Shock held Maggie immobilized as his words bounced around inside her head. "Fired?" she whispered.

"Gather your belongings." His voice was as cold as his eyes. "I'll escort you out."

"You can't..." She shook her head. "You can't mean this."

"Oh, I promise you, I do. From the beginning, I've told you I wanted to work together. And you've fought me every step of the way."

There was no softness about him, no trace of the man who had tenderly bathed, cradled her during aftercare, carried her up the stairs, snuggled her, made sweet love to her, crafted a coffee-house worthy latte.

At work, he'd been patient, and more than fair, even when he overheard the whispers about him.

"I thought you'd be pleased that we saved that Hoskin's account."

"Honestly, Maggie, I might have done the same thing in your place. I recognize that the Peak Imaginings acquisition is taking more time than anticipated and that I'm not easy to reach. It would be unrealistic to expect that you wouldn't make decisions in my absence."

And so?

"You owed me the courtesy of at least telling me about it, so I wasn't surprised when Cindy mentioned it. A voicemail would have taken you thirty seconds."

She winced.

"The fact you didn't come to me indicates there's a greater problem. From the beginning you've made it clear you didn't want to be tied up in my golden handcuffs, as you *call them.*"

How do you know I've called you that?

"Congratulations. You've gotten everything you want. You're no longer constrained by an onerous employment contract, and you'll never have to wear my collar again."

Frantically, she shook her head. None of this was what she wanted.

"There's a box in the break room. I will get it for you."

While he was gone her shoulders fell, and she pulled her hair into a ponytail. In school she'd been a straight-A student, and at every job she'd ever had, she'd received glowing commendations. And now she was being fired from her own company.

Before she knew it, he was back, as implacable as he had been a few minutes ago.

Mechanically, under his watchful eye, she stood and began to gather the items that were part of her everyday life. Photographs. Small gifts and souvenirs. Her favorite pens and notebooks.

She reached for her calendar only to realize that it was company property.

How could this be happening? Everything she had fit inside this one small box.

Automatically going through motions, she glanced around, then double-checked her desk drawers to be sure she hadn't missed something.

"You'll receive six weeks' severance pay. I'll have Barb cut the check tomorrow."

Unable to find words, she settled for nodding.

"I'll need your keys before you go."

Had she ever been more humiliated in her entire life?

Her fingers shook as she tried to pry apart the tiny metal ring that they were on.

Finally, they came loose, falling onto the desktop with a loud clatter that echoed a sense of finality in her ears.

"I have one piece of advice for you, Maggie."

She wasn't sure she wanted to hear what he had to say.

"Be honest with yourself, if not me."

Feeling a little wobbly, she slung her purse strap over her shoulder and then clutched the box tightly to her chest.

He moved aside as she walked past him, and damn it all, she still had a powerful, feminine reaction to him as his scent wrapped around her.

Staying upright required all of her concentration, and all she heard was the finality in his footfall as he followed her to the entrance.

In the doorway, he reached around her to push the door open, and he held it while she walked past.

"Goodbye, Maggie."

Swallowing deeply, she stood on the sidewalk, momentarily immobilized as he locked her out.

Somehow she kept it together until she got to the car where she broke down.

Then she sat there, staring absently at the mountains, trying to process what had happened.

Maybe fifteen minutes later, David passed her in his car.

If he saw her, he never acknowledged her.

She blew out a breath as the shock receded and reality began to set in.

At some point, she needed to let her mother know what had happened, but she wanted to put that off as long as possible.

But first, she needed a friend, so she called Vanessa who immediately invited her up to her place in Evergreen.

The drive was more than Maggie had the energy for.

"Come up tomorrow, then. I'll finish work early. We'll have margaritas and chocolate, and you can plan on spending the night."

"Are you sure it won't cramp your style?"

"Honey, right now, no one matters more than you do."

They spoke for a few minutes, with Vanessa being indignant on Maggie's behalf.

"Asshole doesn't realize what a great person he lost."

She was grateful for Vanessa's friendship and to have something to look forward to because right now,

Maggie's future loomed in front of her, dark, and lonely.

* * * *

"Oh, honey! You look like you need a gallon of margaritas."

"Maybe more." Outside a local Mexican restaurant, Maggie fell into Vanessa's welcoming hug.

Still holding Maggie's shoulders, Vanessa took a small step back to study her. "You're still not sleeping?"

"Is it that obvious?"

"Only to someone who knows you really well," Vanessa replied loyally. "Let's go inside and get started."

Because it was still earlyish, they didn't have to wait for a table, and the dining room wasn't too noisy.

Almost immediately, chips and salsa, along with glasses of water, were delivered to the table, and they were asked for their drink order.

Maggie didn't even need to study the extensive cocktail menu.

Needing a little jolt, she went straight for the spicy, jalapeño-flavored margarita. Even though that was her favorite combination, she'd never found another restaurant or bar that came close to matching the flavor of the one they made here. They made it better by rimming the glass in their secret blend of salt, sugar, and ground chili spices that lit the drink up even more.

When they were alone, Vanessa studied her. "Spill the tea, girl."

"I hadn't realized how long a day can seem when you have nothing to do." She wasn't sure she was doing a good job of explaining herself. "Ever since high school, weekends and vacation time seems to fly by. But today seemed to be the longest day of my life. I feel adrift. Cutoff. I was wondering what everyone was doing, and how the employees took the news that I had been let go."

She pushed her hair back over her shoulder. "Being home on a weekday while everyone else was working felt brutal." Made worse by the fact that when she returned home sometime tomorrow, she had endless blank days on her calendar. She'd spent part of the morning canceling all the events she had scheduled for the next month.

"What did Gloria have to say?" Vanessa asked as she reached for a chip and crunched into it.

"She was her typical self. Focused on how it impacted her mostly—fretting how she would handle managing even more accounts. She's furious since it seems unfair that everyone screws up, but now she has to work harder."

"Nothing about how it impacts you? Or the fact the situation wouldn't have happened at all if she'd done her job properly in the first place?"

"Is that a surprise?" Maggie shrugged. For as long as she could remember, everything revolved around Gloria's world. "She said she was going to call in sick today. But since she was planning to go to LoDo and drink vodka with Barb's mom last night, I think it was a convenient excuse not to set an alarm this morning."

"I'm sorry. That makes it worse."

"She's never been the warm, rah-rah type of parent."

"Doesn't make it easier," Vanessa insisted.

"I appreciate that." She picked up a chip. "Barb sent me a message that she was going to call in sick, as well, as her form of protest." But it bothered her to know everyone was talking about what happened to her.

And now that she was gone, she worried that no one was paying attention to the upcoming open house. Not that it was her concern any longer.

"Earth to Maggie. You seem lost in thought. Thinking about work?"

"Yeah. I think it will take me a while to stop doing that." She dipped the chip in the salsa.

Vanessa nodded. "You've been there for a long time, and most of the responsibility has been on your shoulders. Makes sense that it's on your mind."

How long until those random thoughts became less intrusive?

Their massive, happy-hour size margaritas arrived, and she took a long sip. Almost instantly the tangy, sharp sweetness hit her tongue and sent a wave of relaxation through her.

"Do you have any idea what you're going to do next?"

"Honestly, I haven't even thought about it. I spent most of the day sitting on the couch, watching television — or I should say staring at it but mostly worrying." About her mom, the business, finances, even David. With running a company while trying to buy another, he had a lot on his plate.

"I should have started looking for another job, but I didn't have the energy." Maggie stirred her straw into the drink. "And I don't know where to start." In the past, she might have considered applying at Peak Imaginings. But David was adding that company to his empire, as well.

"Take some time. I mean you've worked twelve-hour days and most Saturdays for years. It's an adjustment. A big one."

She'd spent so long being needed that having the responsibility taken away left her disoriented.

"Be gentle with yourself. If you can afford it, you might want to take a vacation. Go somewhere you've always wanted to visit, or just go to the mountains for a few days. Peace and quiet fixes a lot of things."

"Or it will make you crazy."

Vanessa laughed. "There's that."

Their meals arrived, and still she'd avoided talking about David. She didn't want to get into that kind of personal conversation until they were alone.

Dinner was wonderful, and she followed Vanessa back to her place where they changed into comfortable clothing, then flipped the television on and found a true crime drama.

"Now that we don't have to drive, it's time to get serious," Vanessa said, heading for the kitchen.

With a grin, Maggie followed, grabbing two glasses from the cupboard while Vanessa arranged all the needed ingredients for killer cocktails on the kitchen island.

Soon, the blender whirred. When the ice was pureed, she poured the frozen concoction into the glasses.

Before leaving the kitchen, she grabbed a bag of chocolates and another filled with pretzels.

Then they plopped onto the couch next to each other and put their feet up on the coffee table.

Vanessa raised her glass toward Maggie. "Bring Mama V up to date."

Choking, she sputtered, "Mama V?"

"I spent last weekend with twins. One of them called me that, and I kind of like it."

Blinking rapidly, trying to process what her friend had said, she repeated, "They're twins?"

"Fraternal."

"And... You were the Domme?"

"It was fun. And it turns out I look pretty good in boots and holding a whip."

"I bet you do." Shaking her head, Maggie took a drink.

"Let me know if you'd like me to practice on you. I mean, now that the Tyrant is in the rearview mirror, you're going to want your butt spanked." She tapped a polished fingernail on the side of her glass. "Or come to the dark side with me. I can show you a few tricks to get your man to lick your boots."

Choking on the drink, Maggie frantically shook her head. "None of the above, thank you." But she had to admit, she was no longer feeling sorry for herself.

When she finally blinked back the tears of laughter, Vanessa regarded her. "Let's get serious," Vanessa said. "I know you've been playing with him, and you spent the weekend together. So I feel like there are a whole lot of things that happened between Friday and today that led to this. Because to me, it makes no sense that he would fire you over this."

Especially since he admitted he might make the same decision.

Maggie brought her friend up to date over the next hour or more, leaving out very few details.

"You left his house early on Sunday?"

While he was still on the phone.

"Because...?" She tipped her head to the side. "He wants something more serious with you, and that scared you?" Vanessa guessed.

"It's not that easy."

"No relationship is, especially with someone as demanding as he is. The man is all Dom from the inside out."

Demanding and rigid.

"Ever since Samuel, you haven't gotten serious with any guy."

"I'm not sure I'll ever be ready to take that kind of risk again. And I'm very much happily single right now."

"Are you?"

With a scowl, Maggie faced her friend. "What do you mean?"

"If David didn't matter to you, would you be bothered at all by what he asked or what he thought?"

Her scowl deepened.

"For example, Master Lance..."

Quickly she put down her glass so she didn't slosh the contents over the side. She'd played with the man once. Though he was competent, he was puffed up, full of himself.

"If he wanted to collar you, you'd politely refuse." Vanessa cleared her throat. "Or maybe not so politely."

Shaking her head at her friend's ridiculousness, she laughed. "True."

"So it makes sense that someone like David would freak you out."

The man was overwhelmingly masculine, demanding, but giving as well.

"I guess at some point, you have to ask yourself some questions."

Vanessa's offhanded comment was so similar to David's that a chill raced down her spine.

"Why did you run? And if you say he's anything like Samuel I'm going to roll my eyes so hard that I'll be able to see last week."

She had a point. David's work ethic was incredible, and his expectations of BDSM were exactly what she wanted. He wasn't afraid to give her everything she wanted, push her in ways she'd dreamed of. He found her attractive, not lacking. And he was willing to protect and care for her, rather than just expecting her to serve him. "Maybe it was just all too much, too fast."

"And it would have been better if you had no idea where you stood with him? I mean, girl. You were at his house. He was spanking you and fucking you. Held you half the night."

True.

"What if the situation were reversed and he was too scared to get into a relationship or even admit how he felt? If you wanted a commitment, and he was scared to give it?"

"It was still kind of sudden." She pulled her feet back onto the couch, then tucked them beneath her to face Vanessa. "You have to admit that. Right?"

Vanessa sighed. "You wouldn't have let him spend the night at your place if you didn't like him. Am I right?"

She blew out a breath. "You have a point."

"And you would never have gone to his house. If you wanted a flogging, you could have gone to the Den."

"Also true."

"Look, Maggie. I'm not saying you have to forget your past and drop to your knees and worship any man. God knows I don't plan to. But you broke a lot of your self-imposed rules with him. Maybe there's a reason for that?" She leaned forward to grab a chocolate, candy-coated peanut and popped it into her mouth. "And maybe I'm completely wrong about all of this and you should ignore everything I said. Only you know your heart."

Even though they talked about Vanessa's business and watched parts of the television show, Maggie's thoughts kept straying back to David.

As usual that night, she had nightmares, with David and his haunting eyes at the center of them.

When Vanessa finally rolled out of bed a little after eight, Maggie had been awake for hours, had played a hundred games on her phone, and even read a book. She was definitely ready to head into town for a specialty coffee.

Not even trying to swallow her yawns, Vanessa pulled her hair back and pulled on a lightweight jacket.

"You're not getting dressed?"

"Why? I'm not trying to impress anyone. Besides, the baristas would be shocked if I showed up looking all put together on Saturday morning."

Maybe in her next life, she could be as confident as her friend.

After grabbing a completely decadent extra-chocolate mocha with syrup drizzled on top of the whipped cream, and a fine, Belgian truffle dropped in the bottom, she returned to the counter for breakfast burritos.

"Something with some nutrition," she explained to Vanessa when she carried them back to the table.

"Pfft. Chocolate has antioxidants. Milk has calcium, which we need for our bones."

"You're going to convince me this is health food?"

Sitting back, legs crossed, Vanessa smiled. "It totally is."

At least now she had the time for extra workouts. And if she hung out with Vanessa, she'd definitely need to.

Afterward, they took a walk around the lake, and by then the first shops in the quaint, historic area were starting to open.

Though she'd never been much for casually browsing for souvenirs and artwork, she enjoyed wandering around.

"That was more fun than I imagined," she admitted when they were on the way back to Vanessa's place.

"Enjoyment is a lot about how we look at things," Vanessa observed. "I mean, not all of it. Because sometimes things happen that suck."

"Like losing my job?" Or having her father die so young and being thrust into adulthood years before she should have had to take on those responsibilities.

"Exactly." Vanessa stopped at a red light and looked at Maggie. "I hate that this happened to you. But maybe David was right?" Quickly she raised a hand to cut off Maggie's instant objection. "You were counting down the days until you could be free of him."

In fact, she had a countdown app on her phone that was still running.

"A few weeks ago, you were trying to find any way you could to get out of his golden handcuffs."

I was.

Vanessa grinned wickedly. "Though his silver ones that night when he was the HM were kind of hot. Admit it."

An image of him wearing that band on his biceps and the metal winking in the light sent an illicit thrill through her.

"I would have never wanted this to happen to you, but this gives you a chance to look for something that's a better fit for you."

She wasn't sure she was ready to be that optimistic yet.

"Think of it this way…" The signal turned green, and Vanessa began to accelerate. "You don't have to stay in the same business. Maybe consider trying something entirely new. With your business degree, you can work anywhere you want. If you want, you can even move. You've talked about wanting to live near the beach or something. This could be your opportunity."

Maggie's practical mind instantly cataloged a thousand objections. She needed to be close to her mother. Most of her friends were in the Denver area. There were great employment opportunities, and she owned a home she'd need to either sell or rent out. If she left Colorado, she wouldn't be able to scene at the Den. More than anything, though, she loved the mountains…*especially the view from David's backyard and hot tub.*

"Think about it."

Now that her life had been upended, she had an abundance of time to do exactly that.

"You know, we could go to the Den next weekend, if you want."

Frantically, she shook her head.

"We can stay at the Chalet again. Or maybe find somewhere new and exciting."

The fact she'd considered an event without him was another thing they'd disagreed about.

But now that she had the chance, she didn't want to seize it.

The truth was, he was the only Dom she wanted.

The idea of sceneing with anyone else left her cold. "Thanks, but I think I'll skip it."

"You've spent years refusing to play with the same Top twice." Vanessa parked the car. "He matters to you," Vanessa said softly, with no hint of judgment. "Maybe more than you're willing to admit."

Around lunch time, after packing her bag, she headed back home, but first stopped at the grocery store.

By six o'clock, she'd finished all her weekly chores. The house was spotless. And she was restless as some of her recent life choices returned to haunt her.

As she hugged herself and stared out of the window, Maggie told herself maybe he'd made the right decision in firing her.

They were free of each other, which meant her life was considerably less complicated. She'd been planning to stop sceneing with him, and his ruthless action had ensured that happened.

As for her job, sometime over the last few weeks, she'd stopped resenting it—and him.

Now that she had everything, she thought she'd wanted, she was unhappier than she ever remembered.

In this moment, she'd give anything to turn back the clock and earn a second chance at happiness with the man she just realized she was in love with.

Chapter Nineteen

Gregorio offered David a HM armband, and he held up a hand to refuse it. "Not tonight."

"Oh?"

More than a week had passed since he'd banished Maggie from his life. A long, fucking, stupid miserable week.

And he wasn't taking any chances of missing her if she showed up tonight. After all, she'd had the day circled on her calendar.

At his house, he'd been furious at the idea she might attend the Den without him. That feeling hadn't diminished. If anything, it had intensified.

Maggie—damn her—belonged to him. And only him.

"You listening?"

At Gregorio's question and raised eyebrow, David shook his head. Wasn't the first thing he hadn't been paying attention to in recent days.

"We're short a couple of volunteers," Gregorio repeated.

"Figure it out." This was the first time he'd ever turned down a request to help.

"Something on your mind?" Gregorio persisted.

Nosy fucking bastard.

"Someone, maybe?"

"Don't you have someone you need to check-in?" Without waiting for a response, David strode to the living room.

Senses on high alert, he swung his gaze around. Took seconds to realize his petite, dark-haired obsession wasn't anywhere around. Not that he'd need to see her to confirm that. When she was near, every sense slammed into high gear.

Annoyed, impatient, he went outside.

Tonight, no band was in attendance, and a DJ spun tunes.

Maggie wasn't here, either.

Returning inside, he prowled through the entire main level. When he didn't see her, annoyance knotted his gut. That left only one other option.

The dungeon.

Fuck it all to hell and back.

If he found her there, he'd tear her Dom from limb to fucking limb before forcing her to admit the truth.

She belonged with him. *To him.*

Forcing restraint he didn't feel, he headed down the stairs.

Maggie wasn't in the main area.

Which left the private rooms.

"Didn't expect to see you here." Damien intercepted David before he got very far.

Moments later, Gregorio joined them.

"She isn't here," Gregorio said quietly.

He balled his hand into a fist. "You trying to stop me from looking?"

Damien, dressed in all black, his hair pulled back and secured by a thin strip of leather, shook his head. "Trying to stop you from making an ass of yourself. You've got the energy of a caged animal. And we discourage that here."

He exhaled.

"I'm not fucking with you," Gregorio said. "She is not here, and she didn't RSVP."

At the information, Damien raised an eyebrow. "We don't normally disclose the habits of our members."

"Yeah," Gregorio agreed. "But you think he's fucking listening to either one of us?"

"Look, David. We've been friends for years, known each other for even longer." He paused, as if making sure David was paying attention. "I've always been straight with you. She's not here. If she were, she would have every right to privacy and to scene with whomever she wanted."

"And protected from anyone she didn't want to be involved with," Gregorio added.

"Friendship or not, our rules are not flexible. You will be escorted off the property. And risking a lifetime ban."

Fuck your adorable rules.

"Take my advice." Damien leaned forward. "Go home. Work off some of your energy."

The only thing he planned to do was put his fist through some solid object.

"And pull your head out of your ass." Gregorio exchanged glances with Damien.

"Seems to have been a lot of that here this year," Damien observed.

Because he often served as a House Monitor, David had seen evidence of that, from Tops he figured were in total control of themselves.

Until now, he'd never understood how a Dom could lose his damn fool mind over a wisp of a seductive submissive.

"Look. Join me upstairs for a whiskey."

He didn't need alcohol. He needed to be buried balls-deep in Maggie's pussy.

Gregorio folded his arms. "I believe the man issued an invitation. You might want to accept before I escort your ass out of here."

He tightened his fist, and Gregorio considered him for a moment, long enough for David to get a grip.

"Stand down, Tomlinson."

The man had been part of some special forces team — a foreign government if rumor could be believed. No doubt Gregorio knew several ways to silently kill an enemy. Dropping David to the floor and restraining him would be less effort for Gregorio than a stroll in the park.

Common sense finally prevailing, David nodded.

"I've got a fine Bonds whiskey," Damien said, eliminating the lingering tension.

"I can't get the bastard to send me any."

"Perhaps I'll put in a good word for you."

They made their way through the house to Damien's private office and command central.

True to his word, he poured them each two fingers of the remarkable single malt before taking a seat next to David in front of the desk.

David raised his glass toward his friend. "Saved me from acting an ass." He winced. *Or from acting like a bigger one than I did.*

"Saw you go through a divorce without losing your shit."

But Sandra wasn't Maggie with all her perfect, submissive and defiant ways.

"She must be important to you."

Until she was gone, he hadn't realized how much she mattered to him. "Yeah."

Without saying a word, a master of his emotions, Damien allowed the silence to stretch, then grow.

"It's complicated."

"Matters of the heart often are. Especially when work is involved."

"Fucks it up."

Again, he waited for David to go on.

"I wanted too much. Moved too fast."

"Neither are unrecoverable errors."

"And I fired her."

Damien slowly nodded. "That does complicate things."

Rolling the highball glass between his palms, he outlined the events that had led to his decision. "I thought that was what she wanted."

"You gave no consideration to what you wanted?"

"I did. Maybe too much."

"You acted from anger?"

"Yeah. I was fucking pissed when she said she might come here without me and refused my collar."

"You can't force the river."

He snarled. "When did you become a fucking Zen master?"

Damien lifted his glass and quirked his lips. "Easy when it's someone else's life involved rather than my own."

"That's honest, at least." Much as he hated to admit it, his friend was right. Instead of exercising his customary patience, waiting for her to come to him, he'd acted to claim her before anyone else could.

"And how are things running at the office?"

"They're a damn disaster. I'm working on acquiring another business, and I was already stretched too thin. Her mother's a nightmare at organization and shows up whenever the hell she pleases, whenever she pleases."

"But she's the creative genius behind the company's success?"

"Yeah." And he'd had no idea how much work Maggie had done to keep her mother focused and meeting her deadlines.

This week alone, Gloria had missed a client meeting and two deadlines.

In addition to being sick a week ago Friday, she hadn't shown up at all on Tuesday. No call, no excuses. And she'd apparently turned off her phone and refused to respond to emails and texts. However, on Wednesday morning, she had pink hair, a glowing complexion, and a fresh pedicure that she showed off to Barb.

Which was another story. She, too, had been ill the same day Gloria had called in.

The woman he'd promoted to manager had quit after several hours of trying to deal with Gloria and Barb.

And then yesterday, half the staff had opted to take a three-day weekend.

This was an out-and-out mutiny.

He'd be furious, except for the fact he missed the hell out of Maggie as well. And he wanted her back as desperately as everyone else on the staff.

If something didn't change quickly, he'd have to back out of the Peak Imaginings acquisition, and the kill fee would cost him a chunk of change.

"Out of curiosity, what would you have done if she'd been here?"

"Talk some sense into her." Then thrown her over his shoulder, taken her to a private room, spanked her until she screamed his name and admitted the truth — that they belonged together.

"I see."

He took another drink. "The hell does that mean?"

"You might want to talk some sense into yourself first."

Had he always been this annoying?

"Do some soul searching. What is it you want, David? And what's the best way to get it?" Damien leaned forward. "I have it on good authority that being a domineering ass isn't always the best approach."

"Any other words of wisdom?" He came to his feet and thumped his empty glass on Damien's desk.

"Yeah. Maybe try to find a way to apologize that doesn't involve being a dictatorial, sanctimonious prick." He grinned. "I think that about covers it."

David left, not just the office, but the Den itself.

The drive back to Castle Pines took forever, making him regret his impulsive decision to come up here.

But when it came to Maggie, emotion had obliterated rational thinking.

Damien was right.

He'd never behaved this way with another woman, even his wife.

And maybe because…

Fuck.

He'd never been in love before.

Love?

Where the hell did that thought come from?

According to his ex-wife, he didn't know the definition of the word. Maybe she'd been right. He'd certainly never uttered it to her. When she asked, he'd told her he cared for her and was loyal, which was the absolute truth. Beyond that, he hadn't been sure what she needed to hear.

Wasn't that what mattered?

That he'd be there for her and provide for her every need?

To him, marriage had been a logical decision. Eventually he'd want children to carry on the family name, and it made sense that they had a mother and intact family.

To his mind, Sandra had been a perfect choice for the role.

Except for one missing piece.

Love.

The thing he hadn't believed in and had scoffed at.

Now he knew. It was a terrible, wonderful, consuming, all-powerful emotional connection, more powerful than the need for air.

And he felt it for Maggie.

One thing was certain. This obsession would never diminish, which meant one thing. He had to get Maggie back, as his partner, his submissive, his wife.

He didn't care what it took.

David would pay any cost, demolish any obstacle until she was his. In every possible way.

Chapter Twenty

She couldn't do it.

With a sigh, Maggie put down her phone and picked up her latte.

Around her, the coffee shop buzzed with businesspeople and medical personnel grabbing to-go cups and treats.

Only a few people, like her, were actually seated at tables.

One appeared to be a student, others seemed to be working at their jobs. A gentleman read an actual newspaper. But she was the only one who seemed to have nothing to do.

Which wasn't true.

She had something to do—find a job—but she couldn't bring herself to do it, despite the fact she'd opened her professional networking site and mindlessly scrolled through it for at least fifteen minutes.

The truth was, she longed to be back at Elevated Edge. With David.

Frustrated with herself since she'd done the exact same thing for three days in a row, she grabbed her cup and drove back home.

A courier was standing outside her door, poised to knock again.

"Maggie Carpenter?" he asked.

Blinking, she nodded.

"I have a delivery for you."

"Thank you. Let me get you a tip."

"It's already been handled." He handed her the envelope, and after she signed for it, he jogged down the stairs.

Since there was no return address, she had no idea what was inside or who it was from.

Inside the condo, she put down her coffee and purse, then carried the envelope to the kitchen, slit it open, then turned it upside down to empty the contents. At least a dozen small pieces of paper floated out.

She turned one over, and a few words jumped out at her, enough to let her know exactly what she was looking at. A torn-up copy of her employment contract.

Confused, she looked in the envelope again, but there was nothing there.

It had to be from David. But why? He'd already fired her which voided their contract.

An hour later, the man was back, this time with a small box.

She used a pair of scissors to cut through the packing tape, then she parted the flaps. Her breath seared her lungs.

A pair of golden handcuffs lay nestled in black velvet.

There was no doubt David was behind this, but she had no clue as to why.

She was standing there, perplexed, watching the overhead light reflect off the metal when the doorbell rang again.

Shaking her head, she signed for another envelope. "Do you have any idea who's behind this?"

"No, ma'am." He shook his head. "All I know is I was paid a lot of money to deliver these at certain times."

"Oh? Are there any others?"

"Not that I'm allowed to say."

Curious.

This one contained a folded, handwritten letter.

Maggie,

I know I have no right to send this, and I don't deserve a reply.

I owe you an apology.

Maybe we should not have combined personal business and pleasure.

I fucked up. I own that.

But I'm not sorry it happened.

If we hadn't spent time together, I would never know the softness of your sigh.

This sweet temptation of your surrender.

I wouldn't know the sound of your gasp, or the way you soar when you reach subspace.

Stunned, hardly able to comprehend what she was reading, her knees weakened, and she sank down onto the floor where she tucked her knees close to her chest and clenched the letter in her hand.

Finally composed, she continued to read.

I was a complete and total bastard to you.

The truth is, Maggie, somewhere along the line I fell for you, and the idea of allowing another man to touch you drove me a little mad. Yeah, I was an ass. But I'm human. A man with many failings.

Tears stung her eyes, blurring the words.

My actions were unforgivable. And yet here I am asking your forgiveness.

I would rather say these words to you in person. But I do not want to invade your personal space.

Firing you was one of my biggest fuckups ever.

The business needs you.

I need you.

The letter continued on the back side of the paper.

If you're still reading this, the courier is waiting outside with another delivery.

He'll be there for an hour. And you're free to send him away, if you wish.

David

Hurriedly, she dropped the letter, pushed to her feet, then took a deep breath to steady her nerves.

The man was on the sidewalk, and she dashed down the stairs.

"Not sure what's going on, but this is one of the most interesting days I've ever had."

"You don't have any other instructions?"

He shook his head. "No ma'am. I'm as interested by this as you are."

After thanking him and once more scrawling her signature, she hurried back to her condo.

This time, she found three pieces of paper inside, each folded in half. She opened the first that had the number one written on the outside.

There are no strings attached.
I have complete confidence in you.

Fingers shaking, she unsealed the second one to see the words Business Proposal. She read carefully, not wanting to miss any detail.

David was offering her the position as CEO of Elevated Edge, and if the acquisition went through, of the combined entity that included Peak Imaginings.

She would have full autonomy. He offered to double her salary, provide remote work options, and included six weeks of vacation time, in addition to a generous benefits package and profit sharing.

Her only requirement would be quarterly meetings with him and the board of directors of Tomlinson Enterprises.

Finally, she unsealed the final missive.

I will move out of the LoDo offices.
Other than the board meetings, you will never have to see me, but I will be available to lend all the support you want and need.
If you would like to talk, I'm available by phone or text.

This should have made her deliriously happy. If she accepted, she would return to her company triumphant and in charge with no interference.

But in reality, she didn't want a future that didn't involve David. They made a good team, and the business was better for his involvement.

At that moment, her phone rang.

Expecting to see David's name, she frowned when she realized it was her mother.

Did she have any idea what David was up to?

"What's going on?" Gloria demanded without even saying hello.

Frowning, Maggie repeated, "Going on with what?"

"I just checked my bank account and every penny the Tyrant promised me is in there. And I wasn't supposed to get it for another eighteen months."

He'd given her mother a serious lump sum of cash? "Are you serious?"

"Every penny," Gloria reaffirmed. "Not that I'm complaining."

Maggie opened her banking app on her laptop, then gaped at the balance. In addition to her severance pay, her bonus was there.

This can't be happening.

"Did you have anything to do with this?" Gloria demanded.

"No." Even though her mother couldn't see her, she shook her head. "I haven't been in contact with him since he fired me."

"Well, he admitted he made a mistake."

"Did he?"

"At our staff meeting."

In front of everybody?

"And he said he was going to try to make it right. Barb said she was quitting if he didn't hire you back."

Despite herself, Maggie smiled.

"Though I find it rather pleasant when he has to sit behind the receptionist desk and answer the phone. Listening to him give directions to Myrtle Datsun for the fifth time is God's own gift." She all but cackled.

David's talents were much better spent acquiring businesses and building them into an empire.

"Anyway, he's trying to fix the copier, and everybody is standing around watching him. This is too good to miss." Without saying goodbye, Gloria ended the call, leaving Maggie gaping.

Wondering if he had anything else in store for her, she went outside and leaned over the railing to look at the sidewalk, but the courier was nowhere in sight.

Back inside, she paced the kitchen and living room, trying to figure out what to do.

Before she could make a decision, the doorbell rang.

The courier was back with an enormous bouquet of roses, countless balloons, and the biggest box of chocolates she had ever seen.

David was as persistent as he was relentless. "Is there another envelope?"

"No, ma'am, this is really it."

It took her two trips to get everything inside and to secure the balloons so they didn't soar to the ceiling.

Her phone lit up once more, this time with a text message from Barb.

When she clicked on it, she saw a picture of David, dressed in shirtsleeves, his tie slung over his shoulder. His face was streaked with blue ink, and so was his white shirt.

While she was still taking in the sight of David, Barb sent another message.

We need you. The caterer for the open house just canceled our order. And the coffeemaker died. Everything is falling apart without you.

Despite everything, Elevated Edge was still the business that she and her mother built, and she loved everything about it, from the employees to the clients.

Resolved, she squared her shoulders and typed her response.

Call Chelsea Barton, explain the situation and tell her we need a recommendation for a caterer.

Get a coffee order together for all the employees and place an online order at Grounds for Thought and have them deliver it. Order a new coffeemaker through the magic cart company and pay for expedited delivery.

A few seconds later, Barb replied.

Got it.

Then a second message came through.

I knew I could count on you. Welcome back.

Yeah. I'm back.
Since she still had her phone in hand, she scrolled to David's name and typed in two words.

I accept.

Then, drumming her fingers on her thigh, she smiled and decided to second a follow-up.

My office. One hour

His reply was instant.

Yes, madam president.

Things were close to being the way she wanted them to be.
Close.
Now she just needed to nudge them over the edge.

Chapter Twenty-One

By the time she had dressed for work and driven to the office, Maggie's nerves were frayed.

Even though she was the company's new CEO, when it came to David, she was still a woman and a submissive. That part, she didn't want to give up.

As much as she missed the job, she missed sceneing equally as much. She just prayed she had the courage to ask for what she wanted.

Fortunately, she found a nearby parking spot right away, but as she parked, a fresh wave of butterflies assailed her, and she sat in the car for a few seconds, drawing deep breaths before exiting and forcing a confident stride into her walk.

When she arrived, David was perched on the end of the reception desk, and a whole tray of coffee cups occupied the center section. One contained something that was bright green and had purple blobs floating on the top. Clearly that belonged to her mother.

"Better not let the boss catch you lazing around, Mr. Tomlinson," Barb teased.

She only had eyes for him. And now that he was in front of her, all pure male spice and Dominance, her longing bubbled to the surface.

With a slow, appreciative smile, he swept his gaze over her. "Maggie."

She gripped her purse straps so tightly that her knuckles whitened, and there was no way he would have missed that gesture.

Barb stood and came over to hug her. "Oh, Mags! It's good to have you back. This place has been a mess without you."

"Thank you for saying so." Smiling, filled with genuine warmth, she returned the embrace. "I've missed you."

Barb offered her a latte. "I figured I'd get you one. You've got so many, many messages to get through that I'm sure you'll need the caffeine."

"You're right." She accepted it. "And it's even a large one." Between this and the one she'd had at the shop near her house, she'd be flying until midnight.

David pushed off the desk into a standing position. "You wanted to see me?"

Being in control was easy until she got within ten feet of him and his sizzling masculine energy. She craved his touch and his possession. She ached to fall to her knees or drape herself across his lap. Maybe both.

"Have we talked to Chelsea?" she asked Barb.

"She's talking to caterers and promises you don't need to worry about a thing."

Definitely the type of company they needed to work with.

"Perfect. Thanks. If you'll excuse us," she said to Barb.

"Absolutely."

She walked down the hall to her office, and he followed.

"I moved out of the one I was using. You should take it."

"Let my mother move back in."

"I offered. She doesn't want it. Something about the light being better on the other side of the building."

Artistic temperament? Or closer to Barb where she could listen in to the office gossip, as well as the comings and goings. "Speaking of... Is she not here?"

"Something about a sale at the Cherry Creek Shopping Center."

"Ah." The bonus money. No doubt she thought she deserved a gift to celebrate. And she was right. "And you had a mishap with the copier?"

"Had to change my shirt and wash my face. Needs servicing."

"Did Barb call?"

"She was waiting for approval from the new CEO."

Which was something she would be working on — giving Barb and other employees more authority to make decisions so that business didn't grind to a halt.

They arrived at her office, which was barren and empty without her belongings, and she hadn't thought to bring her box back.

She walked to the far side of her desk, put her latte on top, then tucked her purse into the bottom drawer before taking a seat. "Anyway, as far as your office, I vote for turning it into coworking space. That will be a bonus if we add staff."

"There will be a lot of details to work through as far as consolidating offices. But those decisions will be in your capable hands." Once he'd closed the door, David dropped into a chair across from her. "I'm glad you're back."

After the absence, it felt odd, but Barb had done a great job of not making things feel awkward.

"I want to apologize in person for being a sanctimonious prick."

"A..." She blinked. "Sanctimonious prick?" she repeated.

"Damien's words." He winced. "Not mine."

"Ouch."

"Sometimes friends need to tell us things we might not want to hear."

"I get it." She nodded. Vanessa had done the same for her. It wasn't until she spent time with her friend that she was able to admit to herself that she truly did care for David.

"I know I don't deserve forgiveness."

She smiled. "I think you do."

"Maggie..." He stood and shoved his hands into his pockets. Then he paced the room several times before stopping to face her. "I'm fucking this up."

"Keep going."

"What I'm trying to say is, I moved too fast. And I have one massive sin to confess."

Her mouth dried, and as she had so many times with him, she twisted her hands together beneath the desk.

"I fell in love with you." Barely taking a breath, he went on. "I've never experienced anything like it. As I said in that note, I might have lost my mind a little bit. Goddamn it, Maggie, I've never had a jealous moment in my life until you." Hs jaw tightened. "The idea of another man touching you..." He shook his head and exhaled sharply. "I hate this, but I'd rip his fucking head off."

She swallowed deeply. "It wasn't just you... I came from a place of fear, scared to death of getting involved in another relationship, terrified of being hurt."

"That's the last thing I would ever do to you."

"I know that." She pressed her hands even tighter. "That's not about you. That's about me."

"I'm sorry, Maggie. For pushing, for overreacting."

She gave him a quick smile. "For being a sanctimonious prick?" she finished.

"Yeah. That. All that."

Her mind reeling as she tried to process everything he said, she asked, "Can we go back to the part where you mentioned you loved me?"

"I do, Maggie. I love you. But I have no expectations, and—"

"David?" she interrupted.

He raised a questioning eyebrow.

"I love you, too."

He went still, very, very still. "You...?"

"Yeah," she admitted softly. "And I wasn't honest with you that Sunday morning. Because I wasn't honest with myself." Suddenly, a memory of her nightmares plowed into her. And she recalled Vanessa's words that maybe the terrors were telling her she needed to face her own fears.

And now that the chance was here, it was every bit as terrifying as she imagined.

She met his blue eyes, as startling as the ones in her dreams. "I didn't want any man to touch me except for you. In fact, I don't want any man, except you, to ever touch me again."

"Maggie..."

"I would have never gone to the Den without you. It's just... After my ex, I didn't want to get involved with anyone."

"I've fucked up with you, Maggie. By letting my emotions overrule my restraint. I can't promise it won't happen again, but I can swear I'll try my best."

"I will forgive you, if you give me a second chance in return."

"Damn, woman. Come home with me after work. Stay this weekend?"

"How about my place?" she suggested. "It's closer."

"I was hoping you'd ask." He took his hand from his pockets. "How does the new boss feel about fraternization?"

"She has no rules against it."

"In that case, come to me, Maggie Mine."

She didn't walk, she ran.

With a laugh, he scooped her from the floor and devoured her with a hungry, demanding kiss. "That will hold you for a while."

"No, Sir," she disagreed. "I don't think it will. I think we should do it again to be sure."

"Maybe we should." He propped his knee, angling it toward her. Accepting his unspoken invitation, she leaned into him, grinding her pussy against his thigh as he held her tight, digging a hand into her buttocks and hungrily staked his claim on her.

After several short seconds, her orgasm built, and he swallowed her cry with his mouth.

"We may need to leave early for an offsite meeting," she murmured against his ear.

"Whatever the boss says." He grinned. Then it faded as he dug his hands into her shoulders. "I will never get enough of you, Maggie. Say you'll be mine."

"Yes." Tears stung, and she frantically blinked them away. "A thousand times, yes, David. I'll be yours."

"Forever?" he pressed.

"Forever, Sir. Forever and ever."

Chapter Twenty-Two

Yawning, Maggie stretched and slowly opened her eyes.

Even though she was waking up alone in her Dominant's bed, she smiled.

A little over two months ago, he'd hired her back, and her life was happier than she ever remembered it, especially now that they had a lot more time together.

When he'd invited her to move in with him a few weeks ago, she'd unhesitatingly agreed. Even though her condominium was closer to her workplace, he had plenty of room and she loved seeing the sunrise paint the sky pink and watching the sun descend behind the mountains at the end of the day. The hot tub was a glorious benefit.

If all went according to plan, the deal with Peak Imaginings would close at the beginning of the year, which wasn't as soon as she'd hoped. But it gave her extra planning time.

David had already bought the building that housed their offices, and she was considering a complete remodel so that he could lease out part of the space.

If they adopted her design, incorporating elements of a coworking space, complete with coffee bar and a small restaurant, the employees of the joint company could work at either location. The entire entity could now serve a greater client base. Now all they needed was another satellite in Northern Colorado.

Since David rarely visited Elevated Edge, her mother had become even more creative, and Cindy Hoskins had finally given them all of her business. The triumph had been partially related to her mother's excellent work, but Maggie was convinced that Cindy had a secret crush on David.

They'd met in person at the ultrasuccessful open house, and the two had hit it off.

He was a natural-born socializer, making customers feel valued. He was an asset to the business, and she often brought him into client meetings.

He'd been right that they made a good team.

And the best part? He always made sure that everyone knew he had eyes for only one woman. And a spanking for one as well, she realized, wincing as she turned over.

She loved the paddle that had his name on it, and last night he'd wielded it with great skill.

The scent of brewing coffee wafted in the air, and the unmistakable sound of milk being steamed pulled her from the bed.

Rubbing her bare arms against the morning chill, she hurried to her closet to pluck her terrycloth robe from a hook. He'd bought it for her after getting tired of watching her struggle with the extra-long sleeves on the one she borrowed.

Knotting the belt, she descended the staircase, appreciating the fact she had her own personal barista.

On more than one occasion, she'd stayed in bed, pretending to be asleep just so she didn't have to be the first one in the kitchen.

She knew how to operate the coffeemaker, but the pots she brewed weren't as strong or rich as his. And frankly she was too lazy to make her own lattes.

When she neared, he turned to face her, holding her cup in his hand.

A slow smile curved his lips.

No matter how many times she saw him, he took her breath away.

More than once, she'd worked in his home gym so she could enjoy the sight of his muscles rippling as he lifted weights or exercised on the rowing machine. The combination of his intensity and pure male exertion did strange things to her libido.

He was a distraction, all right. One she could not imagine living without.

When she thought about it, it scared her to realize how close they had come to losing this chance at happiness.

Maybe because of that she never took it for granted.

"Morning, Maggie Mine."

"David." Her heart fluttered. He wore a tight, black T-shirt that snuggled his well-honed body. The erection pressing against his pants showed he was already thinking about how they would spend at least part of the day.

At one point in time, she'd realized that the more she got of him, the more she would want. And it was true. She was obsessed with him.

Fortunately, he seemed to feel the same way about her.

When he beckoned, she willingly went to him, accepting his offering, and then lifting up onto her toes to kiss him. "You spoil me."

"Get used to it. You deserve it."

She took her first sip, then sighed. "I appreciate you saying that."

"I mean it. No one works as hard as you do, or gives herself so completely, or whimpers my name so perfectly."

Response fluttered inside her.

"I don't want to rush you…"

Wondering what he was talking about, she tipped her head to one side.

"About our future."

Her heart skipped over its next few beats.

"Living together has been a great first step."

Searching his eyes, she repeated, "First?"

"Toward forever."

A few months ago, those words would have terrified her. But now, she was no longer scared. Yes, he had a possessive streak, one she'd seen at a party where he made it clear by keeping a hand in the middle of her back for most of the night.

Recently, they'd attended the Den together.

While she was getting ready, she'd gone down to the basement and opened the storage trunk to find the collar that he'd bought for her.

With determination, she'd picked it up, then walked to his office and knocked on the door.

Smiling, he'd waved her over.

In front of him, she'd bravely knelt, offered him the thin strip of leather, and asked him to secure it around her neck.

He'd caught his breath, recognizing the importance of her gesture.

The flare of approval in his eyes when it was in place made everything worthwhile.

She belonged to him.

They both knew it, and she wouldn't want it any other way.

Now, stunning her, he reached behind a bag of coffee to grab a small box. Its shape was distinctive, but she couldn't believe what she was seeing.

Slowly, he lowered himself to one knee.

"Maggie..." He looked up at her, and then, because the latte was in danger of slipping from her grip, she slid it onto the counter.

"Will you do me the honor of becoming my wife?"

Emotion rushed through her, and she couldn't find the words to respond.

"If this is too sudden, I understand. We can take as long as you need to set a date, but I want you to know that I love you completely. I didn't know it was possible to feel this deeply about anyone. And I vow, that if you give me the chance, I will spend the rest of my days making you happy."

Hot tears stung her eyes.

"Please." He smiled charmingly, entreating her. "Put me out of my misery. Say yes."

"Yes!" She choked on a sob. "Yes, David. I love you so much. I can't imagine a future without you in it."

He slipped the exquisite diamond solitaire onto her finger.

The fit was as perfect as their relationship.

Once it was nestled in place, he stood and claimed her mouth in a hot, hungry kiss that promised forever.

"I love you, Maggie." He raised her hand to his lips. "You'll be my bride, my sub, my partner for the rest of my life."

"For eternity," she agreed, a fat tear clinging to her eyelashes. "You've made me the happiest woman in the world."

This time, his kiss was demanding as he tasted her, hungrily, as if he'd never be able to get enough of her.

Then he lifted her from the ground and sat her on the counter while he lowered his pants.

Since she was now on birth control, they no longer used condoms, and she adored the way he felt inside her.

"I have to have you."

Gripping her hips, he drew her toward him, and she clutched his shoulders, hanging on for dear life as he eased her ass off the countertop, holding her, fucking her hard and deep.

Somehow, he managed to move them to the living room, and he placed her on the couch. Moving her onto her back, he claimed her with hard, possessive strokes.

"Forever," he reaffirmed. "Mine."

"I've never been anyone else's, David," she promised, tracing a finger across his forehead. Her words had never been more honest. Compared to this relationship, everything else had been meaningless.

Their joining was fiercer than ever before. "Yes," she whispered. "Yes, yes, yes."

He dug his hand into her hair and pulled back her head, holding her imprisoned, looking at her eyes, staring into her soul as he demanded her total capitulation.

Happily, screaming, she offered it.

Everything he wanted, she would give. And more.

Groaning her name, he came, filling her with his hot seed, claiming her as his.

"I'll never get enough of you."

Shocking her, he hardened, and began to move again.

"But this will do for a start..."

"Yes, Sir." She smiled happily. "Bring it on."

Want to see more from this author?
Here's a taster for you to enjoy!

Mastered: For the Sub
Sierra Cartwright

Coming April 2024

Excerpt

"Another drink, Sir?"

Startled out of his reverie by the softness of a woman's voice, Niles Malloy looked over the rim of his empty glass. Brandy, one of the house's submissives, stood in front of him, her legs close together, her shoulders pulled back in a sexy way that thrust her chest forward.

Had he been so lost in thought that he hadn't heard her approach? Or were her movements so graceful and perfect that she'd managed to silently cross the Den's patio?

Given her seductively high stilettos, he doubted the latter.

Her long blonde hair flowed over her shoulders and tumbled down her back. Tonight she wore a short, slinky black dress that covered everything, but she seemed more intriguing because of it. The material clung to her, highlighting her ample breasts, trim waist, and curvy bottom. This woman—sub—appealed to every one of his masculine sensibilities.

Her legs were bare, and her black heels emphasized the feminine shape of her ankles. For a moment, he fantasized about placing her on her back, removing her shoes then stroking his fingers against her instep before applying a cane to the soles of her feet.

He shook his head to banish the image.

It had been years since he'd played with a woman in anything other than a detached way. In fact, it hadn't happened since the death of his wife and the unraveling of the devastating secrets she'd hidden.

But right now, he was thinking about touching Brandy in a way meant for their mutual satisfaction.

"Sir?" she asked, tipping her head. "Master Niles?"

The motion swept her hair to the side, snaring his interest. The locks were long enough, he mused, to be used as part of a hot bondage scene.

"Would you prefer to be alone, Sir?"

"Actually, no." The answer surprised him.

A month ago, he'd declined the invitation to tonight's party. Every fall, Master Damien hosted a get-together for Doms and Dommes who had been members of the Den for at least seven years. It was a small, select group, and they gathered to play poker, sip the finest single malt on the planet, enjoy conversation and, if they chose, scene with house subs. Not many people availed themselves of the playrooms, however, as most were in relationships, and this exclusive gathering focused on socializing, which was not his strong suit.

This year, Damien had pestered Niles to the point of annoyance.

Despite his reluctance, and tired of his own company after spending a week at home by himself, Niles had agreed.

But after half an hour of mindless white lies, telling his friends and acquaintances that he was well, he'd made his escape to the solitude of the patio. He'd dragged a chair close to the crackling firepit to enjoy the sunset. Today had been a mild day, and summer was breathing her last gasps before surrendering to the inevitable shorter, colder, bleaker days.

Brandy, a natural submissive, rather than one who'd been trained for it, cast her gaze down at the ground before looking up him. "I never said thank you for what happened at the last Ladies' Night."

"No thanks necessary," he assured her. "Any Dom would have done the same thing."

There was often an assumption among new Doms that subs wearing the house's purple wristband welcomed any attention. A first-time visitor had made that error with Brandy.

Master Damien had not served alcoholic beverages at Ladies' Night, opting for froufrou, sugar-laced umbrella drinks that the ladies seemed to like. But that hadn't stopped the guest from drinking before he'd arrived.

Even when Brandy had used the Den's safe word, the asshole had continued on, forcing her to her knees and shoving his dick in her mouth. Niles had noticed her distress and stepped in.

"You were my hero, Sir."

"I don't know about that." He'd enjoyed throwing the sonofabitch out of the front door. The physical altercation had dissipated some of the angst churning in his gut, emotion he hadn't been able to get rid of otherwise. If Master Damien or anyone else had witnessed the uppercut Niles had delivered to the guy's jaw, no one had mentioned it.

Seeing his bruised knuckles the next day had satisfied him deeply, but it wasn't nearly as rewarding as seeing the current, exquisite expression of gratitude on Brandy's face.

He rolled the empty glass between his palms, keeping his hands busy so he didn't yield to the temptation to reach out and touch her.

After all, he didn't have the right.

Cocking his head to one side, he studied her.

Though he'd seen her around the Den for years, he knew next to nothing about her. She was always unfailingly obedient, but she didn't stand out. No wonder Damien continued to have her at his events.

She met his eyes, then she shifted.

Very much not like her.

"Something on your mind, Brandy?" he asked.

Gently, she released a breath. "If you'd like to go to one of the private rooms, Sir, I'm available."

His cock hardened.

Her pretty blue eyes were wide open, and she gave him a quick smile that slammed into his solar plexus. *Fuck.* Why had he never appreciated how attractive she was? *Maybe because you're not the type I usually go for.*

He was over six feet tall, and his deceased wife had looked him in the eye when she had donned the heels he liked. She'd been runway-model thin, with deep brown eyes, and raven hair styled in a sleek, no-nonsense bob.

The two women couldn't have been any more different.

Hopefully in many more ways, as well.

Suddenly, the thought of bending Brandy over, making her scream as she came, stoked every one of his dominant urges. Still, he didn't want to scene just because she had a misplaced sense of gratitude. "You owe me nothing."

"I think you misunderstand, Sir. It's an invitation." She linked her hands at her back.

Interesting. If he wasn't mistaken, she'd tucked her hands out of sight so he couldn't see the way she was fidgeting.

"I'm afraid I was being bold," she said, momentarily casting her gaze at the ground. "Forgive me."

So she was nervous, and he understood why. Though she was often summoned to the dungeon, he was certain she initiated few, if any, of the scenes, and suddenly he wanted to soothe and reassure her. "I respect a woman who asks for what she wants."

As he stood, he put down his glass. Brandy—so very perfect—didn't glance up.

He placed his forefinger beneath her chin and gently tipped her head back, and their gazes met in a collision of need and desire.

Fuck.

She smelled of cinnamon with a tangy undercurrent of arousal. The spicy scent intrigued him, consuming him with sensual fire. "I'd be honored."

The answering slow, sensuous curve of her lips melted ice from his emotions. "After you," he encouraged, dropping his hand.

After scooping up his glass, she started toward the main house. Her hips swayed from side to side, not in an exaggerated movement, but with natural feminine grace.

He couldn't look away.

Responding to a male instinct as old as time to mark her as his, he placed his fingers against the small of her back.

Gregorio, the Den's caretaker, opened the patio doors for them.

"We'll be availing ourselves of one of the playrooms," Niles informed him.

Obviously surprised by the news, Gregorio drew his dark eyebrows together.

"I see." He accepted the glass from Brandy and spoke directly to her. "Let me know if you need anything."

Niles gritted his teeth. "I'll take good care of her."

"See that you do," Gregorio replied, sparing Niles a glance.

His overt concern annoyed the hell out of him. Niles hadn't participated in a personal scene in years, but that didn't mean he couldn't be trusted.

With a nod toward the watchful Gregorio, Niles guided her through the kitchen then down the stairs that led to Damien's elaborate dungeon.

Then it occurred to him that there might be something he didn't know. He'd been so lost in his own past that he wasn't being considerate enough of Brandy. "He's protective," he observed, guiding her to private corner.

"I'm an employee as well as a friend," she replied.

He studied the emotion in her eyes. "Anything special I need to know?"

"No, Sir."

So Gregorio's looking out for her.

Good to know, even if the knowledge rankled.

"Any preference on which room you'd like to use?" Niles owned a production company that often filmed at the Den. He knew the rooms well, all the apparatus that was available and each of the implements he could apply to her body.

"Sir?"

Clearly she expected him to make the decisions. Under normal circumstances, he would. But this evening was anything but ordinary. "This was your suggestion," he reminded her. "So I'm betting you have an idea or two about what you'd like to have happen."

"In that case, Sir…"

Her soft smile knocked him on his ass.

"First door on the right," she finished.

Pleased with her answer, he grinned. "Most excellent."

Because of its sparseness, this was one of his favorite playrooms. A hook hung from the ceiling, and a chair stood off to one side, tucked beneath a padded bench. The far wall was dominated by crops, whips, floggers, and a tawse handcrafted by Master Marcus. As with all the rooms, there was a small sink and counter, and a cupboard stocked with necessities, including wipes, lube, condoms, and towels.

After he'd grabbed them each a bottle of water from the bar, they entered the space.

He paused to close the door, sealing them in relative privacy. At the Den, all rooms had an opening so that Gregorio or Master Damien could observe any scene. The lack of total seclusion added a layer of security that he appreciated.

When he turned back to her, Brandy was kneeling in the middle of the room, head bowed, hands on her thighs.

The subs — male and female — that he professionally dominated were actors and models. Each act was scripted and choreographed, and each response was exploited to ensure maximum effect. Screaming, whimpering, and begging were all expected from the participants — after all, no one wanted to pay money for a download in which the spankee was silent.

Brandy, too, submitted for a living, but there were no cameras, directors, or second takes now. Whatever happened in her was between them, for no reason other than pleasure.

This was all-too real, and so very damn special.

How long since a woman had done this for him, because of a desire to please?

Jesus.

For a moment, he couldn't breathe.

Hands balled into fists at his sides, he took her in, savoring, appreciating the moment.

Finally, he expelled hot air from his lungs. When he was fully in control of his emotions again, he offered his hand and said, "Stand for me, beautiful Brandy, with your hands over your head."

Trustingly she slipped her small palm against his, meeting his gaze as he drew her dress up, exposing her body, inch by perfect inch. She wore a scrap of material that served as panties, and she had on a black shelf bra that lifted her breasts.

"I'm a fortunate man tonight."

"Thank you, Sir. I feel the same way."

About the Author

Born in northern England and raised in the Wild West, Sierra Cartwright pens books that are as untamed as the Rockies she calls home.

She's an award-winning, multi-published writer who wrote her first book at age nine and hasn't stopped since.

Sierra invites you to share the complex journey of love and desire, of surrender and commitment. Her own journey has taught her that trusting takes guts and courage, and her work is a celebration for everyone who is willing to take that risk.

Sierra loves to hear from readers. You can find her contact information, website details and author profile page at https://www.totallybound.com

Home of Erotic Romance

Sign up for our newsletter and find out about all our
romance book releases, eBook sales and promotions,
sneak peeks and FREE romance books!